Heidi W. Boehringer grew up in the countryside outside of Valley Forge, Pennsylvania. She graduated from the University of Florida, which she attended on an honors scholarship and studied creative writing with Harry Crews. She has had essays published in *The Tropic* of the *Miami Herald*, has appeared on TV and has been a speaker at conferences about writing, getting published, and working with writers' groups. *Chasing Jordan* is her first novel. She lives in southern Florida with her three dogs and two cats.

chasing jordan

heidi w. boehringer

A complete catalogue record for this book can
be obtained from the British Library on request.

First published in the UK in 2005 by Serpent's Tail,
4 Blackstock Mews, London N4 2BT

website: www.serpentstail.com

Designed and typeset at Neuadd Bwll, Llanwrtyd Wells

Printed by Mackays of Chatham, plc

10 9 8 7 6 5 4 3 2 1

For my mother, Dottie Boehringer, who taught me to love the written word. xoox

Children are the anchors that hold a mother to life.

Sophocles

Acknowledgements

Gratitude goes to my sister, Robin Watson, for her role as the midwife of *Chasing Jordan*. Without her almost daily prodding for a chapter to read over morning tea, this book would never have been birthed in quite the frenetic pace necessary.

To my consummate friends, Brett Horn and Joyce Sweeney—love ya, man.

My family, whose encouragement means volumes: Dottie Boehringer, Kim Kiser, Betsy Linen, Robin, John and Isabella Watson and Amy, Don, Zoe and Mia Schenk. I love you all.

Harry Crews for his gracious willingness to read the novel in manuscript. Janell Walden Agyeman, my first agent, who validated that I could do this. Janis Nelson for her insight and solid counsel, without which I may never have pushed so hard to find a publisher.

To friends who read the manuscript and provided critique and support: Joan Mazza, Mary DeMayo, Martha Clark, Marcia Braff. To the years of encouragement from my writers' group—Lois Avrick, Dorian Cirrone, Gene Cryer, Ellie Eckardt, Alex Flinn, Marjetta Geerling, Kingsley Guy, Christian (in name only) Henz, Kathy Macdonald, Mary Mastin, Gale Payne, Audrey Roberts, Gloria Rothstein, Lucille Gang Shulklapper, Cher Souci, Mel Taylor and, of course, group leader Joyce Sweeney, who always knows how to vary her mentoring style to fit the person. A special thanks to Mark D. Smith for his superb editing of the first draft and his tireless quest for a title.

To Jim DeCesari, unwitting father figure, mentor and a damn fine person—thanks for always letting me give agent and book publishing updates in your staff meetings.

Amy Scholder, my editor, whose meticulous excision kept the

heart of the novel and made it stronger. And, above all, thanks to my renegade shepherds at Serpent's Tail publishers: Ben Cooper, who was so good-natured about my heckling to get an audience, Martin Worthington, who agreed my manuscript had merit and kept it in play, and Pete Ayrton, who gave the manuscript a quick turnaround when I was at wits' end and said, "Yes."

chapter one

There's that damn Susie Richardson on her hands and knees again. Her back sways down like a twenty-year-old pack mule, except the only thing she's packing is her ass—propped up high in the air. Cheeks looking like two ice cream cones, good enough to lick. I'm sure my husband Paul would just love to bury his tongue right in there. I see the way he looks at her— especially when she wears those jean shorts, cut at just the right angle to make you think you're going to get a glimpse of bush. I can't really blame him, who wouldn't stare? Even I can't help gawking at her to see if you can—see her bush, I mean. I'm like that. If people put that shit out there, well, I'm gonna look.

Paul rode his Harley out to…what's the name of the city where all the bikers converge in August for that motorcycle rally? Sturgis. That's it. Anyway, Paul rode his bike out to Sturgis this year, coming back with a story about a teenage girl in a tattoo parlor window, legs spread wide, getting her clit pierced. He said people were lined up pushing and shoving in front of the window to get a look at her. Take a piece of her away with their eyeballs. I asked him for details on what he saw, but he said after he pushed his way up to the window and saw what the spectacle was, he had to walk on by. He said it made him feel funny to think that maybe one day it would be our daughter Madeline people would be looking at. I don't really believe him, though. I think he just didn't want to give me the details—admit to me that it was another woman's crotch besides mine splayed out in front of him. I swear, sometimes he needlessly chokes himself with his own wedding band. And other times...well, let's just move on.

It's her rose bushes Susie's tending to. She's got all kinds: Angel Face, Peace, Circus. If there is such a thing, I think all her rose bushes must be of the male species. I've never seen roses grow like hers before. Maybe she's got a special brand of fertilizer—dead people buried under each bush, like that old woman up in the northeast that took in elderly people, then buried them in her yard when they died of purportedly natural causes. She'd give them the decency of a rose-bush burial, then continued collecting their Social Security checks. Beats eating cat food, I suppose. But I wonder how an old woman like that could dig a deep grave, then drag the bodies into them and cover them back up with a rose bush on top, like it was a cherry on a sundae.

I look up in my rearview mirror at Madeline cooing in the backseat. We call her Maddie for short. Love bug, goozie girl—she's got lots of names. She's only eleven months old. I look at her reflection. She's so cute, with her black curly hair like Paul's, chunky cheeks, green, green eyes and milkmaid skin like mine.

"Hey, baby girl. Mommy sees you."

I spot Paul in our front yard, hands on hips, looking over at that witch Susie like he's Tam O'Shanter staring at the winsome wench dancing in her longitudinally sorely scanty shirt. Any second, I know he's going to yell out, "Good work, short shift."

Susie stands up; I roll my window down to wave at her. I don't know why I bother, she never waves back, has barely said five words to me in the three years we've lived here.

Yep, she doesn't wave. Turns her back when she sees my car.

There's Paul, he spots me spotting him spotting Susie. Madeline starts "Da-da-da-ing", like she knows we're home.

Susie rubs the small of her back, shoving her ass out like it's a damn shelf. And there's Paul, mopping his forehead with the front of his T-shirt like he's been pumping away at her for the last fifteen minutes, instead of just eyeballing her.

I hear Paul yell something. I swing my attention away from Susie's ass.

Oh God. I've hit something. Paul rushes towards my car, shrieking. His arms are flailing toddler-style, outstretched as he runs across our yard.

Did I hit our cat, Susie's dog? Paul's still shrieking. Paul's shrieking and shrieking and I can't get the damn SUV in park fast enough. Madeline's wailing, matching Paul lung power for lung power. Susie's yellow lab is pounding against her front picture window, bellowing along with Paul and Madeline.

I swing my car door open. What have I done? I can feel my feet clamoring for the running board, but my seat belt deadlocks me in place. I slam my body back into the seat, struggling to free myself.

Rounding the corner of the car, I see Paul kneeling, cradle-scooping up our son Jordan's tiny body. Blood's coming from somewhere—everywhere—spreading out all over Paul's T-shirt.

"Oh, God. Don't move him, don't move him—you could paralyze him," I say, feeling myself sag to my knees. The baby in the car is screaming. The baby in Paul's arms isn't making a sound.

"Call an ambulance," Paul orders.

I'm numb and I can't move. Someone has stitched my knees to the driveway.

Paul yells, "Look what you've done, Meg. Call an ambulance."

"Is he breathing? Don't move him. Let me hold him."

Paul shoulders me away. I'm an octopus, tentacle arms wrapping this way and that way around and over Paul, pawing for my son.

Susie is running towards us. "My God. I'll call the ambulance. Get Madeline out of here."

I wonder how it is she knows Madeline's name.

She grabs her cell phone holstered on the band of her shorts. Dials 911, tells the dispatcher that Jordan has been hit. The next thing she says is that he's about two years old.

"He's twenty-seven months," I hear myself say. I rock back and forth on my knees, snuggling Madeline, breathing in her sweaty sour milk smell, not minding her screaming directly into my ear. It's a sound I can understand and fix, but not at the moment.

Paul relinquishes Jordan to Susie's arms. My stomach jumps when I see the trusting look in his eyes. Susie gently lays Jordan on the blacktop.

I'm thinking that the blacktop is too hot and will burn his little legs, but it's like I'm an actor in a play that has forgotten her lines and there's no prompter to tell me what to say and how to act.

"I think he's still breathing," says Susie.

Right then, I know I will forgive any indiscretion with my husband if she is the Savior come to raise Jordan from the dead.

Home from the funeral, I drop my black suit jacket by the front door, take Madeline from Paul's sister Julie, who flew in from Utah. Paul didn't want Madeline at the funeral, so Julie stayed home with her. Paul comes in the door behind me, kneels and pets Sasha, Susie's dog, who has wandered into our house. I wish I had some magic incantation to make this all disappear.

Julie says, "Paul, take the dog back to Susie's so she doesn't bark at the company."

"Let her bark," says Paul walking from the room, banishing himself out to the garage without looking at me.

Julie tisks and says, "Meg?"

I shrug my shoulders. She huffs and stomps out to the kitchen. I hope she's able to keep her bad temper under control—there's enough dissension flying around already.

Here we go. Paul's mother's raised voice carries from the kitchen. She says, "Julie, don't be like that. They're under a lot of stress."

I can picture Paul in the garage sitting on his Harley Road King. Just sitting.

Madeline and I sit on the odd-shaped barrel swivel chair— the one with the back that was high on one side and spiraled down low on the other side. The one Jordan had laughed at just one month ago in the store. Even though I knew Paul would say it didn't match anything else in the house, I had impulsively bought it after Jordan sat in it the entire time I browsed around the store.

I know it's going to be like this now—recounting minute-by-minute Jordan's twenty-seven-month life. Sad for all the minutes I hadn't been with him. Angry at all the minutes he would never be with me again.

Madeline starts squirming and nuzzling at my breasts. I know she's hungry, but I don't have the energy to get up and go in the bedroom to breastfeed. Besides, I've gotten to where I like the sound of Madeline's crying—at least then, I know she's breathing and still needs me.

People are beginning to fill our house now, bearing casserole dishes of food I'm never going to eat and bottles of alcohol. Ordinarily, I don't permit alcohol in our house, but I'm too tired to say so. Besides, I could use a drink.

What time is it? I glance at the clock above the dining room table. 11:00 AM. My mother used to say, "It's always happy hour somewhere in the world, dear," when I'd try to take away her Tanqueray and tonic because it was only 9:00 in the morning.

Here comes Susie. She's a fixture in our house these days. Talks to me till she's blue in the face or I give her the finger—whichever comes first. She breezes in like she belongs here.

It's all her fault. If I hadn't been waving at that short-shifted bitch for the two millionth time, knowing full well as I did that she would never wave back, then maybe I would have seen Jordan chase his orange ball into the road. Maybe I would have been able to slam on my brakes and swerve away. I had to be gauging whether Susie's shorts were actually legal or not while my car was crushing my son's skull. What kind of mother am I?

"How are we today, Meg?" She lightly touches the top of Madeline's head.

"Fine, fine. Just like you'd be after burying your son." Does she have to pat me on the back and bend down with her hands on her knees like she's addressing a child?

"Do you want to help us in the kitchen?" She says the word "us" like she's part of Paul's family now.

"Pass."

Enter Mrs Rutherford, the neighbor from down the road, toddling in on her three-inch heels. I hope she falls and breaks her damn neck.

She zeros in for a kiss. I jerk my face away. Her kiss lands on my shoulder. I know without looking she's left her mark on me—a smudge of red. Paul wouldn't let me throw out his T-shirt smudged and soaked in places with Jordan's blood.

Susie says, "My, Mrs Rutherford, don't you look nice today. The kitchen's this way. We could use some help setting the table."

The old biddy. I heard Mrs Rutherford and her crony loud and clear in the church this morning. The two of them, sitting prim and proper, knowing all the calls and responses just like they know their rosary beads—which is better than they know their own vaginas, I am sure. They think they're pious, but I swear it was blasphemy spewing out of their red-crayoned mouths. Following Jordan's tiny casket, the last thing I expected to hear was Mrs Rutherford saying, "Good Lord, what the devil is she doing wearing pants to her boy's funeral?"

Then Mrs Casey whispered, "For Christ's sake, you'd think she'd have more sense."

"If she had any sense, we wouldn't be sitting here."

Mrs Casey clucked, "At least her pants are black."

Now I'm not what you'd call a regular church-goer, but I know that the good Lord wouldn't have cared if I came naked. I thought about stripping out of my pants right then and there and throwing them in her face. I craned my neck higher as my response. My mother always said, "Silence is the hardest argument to refute." I had to pull on Paul's elbow a little to straighten him up. He didn't resist, but he didn't adjust his posture either. I was sure at any second he would melt into the carpet and all the people in the church would become flying monkeys, surrounding me like Dorothy in *The Wizard of Oz*, accusing me of Paul's death too. I must be the most sinister woman on earth. A water-bearing woman who would melt her husband into the carpet and kill her baby. I wish I could stretch my head up, up and through the roof of the church. *Nearer, My God, to Thee*. I wouldn't have to smell the incense and the bad perfume and everyone looking at me for a reaction, judging whether I was contrite over killing my son. For God's sake, what do they think? What kind of person—mother—do they think I am?

I'm dreaming. I see my brother and my father running towards me, arms stretched out, trying to catch me. I'm sailing through the air in a hammock, swinging recklessly, unfettered to tree or pole. The hammock flies above their heads. But I know they will save me. Their arms become like rubber, stretching forty feet in the air, grabbing at me. They catch my left hand, but the purchase they have found is my wedding band. It slips easily from my finger. I am left alone, helpless in the cocoon of my hammock.

I see their eyes as I fly over them. They're looking up through the glinting gold of the wedding band my brother holds above his head, like I'm some kind of circus dog who will obediently jump through the hoop. Both my father's and brother's eyes are filled with yellow neon light. Every time they blink, the neon light of their eyes waxes and wanes like a blinking caution traffic light. Their eyes flicker-light the way; I can see that I'm hurtling towards a head-on collision with some object. I'm coming up on the object at mach speed now. The object looming large, rising up like the way the ground rises up to meet a parachuter. The object, the object, I can't make it out. I want to see what it is that will kill me. The likelihood of being saved is small.

"Meg, are you ok?" It's Paul's voice reaching out to me in the darkness in a way he can't during the daylight.

I hold my breath. I'm scared if I speak, he'll remember that I'm our son's murderer and the gentle concern in his voice will go away.

He rubs my back. "Meg? I'm here."

I roll over, place my hand on the side of his face, tuck my head so he can't see my tears in the streetlight filtering through the curtain.

"You were crying and yelling 'Save me,'" he says.

"I'm ok." My voice goes into the upper register with a question like it does when I'm upset.

"Ok." He kisses the palm of my hand. After a few minutes of silence, he flips his back to me.

"I was dreaming. A nightmare." I want him to turn and face me again, but the words I have to offer aren't enough.

We lay like that for a moment, breathing in rhythm. The hand he has kissed is limp on the mattress between us. I can feel where he has brush-burned my palm with his lips. I push it against my lips. I hug him from behind. "Forgive me. Please forgive me. God, I don't think I'm going to make it."

He turns, draws me to his chest. "No, forgive me."

"You?"

"How many times did you ask me not to take him out front?" His voice has a huskiness to it, like he has an air bubble in his throat. "A million times you told me he could get HIT with the way cars speed through the neighborhood. A MILLION times."

"Not your fault."

Paul cries hard—loud, tenor cries. When Jordan was born, he cried happy, silent tears. He squeezes me so tight, I almost can't breathe. We fall asleep wrapped around each other, our marriage unraveling about us.

chapter two

Madeline and I have taken to sitting on the side lawn. We have tea parties, except neither of us cares much for tea. Actually, Madeline could turn into a tea drinker one day, but she's too young to have caffeine. I'm one of those mothers I used to hate when I was a kid. The kind that won't allow sodas, sweets or much TV in their house. We sit on the orange, black and red cotton Indian print blanket my father bought me that used to be my bedspread when I was a teenager trying to make a safe haven out of my tiny bedroom. Back when I would tuck myself into bed by staring at posters of Cat Stevens—before he turned to Islam and cut his hair. By day, I used to busy myself by watering, pruning and repotting the sixty-three plants in my room. After my father and brother died, my mother got rid of all our pets. Since my mother rebuked all my attempts at nurturing, I had to throw my energies into some other living thing.

I grew out of my twin bed, but I never could let go of that blanket. It's been with me twenty-seven years—it covered my college dorm bed and then served as my beach blanket. Twelve years ago, it was on this threadbare throw that Paul and I first made love. Except at that time, we were only fucking.

Stretched out on my blanket atop our immaculate St Augustine lawn full of pesticides, but never chiggers or weeds, Madeline drinks Mother's milk and I drink a glass of wine. On days when I don't think I can watch the second hand on the clock for one more tenth of a second, we take a little stroll up to the wine store. It's only five blocks away, which is one of the nice things about living in South Florida—everything's right in your backyard. We drink on the side lawn, the side away from Susie's house, so she can't see us, but we can keep an eye on her. We drink on the side lawn because the fresh air and sun will do us some good. We drink on the side lawn because I still won't allow alcohol in the house. I've got to keep my barriers in place. If I start relaxing on the rules I've set for myself and my family, well then all Hell's likely to break loose.

I threw all the liquor out that people brought for that formality following the funeral. Now I wish I had kept it. There's a world of difference between liquor and wine, though. Liquor is more pernicious. I haven't quite figured out the eating after a funeral ritual. Marriage ceremonies, going to school, to church, brushing our teeth before we go to bed—life's just one ritual after another. Seems a little senseless. Life, that is. Moving from one activity to another.

I've decided to quit my job, spend time with Madeline. Paul doesn't know yet. He thinks I've taken a leave of absence. Really, I know I could get my old job back if I wanted it. But I don't. It's like my mother always used to say, "No one on their deathbed ever said they wished they spent more time at work." Her theory might've been overcompensation for the fact that she couldn't hold a job. She had a hard time holding everything together after the accident—herself and me—much less a job. In the past, I put my job above everything else in my life. I take after my father as far as my work ethic is concerned.

Now I know the value of spending time with the people you love. I guess I've always known it, but I let other things get in the way. I'm sorry now for all the nights I was at work and wasn't home to tuck Jordan in. Sometimes we have to be reminded of the lessons we've forgotten. Some people, like me, have to be broken before they can commit to what really matters.

As I'm pouring my second glass of cab—Sterling Vineyards, moderately priced, because I think I'm worth it—but that's just hair dye commercial wisdom. Anyway, here I am pouring, ready to jump right into the glass with my lips and my liver and then I look at Madeline clinging to my left breast. I probably shouldn't be drinking. I mean, everything I put in my body goes straight to her. When you breastfeed, it's kinda like still being pregnant—you're eating for two. The upside no one talks about is that you can really fork down the food when you breastfeed. I eat twice as much as I did before I was pregnant. Even so, I've been able to get back down to my pre-pregnancy weight. I made it through two pregnancies with no stretch marks. But my boobs are a little worse for wear. You know what happens—how your nipples get big and your once firm fatty tissue deflates. I used to have full, perky boobs, but now after two kids, they're full and flat.

Even with my ruined boobs and all, I think I look pretty good. Not that Paul probably ever wants to look at my body again. We haven't made love since two nights before Jordan died. I monitor things like that—when was the last time, how many times this year did he tell me "No"? I'm always on the alert for sensing and deflecting small, daily hurts. I'm afraid one day they'll all add up into a big hurt that will rock my world. Vigilance will keep me from getting blindsided. If I'm prepared for the hurt, then I won't feel the impact as deeply.

I used to bet with myself on when I thought Paul and I would make love next. What I learned is, you can't ever bet on a cock. In the end, I lost so many bets, I quit. That's one good thing—no one in my family had a problem with gambling. You gotta be happy for the things you can be in this life.

So here I am salivating for my sip of wine when I spy my baby girl eyeballing me. She's so sweet when she's eating, the way she wraps her one arm around my back and push-pounds on my breast with her free hand; the way she looks up into my eyes. And then I know for the umpteenth time that I am nothing if not a bad mother. Drinking wine and breastfeeding. HRS is going to get after me if I keep this up. Why they haven't descended on our household after Jordan and all is beyond me. And what would I tell them? My husband and I were staring at our neighbor's jacked-up ass for very different reasons and lost sight of our son?

My friend Vicki's mother's told me when I was little that her doctor made her drink a beer a day when she was breastfeeding Vicki. Said it was supposed to help her milk come in. Sounds like an old wives' tale to me. Vicki's mom didn't even like beer, but she said she swigged it on down, drinking it over the kitchen sink and then washing her mouth out with warm water, praying all the while for her breast milk to come in. But it didn't and Vicki became just your run of the mill bottle-fed baby.

How Vicki's mom and I got on that subject when I was a nine-year-old girl is beyond me. But then again, how I get on the subjects I do with most people is beyond me. I think I have a digital display running across my forehead that attracts people and tells them to tell me their problems. And then there they go on their way, feeling unburdened and there I am feeling guilty for the rest of the day or week or sometimes longer, thinking I should have done something more than listen. Like the time one of the women at work told me about how she punished her son for calling one of his classmates "Two Changes." I didn't get it, so I asked her what it meant.

"Means he only has two changes of clothes to wear to school."

"Poor kid."

"What's worse is the two changes he has are too small for him. You know, he wears flood pants."

"Can't you give him some hand-me-downs?"

"No, he's bigger than my boy." She holds her empty hands out, like there's nothing she can do.

"What size does he wear?"

"Oh, I don't know."

"Would you find out?"

"It's not like I've got the money to go buying the kid clothes, Meg. He's got his own family. Let them help him out."

"I'll buy him clothes."

Even though I asked her several times, she never followed through with the information. Somehow, I think she resented my wanting to help. She was willing to punish her son for name calling, but wasn't willing to help beyond that. Think what a new wardrobe could have done for a kid like that. Sometimes it's the small, incidental things that change the course of a person's life.

I pour half the contents of the wine onto Paul's prize Don Juan rose bushes, but I save the last sip, drinking it straight from the bottle. He never took an interest in roses until Susie started planting them in her yard. I bury the wine bottle at the bottom of the recycle bin, even though I don't have to worry about Paul finding it. Since I haven't been working, dragging the recycle bin to the curb on Sunday nights is my job.

I'm too tired to push myself and the stroller back up to the store. I haven't driven since, since Jordan, but I think I better pack Madeline in the car, so we can get some formula. Maybe a switch to milk is in order. I don't want to do anything that may damage her physical development. Maybe I better call a cab. Better yet, I'll just tell Paul to pick up some formula on the way home from work.

"Hi, Annie, is Paul around?" I listen carefully to Annie's voice to see if she thinks I'm a bad person. She has a son of her own.

"Hi, Meg. Let me check, I think he's in a meeting. Oh, hold on, he just walked out of his office."

No, she's as professional as she's always been with me. I wait, listening to the same loop of elevator music his company plays for "on hold" background noise. Why have we become a society that always has to have some sort of stimulation—visual, auditory, tactile? Do we think that the world will explode if we all endured a minute of silence? I don't even know what silence sounds like anymore. Even in the middle of the night, there's no silence, what with the way I can hear my own heart pump-rushing away in my ears. If my heart would just stop, then maybe I'd get some rest.

The on hold music is replaced by Paul's voice. "Meg?"

"Hi. I was wondering…"

"I don't really have long to talk. Another meeting," he says.

"Ok. I was wondering if you would stop by the store and buy some formula for Madeline."

"Thought you were going to breastfeed for one year."

"I think, maybe, I should wean her off me. What difference does a month or two more make?"

"Now that you're home for a little while and you don't have to pump your breast at work in a closet, I'd think you'd want to breastfeed."

I twirl a lock of hair. "Yeah, but now I can't breastfeed anymore. If you'd just pick up some formula."

He doesn't ask why I can't breastfeed anymore, instead, he says, "Meg. I work all day. I've been doing the shopping, running to the dry cleaners. I know it's difficult, but you've got to start driving again. Besides, I wouldn't even know what kind to buy. Remember the time Jordan got constipated because of that bad formula I bought?" I hear him cover the phone with his hand and say, "Yes, I know. I'll be there in a few. Get started without me. Meg? You still there?"

"Hmm hmm."

"Sorry," he says. "I didn't mean to bring up Jordan. I don't want to put Madeline on formula until we have a chance to talk and make a family decision."

"Family?" Do two parents who can't look at each other, a dead son and a toddler who can't talk make a family?

"What's wrong with you? Are you ok?" he asks.

"I'm fine."

"Let's talk tonight. What're you making for supper?"

"I haven't thought that far ahead yet."

"How about some pork chops?"

"Would you like that?'

"It would be great. I'll try to leave no later than 6:00."

"Bye."

"Hey. Hug Madeline for me?"

"Will do." I slide the phone back on the hook. Maybe Paul's right. Maybe it is time to pull myself together, get behind the wheel. Madeline is busy pounding buttons on a toy CD player. She could be a mixer one day with the way she's hitting the buttons like she's scratching records. She's got her little lavender dress on with the yellow flowers. The one Jordan picked out. She's going to grow out of it soon. She's going to grow out of all the things that Jordan touched in her life. Her clothes and toys aren't like an Indian print bedspread she can drag around her whole life as a remembrance.

My dad helped me pick out the Indian print bedspread. Mom didn't want me to get it. Told Dad that he was encouraging me to be one of those hippies. Since I had only recently gotten to the place where I actually needed the bra I was wearing, I wasn't about to join the revolution and sacrifice my bras to the feminist bonfire. I told Mom as much, thinking I'd make her laugh like I usually could. But she told me I was fresh and told Dad for the second time to stop encouraging me and told my little brother Jake to wipe the smile off his face or she'd do it for him.

She stalked off, heading straight for the bar conveniently located inside the mall. Mom was always one to drink, but in the last month, she had gotten out of hand. Dad shrugged his shoulders then clap-rubbed his hands together and asked us if we were ready to tear the mall up with shopping. Since a thirteen-year-old needs nothing if not new clothes, I yelled, "Goody," like a damn four-year-old. I let Mom walk away. Normally, I would have followed her, trying to appease her and bring her back into a good mood, but nothing I tried lately would cheer her up. If only I hadn't been selfish and wanted new clothes, maybe things would have turned out differently. I can't count the number of times I rewrote the scene of watching Mom stride away to a scene where I run up to her and bring her back, the four of us shopping like a family in love.

Hours passed, Dad kept reaching for his wallet while Jake and I kept dawdle-shopping as a way of avoiding the unpleasantness of what had become Mom.

When Dad said we better go see after Mom and head home, I asked, "How come Mom's always so mad lately? Doesn't she like us anymore?"

Dad squeezed me sideways to him as we walked along, juggling our bags and said, "She's working through some things right now."

"That means she has to be so mean to us all the time?"

"Things will change, I promise."

When Mom saw us walking into the bar, she yelled, "Now you're bringing our kids into a bar?"

"Come on, Roz, let's go home."

Mom grab-swiped the bags out of Dad's and my hands, tearing through them. "Did you get that hippie blanket? You going to teach her your free love morality now too?"

Dad strong-armed Mom off her barstool towards the door. Jake started to cry.

I knelt down next to him and said, "It's ok. They're just pretend fighting. Ok?"

Jake nodded.

"Let's get rid of those tears then." I wiped his tears away with my thumb and rustled his hair. I picked the bags up from the ground, hoisted Jake onto my hip and scrambled after my parents.

A bouncer had my parents stopped at the door. I heard Dad saying, "It's ok, I'm her husband."

The bouncer stood to the side, holding the door open.

"He is not," yelled Mom.

"We're her kids," I said, ducking my head and rushing through the door out into the rain.

I hustled with Jake ahead to the car, but it was locked. Standing in the rain, bouncing Jake on my hip, I watched Dad and Mom do their strange dance across the parking lot—Mom sitting down deadweight and Dad dragging her. When Dad unlocked the car, Mom started stagger-jogging back across the parking lot. Dad gained on her and they struggle-danced back. Mom put up a real fight trying to stay out of the car. Dad practically did a fireman's carry to get her into it.

On the Interstate, Dad rolled the windows down in the station wagon to drown out the sound of Mom's harangue. The humid air suctioned my wet clothes onto my body. I climbed into the very back with Jake, covering us with my new blanket. If we could make ourselves invisible, maybe the words flying around the car wouldn't land in our ears.

"Baby girl, baby girl. Look at me," Mom pleaded. "Meg, dammit, I'm talking to you. I'm still your mother whether you like it or not."

I poked my head up from the back of the station wagon, "What?"

"Did your father tell you what he's doing with his dick?"

"That's enough," bellowed Dad. He backhanded her so hard her head hit the passenger window.

"Daddy, stop," I yelled.

"Cheating asshole, don't you dare hit me on top of everything else you've done." With that, she grabbed the steering wheel— my father slapping at her hands all the while. The car went into a spin. We were suspended in the space of slow motion, slippery-sliding spin. Round and round we went like an argument, all of us wondering where it would end. The faces of startled motorists came into view—a blue Mustang to the right, a white van to the left and coming up from behind, a black Thunderbird—all gone and miraculously missed.

Impact. Up and over a retaining wall, our car soared through the air. The bags we hadn't stowed under the wheel well were airborne and we were airborne with them. I tried to hold onto Jake, but he slipped from my hands. Someone screamed a scared, guttural animal scream. I thought it was Mom, but maybe it was me.

Impact Two: a metal-ripping, glass-shattering, bone-breaking, rib-ripping, lung-puncturing, skull-crushing impact. Our family of four fades to black.

"Ma, ma, ma, ma. Say it, Madeline. Go to the store with Mommy in the car?"

My new SUV is still on the left side of our circular driveway where Paul parked it after coming home from the dealership. Susie drove him. I know where the keys are because Susie points them out to me every time she comes over. Like she thinks it's no big deal for me to get behind the wheel again. I think maybe I'll pull the SUV back into the same spot when we get home, just to drive her crazy.

With Madeline in my arms, I circle the car like it's going to spring to life. Maybe I should just go back inside and call it a day. I open the driver's door, the new car smell wafts out. My stomach jumps. I can feel myself restrained in my seat, ignorant of the fact of my dying son under my bumper. I shut the door. Breathe. Circle the car again. I open the back door; think about putting Madeline in the seat. Take a deep breath and duck through the doorway. Madeline's little feet are kicking at my back and she's jabber talking. I know she's trying to say words that I can't wait to hear.

I can't do this…I'm not ready. I shut the car door, walk towards the house. At the sound of car wheels screeching, I hold Madeline's head as I run out into the street. Little Teddy down the road could be playing in the yard; I've got to slow that car down. I take one step out into the street; put my hand up like it's a stop sign some speeding motorist will obey. I jump back onto the grass, see the motorist reaching in the glovebox, probably for his cell phone. He never sees me. I futilely yell, "Slow down, asshole," to exhaust fumes as he careens around the corner.

I run back to my car, load Madeline in and do the three-point car seat check—check that the buckle's fastened, check to make sure the seat is secure to the right and the left. I count out loud, "One, two, three," as I check all points. The fourth point check is a kiss for Madeline. Today she giggles when I kiss her. It makes me kiss her again and again, breathing in her baby smell and her laughter.

I idle at the end of our driveway—let cars pass me by, until I see another car speeding in my direction. I ease onto the road. The driver brakes and beeps his horn. I put my hand out the window, making a "slow down" motion. Any time the driver attempts to pass, I edge over the double yellow line, signal with my hand again. The driver finally makes a right turn out of the neighborhood towards Federal Highway. I loop the neighborhood, once, twice, three times…I slow down at least eight cars along the way.

Everyone in life has a purpose, but most people squander their purpose or aren't blessed enough to recognize what it is. I'm more than just Paul's wife and Madeline's mother. I know now what my mission in life is. I can't save Jordan or Jake or my mother or father. But there are plenty of other people out there alive and waiting for someone like me, someone who can help. I just hope there's someone out there left to save me.

chapter three

"Where've you been? It's 8:00. My God, I thought something happened." Paul whisks Madeline out of my arms like I'm some kind of kidnapper caught on the run.

"Driving about in the car."

"I know that, your new car wasn't in the driveway."

"You told me I had to start driving again. Look, I stopped at the store and everything. I got us some pork chops."

"How was it driving? I should have offered to go with you the first time. Sorry. You scared me."

"Because I had Madeline in the car with me?"

"No, no, honey, nothing like that."

Paul's standing there swinging Madeline from side to side so fast, it reminds me of the way I was swinging in the hammock in the nightmare I had the other night. If he keeps up the velocity of his swing like this, I'm afraid he's going to detach her brainstem. That can happen, you know. Babies are fragile. But then again, what the hell in life isn't tenuously stitched together with gossamer threads?

"What then?" I ask.

"It's that you've been acting a little strange lately and I was afraid you might have…"

"I'm not sure how to act anymore."

"Sometimes, Meg, you just have to go on whether you want to or not. Things will fall into place again, you'll see."

"I can't power through things in life the same way you do. I can't just go back to work and pretend nothing's happened."

Paul's really rocking up a storm now with Madeline. I put my hands out. "Here, let me take her. You've had a long day."

"No, I want to spend time with her," he says, nuzzling her cheek, then raises her above his head. At least he's stopped with that incessant rocking. Madeline drools and it plunks straight down into Paul's open mouth. We both laugh, then look at each other, startled at the sound.

"You gonna swallow that?" I ask and Paul laughs again, opens his mouth to show me how Madeline's gob of spit is gone. "It's great to hear you laugh," I say.

Paul swings Madeline over to his left hip and sweeps me close to him with his right arm. We huddle together, the three of us, rocking from side to side. It's as soothing as a lullaby, but then I feel a big cry rising up, ready to burst out of my eyes and my lungs. I squeeze Paul and Madeline tighter, rhythmically rock. Madeline gets excited—laughs and kicks her feet. Paul and I clap our hands and yell, "Yeah Madeline," like we used to. She looks from Paul to me, back and forth, then she laughs and claps her hands together twice in her uncoordinated baby way. We both laugh and clap again. Paul brushes away the solitary tear running down my face and kisses my eye.

I fix dinner and Paul plays on the floor with Madeline. I burn the pork chops, even though I'm standing right over the stove. Paul plucks one of my straight, long blonde hairs out of his rice and eats a second serving of everything anyway. I wonder if second servings are enough to make up for infidelity. I wonder if Paul's infidelity is reality or just a story I tell myself to confirm my mother's teachings. Mom always said if given the choice between maintaining their marriage and dipping their wicks, as she put it, men would always dip their wicks. Men were like animals according to her. You couldn't trust them to make a sound decision once a new piece of muff arrived on the scene. Wick, muff—she was full of euphemisms where sex was concerned. But in the end, she became the new piece of muff into which man after man with other commitments would dip their wicks.

You should have heard her birds-and-the-bees talk. I really missed Dad after that one—he would have handled it so differently. He would have handled everything about my life differently. At least Mom never told me not to enjoy sex. I'd have had a hard time making that one fit into my life.

After dinner, Paul and I bathe Madeline together, then Paul gives her the bottle of breast milk I pumped this morning before I started in with the drinking. I go downstairs, click on the TV because I'm afraid to be alone with my feelings.

Paul stands in the doorway, wags Madeline's empty bottle back and forth. "I think I should have gone to work as an au pair instead of an engineer. I'd have been much happier."

I smile, pat the couch next to me.

Paul turns and goes into the kitchen. I take it as rejection and my stomach jumps. I wish I could shed my skin like a snake, slither into a new life. I don't know how to stand myself minute to minute. I'm not sure what life I'm supposed to live anymore. I think how lucky I am that Madeline can't talk. What if she told Paul that I circled our neighborhood from Sample Road up to Copans Road, not once, but fifty-eight times?

It seemed right that I should stop on the fifty-eighth go round. Fifty-eight is such a nice, voluptuous number. Statistically speaking—that's what I do, well used to do—analyze numbers, project the future as only actuaries and psychics can, so I know that statistically speaking I had an impact on the traffic pattern today. Sure, I bet I made some people late to wherever it was they were rushing off to, but I also bet that I stopped at least one accident. And there were more unattended kids playing in front yards with balls and skateboards and scooters than I would have guessed. If just one mother doesn't have to live through...

"I'm gonna head up to bed," says Paul, leaning in through the doorway in his coquettish way. I see his right leg swinging back and forth. I'm not sure if I should read anything into it, it could just be habit by now. When we first started dating, but hadn't slept together, I busted Paul one night as we were talking in my car at the beach. His leg was swinging back and forth, back and forth. I told him the old leg swing was actually a sub-conscious form of masturbation. His response was to swing his leg wildly, flutter-roll his eyes up in his head and yell, "Save me from myself." It was then that I led him from the car with my Indian print bedspread tucked under my arm to a spot on the beach just outside the range of streetlights, but close enough so I could get a good look at his tall, muscular body.

After that night, whenever Paul wanted to get laid, he'd make a point to get his leg swinging good and hard. I think it was his way of putting himself out there without risking rejection. Funny how after twelve years together—ten of them married—Paul doesn't know that I'm not the rejecting kind. At least not where sex is concerned.

"Ok, good night." Yep, his leg's still swinging. I'm scared at the prospect of making love with him. I have an odd push-pull feeling I've never felt before.

"Are you going to watch TV?" he asks.

"You want some company?" I start to get off the couch.

"Big day at work tomorrow."

I plunk back. "Oh."

Soon as he's out of sight, I know I'll let my eyes well up with tears. I turn back to the TV, swallow rapidly to keep all my feelings stuffed down so they don't spill out in front of Paul. He lingers in the door a moment, then recedes. His footfall on the stairs sounds like he's Atlas wrestling the world up to our bedroom.

❖

I'm dreaming that someone's suck-biting my nipple. I arch my back, pushing my breast further into his mouth, wishing I could fit my whole body in there so I could get tongue-caressed all over—wash my sins clean with sex. But I know I'd only wake up dirty again.

I feel the weight of a body on top of me, a hand fumbling with my underwear. My body's on autopilot, responding and moving. I open my eyes and see Paul. His eyes are closed and there's a pained look on his face. I reach and push my underwear to my knees, then ease them off with my feet.

He gently holds my ankles, spreads my legs open and slowly lets a gob—he calls it drool, because he says I'm so appealing to him, I make him drool, but I call it a gob—of spit spin from his mouth right onto my pussy like it's a bull's eye. The first time he did it, it shocked and turned me on in a way I can't explain. Then he rubs the head of his dick back and forth, entering me on the last stroke with a hardness that makes me gasp. Now he's pushing away in his irregular beat rhythm that I've come to love. I used to tell him that every other guy I knew screwed in three-quarter time, but that he added a little zest with his five-eighths time. I'm so wet, I love the feeling of us moving together—in and out in opposite directions.

I can tell I'm not going to be able to come, though. There's too much noise inside my head and I can't stay in my body. I turn my head to the side. I see Jordan sitting on the floor watching a *Sesame Street* video; he turns his curly blond head and smiles at me. We're bad parents, we shouldn't be enjoying the carnal act in front of him. Every orgasm, every laugh of pleasure is an affront to him and his short life. I have to pay for robbing that life. I'm not sure if misery is payment enough.

My eyes shut and open. Jordan's gone. I raise my legs up higher over my head and Paul pushes my ankles even farther back into the pretzel position he knows I like. Nope, it's not going to get it. I put my hand on his chest and make a movement to sit up. Paul knows what I want, sits back on the couch and guides me on top of him.

Now he's buried inside me and I'm rocking back and forth on top of him—it feels so good. He grabs my hips and quickens my movements, but I'm still not ready. I feel rushed, I feel rushed. I search around for a scene I can play in my head that will tip me over the edge. I sift through image after image like I'm sorting through a pack of cards—the one of two guys and a girl, the one of a woman masturbating in front of a man. I can't find an image to settle on. Paul's moving faster and faster and even though it feels great, it's too much stimulation too soon for me to come. I want to come so bad, I might scream out of frustration instead of passion.

"Come for me." Paul starts his low, guttural growl that signals he's on the edge.

I say, "Wait, wait, wait," and try to slow down our movements, but his fingers dig into my hips and he rotates me back and forth, up and down hard, harder. As he comes, I look down on him, search his face for a hint of love. But he shields himself from me by keeping his eyes closed and turning his head to the side. I sit on top of him, watching him, waiting for him to open his eyes, tell me that he loves me. He sighs with his eyes closed and pats my ass twice as a signal that he wants me off him. I dive to the left, coiling myself up into a fetal position.

He rubs my thigh, cuts his eyes over to me and says, "Sorry, I couldn't wait."

"Next time," I say in a reedy voice, closing my eyes.

I've been lucky. Most of the women I know say they can count the number of times they've come with their husbands or boyfriends. I can only count the number of times I haven't come with my husband. But I'm afraid tonight may be a sign of a new trend. I don't want to become one of those women who fakes an orgasm every time they sleep with their husband—there's no sense in going through the motions if there isn't an orgasm waiting on the other side.

I wake up on the couch with a stiff neck. There's a blanket over me and a glass of orange juice sitting in a ring of glass-sweat on the wood coffee table. Paul never remembers to use a coaster. He's ruined every wood table we have in the house. But still, he did think of me by getting the juice.

Madeline is crying upstairs. I slide my hand between my legs, feel my wetness, rub myself. Paul must be in the shower. Spreading my legs farther apart, I rub harder. I know I can come inside five minutes. My breasts are full of milk and start leaking at the sound of Madeline crying. I look over at the grandfather clock. Shit, it's almost ten o'clock. How did I sleep so late? I didn't even hear Paul leave for work. How long has Madeline been crying? I throw the blanket off and run upstairs.

Madeline's standing in her crib, white-knuckling the rail. Her eyes are swollen, she's gotten herself so worked up with crying. I hope she doesn't get a diaper-rash. It's amazing how fast urine and shit can break down delicate baby skin. I've prided myself on the fact that she's never had diaper rash in her life—I'm fanatical about not letting her sit in soiled diapers. I change, nuzzle and coo to her. I'd sit on the floor and play for a spell, but I know it's already an hour and a half past her breakfast. I hope this isn't one of those early childhood memories that she'll hold up to her therapist as evidence that I'm a bad mother. I breastfeed her. I'll start with the formula tomorrow. Then I warm up her favorite cereal to make up for my lapse in mothering.

Now that she's fed and calmed down, I decide to get her bathed and dressed for a new outing. Most mothers take their kids to Gymboree or one of those other mothers' groups. I never could stand the herd mentality of those types of groups. That's what I call an illegal assembly. Besides, I always gravitated more towards men as friends. Since I got married, though, I let all my friendships slip away. Paul filled me up at first, then Jordan and Madeline came along. Motherhood and work was all I had the time and the emotional energy for.

I dress Madeline in the lavender and yellow dress—the one Jordan picked out—for the fourth day in a row. I call it her little uniform of the day. I don't worry about that, though, I wash it by hand every night when I change her for dinner. I like her to be nice and fresh for Daddy when he gets home from work. She'll grow out of it before I ruin it with over-use.

I wheel around on Susie as I turn from loading Madeline in the car. Susie's on her front porch a whole yard away from me, but I feel like she's three inches away from my face. There's a man I've never seen on the porch with her. He's handsome, with a tall, trim figure and curly black hair. He looks a lot like Paul. I take the confirmation of Susie and I having the same taste in men as another sign. I wonder what Paul will say when I tell him his girlfriend is cheating on him. She ushers him into her house with a flourish and then her big hand is up and waving at me right under my nose. It's like her hand is a missile in a three-D movie, hurtling out of the screen straight for me, trying to make contact, about to destroy me. But the power in our relationship has shifted and now it's me who ignores her.

I shake her off. I have better things to obsess about than her and what acts she might have committed with my husband. I circle the neighborhood five times before heading over to the old Lighthouse Beach High School. The guy's car is still in Susie's driveway. When I make my final turn onto Federal Highway, I am pleased to count a line of ten cars behind me.

I went to LBHS my freshman year, before my mother

thought it best to beg for an academic scholarship for me to go to Cardinal Horn High School during one of her more lucid periods. She said she saw a bit of the wild hair in me and meant to break me before I got too far out of control. As if stepping into a Catholic girl's uniform each day would somehow transform me. I was happy the classes were more challenging, but the academic benefits were overshadowed by the fact that we were poor and everyone at that school was rich. At LBHS, most of the kids did the brown bag lunch routine. At Cardinal, kids spent five bucks on a hot lunch like it meant nothing. I had to scrounge for change every day to buy a packet of thirty-five cent peanut butter crackers to tide me over until I could get home to peanut butter and butter toast. It was bad enough when word got out that I was there on a handout scholarship. My pride kept me hungry because I wouldn't be caught as the only kid bringing their own sandwich.

My mom would see kids smoking at the corner 7–11 and go into a full-tilt diatribe about how if she ever, ever caught me smoking, I'd rue the day I was born. But I did rue the day I was born, what with her daily torture every time I came home to empty gin bottles, piss and vomit on her mattress and had to change her. What was worse was when I came home and found her in bed with a strange man.

In time, I became jaded. It got so I felt powerful as I'd stare at man after man, ducking his head, avoiding my eyes as he dashed for the door. Sometimes I'd count the amount of time I thought it would take for the man to jockey into his pants and shirt, then I'd go to the front door and hold it open, slam it after they ran through it. You can only control certain things in life; if my lot in life was to be the master of the door, then so be it.

As I'd clean up mess after mess, cook something for dinner I thought she might eat, she'd lie in her bed and rant. We had a tiny apartment, so I could hear her loud and clear in the kitchen.

She'd go on about how I should think of myself as having a rope around my neck and that she was holding fast onto the other end. She said that if I were good and she could see I could handle it, she'd give me more rope—a little at a time. On the other hand, if I were bad, she'd snap the rope back. She told me not to hang myself with foolish actions. Every time she said that, I wanted to scream that if she were my role model, I'd be swinging off her gallows in no time. I mean, I didn't think there could be a more foolish act than killing your husband and son, even if it was an accident. But I never said it; some words just aren't meant to be spoken. I took her tirades in silence. Sometimes she'd taunt me and say, "Don't you have something sassy to say to that, missy?" But if I kept silent, she'd finally say, "Good for you. Silence is the hardest argument to refute. Don't forget that."

I didn't understand at the time that she wasn't torturing me on purpose. We just didn't know how to relate to each other after everything happened. I think maybe her badgering threats were actually a misguided, protective gesture of sorts. I make a mental note not to treat Madeline like that. Now that I'm living my mother's life, I wish she were still alive. I'd have someone who would understand how it feels to kill your own, then decay inside your own flesh.

I'd be able to comfort her now. Tell her how sad I was for her ruined life. Tell her I wished I hadn't walked away from her in the mall that day. It's selfish, but I sometimes think about how if I had saved her from sitting in the bar and drinking that day that it would have been me I would have been saving as well. Instead, I watched my mother drink herself to death.

My old high school hasn't changed much—except for the fact that it's now used as an adult education facility, mostly to teach foreigners the English language. I read in one of those local papers about a support group for parents who lost their children and decided to go.

In church, they used to say that God brings people to their knees to learn lessons they're resistant to. I'm not sure what I'm being resistant to or how much further I can prostrate myself. If God's trying to give me the message that the world is one shitty place, I can assure Him I learned that message early on. Except for the time I've spent with Paul. He turned my shitty life into something beautiful. On Oprah one day—during one of those book club discussions that she used to have—they talked about identifying the person in your life who gave you wings. Paul gave me my wings and the courage to be the person I am. Only, now that I'm a baby murderer, I wish I were someone different.

All these years, I thought of Paul as my protector against the world—I looked at him as the person who made the world different, tolerable—no, enjoyable. But I guess God didn't want anyone—most of all, me—to think that Meg O'Hara was allowed a long-term respite. Twelve years of happiness is all I get. Probably more than most people. I shouldn't be so greedy. I need to go back to taking what I get in life without expecting to be happy.

I find the room and take a school desk chair out of the circle that's formed, so I can fit Madeline's stroller next to me. I rummage through her diaper bag—which doubles as my purse— and take out a tissue in case I cry and a book for Madeline. I let her crumple, gum and tear pages in her books. I want her to get the feel for books and have a pleasant association. If I reprimand her for ruining books when all her world consists of at eleven months is the tactile, then she'll grow up to think of them as something to be avoided. So she eats a few pages of her books, I'll get her more when she's ready to devour them with her eyes instead. Sir Francis Bacon said, "Some books are to be tasted. Others to be swallowed and some few to be chewed and digested." I like that quote. Madeline and I have decided to take it quite literally.

People are filing into the room in a ghost-like way, as if they don't exist—or don't want to. I wonder if I look like that: a woman chasing down her shadow, trying to make it disappear. I hope not. I want to be a strong role model for my daughter. I'm ready with a smile for each person because I'm generally a friendly person in spite of my reclusive nature. Each person avoids my eyes. How are we going to share intimate feelings with one another if we can't even look each other dead in the eye? I shouldn't use that word—dead. Dead in the eye; Dead eye Dick; Dead heat; Dead tired. People should be more careful about the language they throw around.

I feel a claw-hand on my shoulder and swivel in my seat. A woman with long, limp brownish-gray hair is at my side. She has a pockmarked, pasty complexion as if she's ill. She smiles curtly, hooks her finger in a come with me gesture. I'm not sure what she wants. Maybe you have to become a member and pay dues or something. I stand, take a step towards her. She walks out the classroom door. I'm not going to leave Madeline, so I take another two steps and halt—standing halfway between Madeline and the door. When the woman realizes that I'm not going to move any further, she shakes her head from side to side in an exasperated way and stalks back up to me.

"Please retrieve your baby and your belongings and follow me."

I obey. It's nice to be told what to do, even if it's at the expense of making a stranger mad. I lean over, stowing the diaper bag back under the stroller. Straightening up, I smile at a woman across the room who briefly looks at me with nervous eyes that remind me of a hummingbird at a feeder. I back Madeline out of the classroom.

In the hall, the limp-haired woman says in a hushed yell, "What were you thinking?"

"Pardon?"

"The baby. You brought a baby."

"Yes, she's mine. I lost my son." My voice catches at the word son. It's the first time I've actually said the words out loud.

"Babies can't come to meetings for parents who've lost children."

"Why?"

"Because they can't. Why don't you go away and think about it and come back when you've got more sense?"

"You call this a support group? Fuck you." I turn and scream into the open classroom and Madeline starts scream-wailing in unison with me, "Fuck all of you."

Madeline and I careen down the hall. At each open classroom door after door, I see accusing faces turn, calling after me, "Can you believe she brought a baby?" I'm validated for the billionth time that it's my cross to bear in this life—I never quite fit in. I've always been a few beats off mainstream. Paul is the only person since my father and brother died who ever made me feel like I belonged to something bigger than just myself.

I kick the outside door open and back Madeline out. A drink would be really nice. Shit, I hate that I'm becoming my mother. I don't want my mother's life, I don't want my mother's life. I don't, I really don't. I have to pull out before the bottom of the bottle calls me for good. Mom used to call me a quitter. She'd say I didn't have the sense to finish anything I started. She'd say I had to learn to muscle through and there was nothing special about me warranting an exemption on doing things I didn't want to. Just this once where alcohol is concerned, I hope she's right. I hope I am a quitter.

I'm too mad to get in the car and drive. It figures when I finally reach out for help that this is the kind of reception I get. God, I'm so full of self-pity, I can't stand myself. No wonder they didn't want me as part of their group, it must be oozing off me. I stride up and down the sidewalk, weaving between buildings.

I stop, wipe tears from Madeline's face and kiss her cheek. I tap the end of her nose and say, "Nose." Madeline goes from crying to laughing just like that. It's a curiosity to me, the way she thinks some words are funny and how she's always so willing to laugh. After I lap the high school grounds, I open the door to a different building, roam the hallway. A woman spots me as she's shutting a classroom door, pauses. As I draw near, she asks, "Are you here for the support group?"

"Which one?"

"She's a cutie," she says, looking at Madeline, then brushes the back of her hand against her cheek. "Children with cancer."

"Yes," I say, hoping my lie doesn't make something shift in the universe in a bad way. I roll Madeline into a room full of women and men seated in a circle on the floor—cuddling and rocking children of all ages and lengths of hair—from bald to patchy to full.

Everyone smiles up at me with love in their eyes. Madeline and I take our place.

chapter four

Paul and I have settled into a tolerable rhythm. I wake him in the morning with an English muffin and orange juice and he asks me when I'm going back to work. We can afford it. That's what I tell him. And we can. I made sure we got on an aggressive savings plan early on. At night, we can actually sit across the table and look one another in the eye without flinching. It's been four months. Maybe time and distance will keep us together.

The support group helps. I had to bone up on cancer. I went on the Internet and did my research. I had to find out what the treatment plan would be for a baby with lymphocytic leukemia. I'm bent towards taking a holistic approach to illness, so I researched what health foods and vitamins would be necessary. It's bad, because I get so pulled into the story I'm telling about Madeline, sometimes I get depressed knowing she could die, although I picked a cancer that has a seventy percent survival rate. Lymphocytic lymphoma used to be almost always fatal. At the health food store one day, I almost dropped $500 on supplements after picking the brain of the vitamin specialist for information. There I was with my cart half full of vitamin bottles and macrobiotic food. I ended up ditching the cart down one of the aisles and scooting out of the store with Maddie in my arms like I was a shoplifter. I felt bad after, wondering what the sales person must have thought when they had to restock the shelf with the contents of my cart. I don't go into that store anymore.

The information proves helpful, though. I go back to the support group, tell them about my trip to the health food store and how now that Maddie is eating solid food, I'm going to purée green, leafy vegetables and make all her baby food from scratch. Several people in the group duck their heads at that, like I had said something inappropriate in mixed company.

The group leader, Marci, says, "How do you feel, about Madeline having cancer?" She pauses and enunciates the word "cancer." It sounds to my ears like she said it into an echo machine.

Now I've had plenty of boyfriends along the way that majored in lying, which means I've had ample opportunity to pick up on some technique. But, I'm not a good liar.

She leans forward, repeating, "Meg, how do you feel about your baby having cancer?"

I scrabble-search my brain, drumming up word combinations that will make for a safe, honest topic. "My friend Kay died of cancer," I say. "It was bad."

Marci nods encouragement.

"By the time they found it, it had gotten into her lymph nodes. Her whole body swelled up in direct proportion to her hope receding. I…" I grit my teeth and flex my jaw so I won't cry.

Marci kneels at my feet, takes my hand that isn't wrapped around Madeline sleeping on my chest. "Meg, I want you to say how you feel about Maddie having cancer. It's okay to cry. Just tell us how you feel."

"Not very fucking good. Not good at all."

I wheeze back a sob and almost shout, "Madeline doesn't have cancer." But I'm afraid they will kick me out. Being with people who have as much pain as me is a comfort. I can't be all alone again. Sometimes lies are better than the truth.

Instead, I wave the question away. "Please, someone else…"

Marci squeezes my hand and bows her head like she's saying

a prayer. I squeeze her hand back, close my eyes, letting a solitary tear slither down my cheek.

After what seems like five minutes of heart-pounding silence, I hear Marci's knees crack as she rises back up. She kisses Maddie on the top of her head, brushes her sleep-sweaty baby hair to the side.

I hear Jackson start to talk. His twelve-year-old son has a neuroblastoma. During the son's third year on the way to the critical five-year mark for remission, he relapsed. Now, he's in the hospital. Marci leads a prayer for him, talking about love and healing and God's will.

The group breaks up soon after. I'm halfway through the door when Marci calls my name out. Pretending I don't hear, I take two more steps.

"Meg, Meg, just a moment of your time."

"I should get home and start dinner." Oh God, I hate how that sounds like I'm some wheedling housewife. I used to be a woman with a high-powered job. I don't know who I am anymore.

"That's what I want to talk about."

"Dinner?" How can I invite her to dinner? She'll kneel down and ask Paul how he feels about Madeline having cancer and I'll be Baker Acted or something.

"No," she laughs. "Your husband. It's Paul, right?"

"Yes."

"Why doesn't he come with you?"

"He works."

"His lunch hour?"

"He's busy. Barely takes a lunch. I don't want to…"

"Burden him?"

"Oh, he's burdened all right."

"I understand. Just think about it."

"Okay. Thanks."

"Meg. You did good today."

"Thanks." I turn, briskly walking away before I have to answer any more questions with lies.

Maddie and I go back home. I pace the floor while she finishes her nap. I gotta get out of the house, but I don't know where to go. Maybe an open-air bar where the smoke won't bother Madeline. Plenty of them in South Florida. Most of them are restaurant-bars, so it won't look like I'm a bad mother to have a baby with me.

I load Maddie in the car. She has her lilac dress on again. I think it's her favorite too. This morning, I heard a seam break loose when I pulled her chunky arm through the sleeve. I'm not ready to let it go yet. When she grows out of it, I'll keep it in a far corner of her drawer. I still have a skirt set that was Kay's favorite outfit before she died of cancer. It's a cool pattern—pink and black oriental splashes on thin white cotton. I can't throw it out, but I don't wear it anymore. I've thought about cutting the fabric up for an art project that could hang on my wall and I'd be able to turn something of Kay's into something beautiful. But I have a problem with finishing things I've started. On days when I'm feeling bad, I hold the blouse in my hands, picturing Kay laughing and eating fresh artichokes—dipping the leaves in garlic butter and lemon, scraping them clean with her teeth; the way the doctors tried to scrape first her skin clean of cancer, then her lymph nodes and later…Kay always said artichokes were the most social food going.

I drive towards the Cove Restaurant, because it's close to home. When I get there, though, I don't feel like going in. I U-turn my car, heading off towards the airport. A bar with people coming and going appeals to me. I put the car in short-term parking. Paul said he was working late tonight, but still, I've got to go home sometime. Well, maybe.

I hand my car and house keys over into a red plastic basket, start to push Madeline through the metal detector machine.

The security guard starts waving me back, the machine beeps at the metal on the stroller. "Back, lady. You can't come through here with that."

He's so expansive with his get-back gesture, that I quickly back up all over the feet of the person behind me.

"Dammit. That's my foot you're standing on."

I look down at his black, Italian leather loafers, see remnants of powder on his upper instep. "Sorry." I shrink my shoulders in, making myself small, trying for invisibility. People brush past me. I unclip Maddie, pick her up. The security guard has stalked me around his booth. He's yelling at me still, but he's lapsed into Spanish and I can't understand. I make a mental note to listen to the conversational Spanish tapes in my car.

Maddie points to a picture on the wall, says, "Boat."

"Good, good girl!"

"G-good girl," she parrots back.

The guard is still yapping at me. When I don't respond, he switches back to English. "Put the baby back. Put the baby back. We'll wheel her around. You go through the machine by yourself." He gestures wildly at the stroller.

I puff up to my full five-foot-five height. "No. I don't hand my baby over to strangers."

"Lady, just put the baby in the stroller."

"No."

"Lady."

"Then get your boss. My baby stays with me." How do I know that he doesn't have some cousin waiting to whisk my baby off, covering her hair with a hat, changing her clothes and shoes within minutes? I had a friend who lost their kid at a fourth of July party once. He went crazy, running all over the beach in the dark, standing at the water's edge. Every time the fireworks lit up, booming behind him, he'd frantically search the crowd for the ten seconds the light afforded him. Then he'd move down the beach, stance like a football player at the line of scrimmage, waiting for the next burst of light. Waiting for his son's face to light up in the darkness amongst the panorama of strangers' faces.

In the end, I walk Maddie through the metal detector machine, while the airport security guy wheels her stroller around and goes over it with a wand. We're dubbed bomb and firearm free. If only the security guy understood what kind of bomb was lying in wait in my heart, ready to explode.

The better bars in airports are down by the gates—more people, more alcohol getting slammed back, courage flying around the room waiting to land on someone. I wheel Maddie right up to the bar. Take a barstool out, place it against the wall, ask a passing waitress for a highchair. Since I've started drinking, I've become a sit up to the bar and have a drink with strangers kind of person like my mother. It's not that I talk to anyone, it's just that I don't want to sit at a table by myself. I'm lonely most of the time. Drinking at home alone is one thing, but drinking alone in public, sitting at a table all by yourself is another thing. I don't want people's pity.

I come in on a conversation between a waitress and a couple. The man is describing how he's so sunburned and parched because he was trimming his elderly mother's trees. I think he's just going for a sympathy drink, but I tune in anyway.

The waitress is saying, "That's good, get off the couch and do something for once. Cut a tree down, mow the yard."

"You've got the wrong man there. I always help out."

"Ah, it's my man I'm talking about." She tips the man's empty beer bottle at his wife. She walks away and serves another customer. Pit stopping, she deposits two steak knives and a replacement beer in front of the couple.

The man says, "Don't give her anything sharp," referring to his wife, who has sat silently through his story looking at her hands.

The woman sharply laughs.

The waitress says, "That means you have to be nicer to her at home."

"That's right, sweetie," the woman says.

All laugh, but the man grits his jaw, rearranges his place setting.

I try to catch the waitress's eye, tell her not to kid with this couple that way. I wonder if later the couple will get into a verbal—or worse, physical—fight. I guess the waitress is trying to do her version of marriage counseling. And who knows, maybe she does have an impact on the world in her own way— besides through serving up momentary alcohol happiness.

It seems like no one is happy with who they're with. I used to be ecstatically happy with Paul. I used to feel blessed, wonder how I got to be so lucky to have the eye and attention of a man like him. But that was before I thought he was cheating.

I take out a wet nap and wipe the wooden highchair down. With a second wipe, I swab the bar. I order milk and spaghetti for Maddie, a glass of Merlot for me. Spaghetti is her favorite food. Just like me, she likes it extra saucy. She shovels forkfuls into her mouth. A third each lands in her mouth, on the bar and on the floor.

I can feel someone staring at me. I turn. A man with black curly hair and big brown eyes smiles at me. I always was a sucker for the Italian look. Automatically, I smile back.

A few minutes later, he pulls the barstool out next to me. He leans towards me. "Cute baby you have there."

"Thanks." I twirl my wedding band around so he can see the diamond and know I'm married.

"Where you off to?" he asks.

Maddie starts to brush spaghetti bits around the bar in front of her. "One more bite, love bug. Nowhere special. You?"

"Colorado."

"Girlfriend?"

"Skiing. Do you ski?"

"In my past life." I gesture towards Maddie. "Are you good?"

"Of course. I'm good at everything." He winks.

"Yeah, well, I'm married."

"Oh, hey, no. I just meant I'm an over-achiever."

"Of course."

He buys me a second glass of wine to show there's no hard feelings. I let him, promising myself I'll only have a sip to be cordial. I can't drink too much. Not when I'm Maddie's designated driver. The waitress raises her eyebrows at me and gives a thumbs-up when he's not looking.

"What kind of work do you do?" he asks.

"I used to be an actuary."

"Actuary. I don't think I've ever met one of those."

"We only come out at night when everyone's asleep, like vampires."

He bears his neck to me and I have to fight back the impulse to bite it. Instead, I say, "Very appealing. Does that mean you're a professional corpse?"

"No, just a humble business owner."

He starts to tell me about his business, but Madeline says, "Poo-poo, Mommy."

I do my index-finger foray into her diaper. I'm a mother with a serious handicap, what with my sinus trouble. "Sorry. I have to change her."

"Listen, I have to catch my flight."

He flips his card at me like a magician. Like it had been living in his palm the entire time. "Call me sometime," he says.

Pausing from unsnapping Maddie out of the highchair, I take his proffered card, quickly glancing at it. "Nice meeting you, Al."

"The pleasure's mine," he gestures with his head like I'm supposed to fill in the blank.

"Emily." My first lie of our relationship.

He places his hand on my shoulder. "Emily, call me, please."

"When do you get back?"

"Saturday after next. I land at 6:45."

"What a coincidence. I'll be here around that time too."

"Great. See you here then? Same barstools?"

"Maybe." I pick Maddie up. "Have a safe flight." I turn on my way to the bathroom. He's standing, pulling his wallet out of his back pocket. I haven't seen that nice of an ass since I first met Paul. Oh shit. Paul. I look at my watch. It's 8:20 already.

I hustle into the bathroom, quickly change Maddie, with her saying, "No way," the whole time.

"Yes way, goozie girl."

"No way."

"We have to change you. Then we're going home and see Daddy."

"Dada."

"That's right. Daddy is waiting for us." I step back up to the bar. My glass of wine is inviting me to take a drink. I pick the glass up, then set it back down again. I can't go home smelling like alcohol. I should pack a spare toothbrush in the diaper bag for times like this. I ask the waitress for the check and a shot of peppermint Schnapps to hide the smell of wine.

"That'll just be four bucks. Al paid for everything else." She laughs. "He's a cute one."

"Yes he is. I mean…"

"Just cause you're married doesn't mean you can't have a little fun." I look at her plain gold band.

"No. I can't. I mean, I'm not a cheater. I've never cheated."

"Sure hope your husband says the same thing." She shakes her head, moves off to a new couple at the corner of the bar.

I lay a ten down on the bar, put Maddie in her stroller and gather our belongings. Out at the car, I can't find my keys. It's 8:35. Shit, shit. Paul is going to be frantic. I don't want to call him until we're on our way home. I take every last diaper, tissue and bauble out of Madeline's Zoe from *Sesame Street* backpack that doubles as my purse and her diaper bag.

I jiggle the stroller back and forth. Madeline is getting restless. Where the hell are my keys? I picture them in the red basket at the X-ray machine. I was so flustered by the guard, I must have forgotten them.

I throw everything into the backpack, career the stroller back across to the airport. Breathless, I ask the new security guard if she's seen a pair of keys in the basket.

She shifts her three hundred pound bulk around her creaking stool, sucks her teeth. "I came on at 8:00, honey. No keys here. Check lost and found." She gestures towards the escalator. "Downstairs to your right."

We skid onto the escalator, in spite of the sign forbidding strollers and pushcarts. Madeline leans sideways out of her stroller at the stairs as they recede. "No, no, baby. That will hurt." I lean forward, putting Madeline's hand back inside her stroller. She flaps both hands and lets loose with a scream that makes people on both sets of escalators turn in our direction.

My heart is pounding. What if I can't find my keys? What if I have to call Paul for my spare? What will I tell him I was doing at the airport?

When I get to the lost and found counter, no one is there. It's now 8:53. I am in so much trouble. I don't want to call Paul with the background announcements of what flight is leaving. I pace back and forth. Go over to the rent-a-car counter, futilely ask if they know where the lost and found person is. I start back over. A woman is locking the door to the small glass office. I run. "Wait. Wait."

"We're closed now. You'll have to come back tomorrow."

"No. I've been here. You weren't here. My keys."

She looks at me.

Madeline says, "Hi."

I say, "Madeline, ask the nice woman if she has our keys."

The woman, purse-lipped, looks at me.

"Please."

"Oh, all right. What do they look like?"

"Thank you so much. They're on a key chain with a big plastic yellow Lego. Her daddy's an engineer. He thinks if he gets her started early...do you have them?"

She finishes unlocking the door. "Yes. They just came in tonight. Did you miss your flight?"

"No. We decided to sit this trip out." I tip the woman five bucks, even though she protests.

Once we hit I-95, I dial our home number. No answer. Maybe he got tired of waiting for me and went to get some fast food. I leave a cheery message on the machine, accelerate, bob and weave through traffic.

I pull into the driveway at 9:30. Our house is dark. I look over at Susie's house, hoping her garage door is open and her car stowed inside. The garage door is shut, the outside light on, her house dark.

chapter five

Just as I'm about to pop the cork on a Latour Puligny Montrachet I had hidden out in the bowels of the garage refrigerator, there's a knock on the door. I've made a concession—I stick with wine instead of liquor. You can't really be an alcoholic if you just drink wine. Look at the Europeans, they drink it every day and no one calls them alcoholics.

Opening the door, I say, "Susie." She comes forward as if to enter. I block the door with my arm. She steps back. The bottle of Montrachet is sitting on the kitchen counter. The absolute last thing I need is Susie telling Paul I've gone to drinking during the day.

"Hi. I thought you might like some company. I brought you these." She shoves a fist full of beautiful angel face roses at me. Some are fully open, others with buds barely unfurling. She has three baby palm fronds stuck in the bouquet, giving the arrangement width to counterbalance the roses' height. They are so beautiful, I want to reach for them, but then I think Paul will ask where I got them. Maybe it's Susie's way of sending him a message—angel face roses for her angel.

"I'm kinda in the middle of something."

"Oh." Her rose hand hangs in the air.

I smile at her, she smiles at me. No one moves. One minute, two minutes, three minutes...I'm impressed by her ability to hold her ground and it makes me cock my head to the side and smile wider. She smiles at me in a way that makes me uncomfortable. I feel like she may just slap a big sloppy kiss on me.

Madeline screams. She's on her blanket. I'm afraid she's hurt herself. In my head, I can see her holding onto the narrow table, pulling herself up and knocking over my bronze nude lovers statue on top of her head. Whenever I hear her cry in earnest, I always picture her with a head trauma. But I know if she did hurt her head…Jordan didn't make a sound. My brother Jake's head was crushed so badly, we couldn't have an open casket. The snapshots in my mind won't go away. A family photo album straight out of a horror film.

Maddie's scream goes up another half octave.

I bolt from the door, passing the wine bottle on my way into the family room. Even with fear in my heart, the wine's delicate, buttery song is calling out to me.

Madeline's pitch rises higher in volume when she sees me, but it's only to scold me for walking out of the room on her. She's been going through a separation anxiety phase. I can't leave the room without her having a down and out scream fest.

"Hey, baby girl, getting yourself all worked up. Mommy's here. I won't leave you. I won't leave you." I bend down and swoop her up in the air, swinging her from side to side. "Weee." We spin round and round the room. The more Madeline laughs, the faster I go. On our last pass, I catch Susie leaning against the family room doorway in my periphery. We halt abruptly. A giggle gets caught in Madeline's throat.

"You love her."

"Of course." I look past her. The bottle is in full view, cooling sweatbeads pooling on the counter. I shift Maddie over to my left hip. "What is it you wanted?"

"Just a friendly visit."

I swallow a sarcastic laugh.

"No really," she says.

"Not my friend."

"What?"

"You're not my friend."

"I could be."

"Look. Before Jordan got hit…before I hit Jordan…" The support group says you have to own your actions by verbalizing them. Verbalization is the first step to healing, they say. At the last support group, they ganged up on me to divest me of what they called, "My cancerous case of denial." They said my denial was spreading, clouding my judgment and that it was time I faced facts. Then they made me say out loud, "My baby has cancer."

I begin again, "Before I hit Jordan, you wouldn't even look at me so much as say hello. What makes you so interested now?"

"I feel bad."

I look at her standing there holding her roses in front of her like a hopeful bridesmaid. "Why?"

"Because I couldn't save him."

"I'm his mother. I was supposed to keep him safe."

"But I was there. I should have done something more, something different."

"So you think you're Jesus Christ or something, is that it? Pretty big ego you got going there. You think you can save the world? He wasn't ours to save. No one can save anyone. You just have to worry about saving yourself."

Her eyes well up, she doesn't say anything. Her wrist has wilted, the roses are pointing groundwards. Then she turns and walks into my kitchen, right past the wine bottle and starts opening cabinets.

"Get out of my cabinets." I run into the kitchen. I consider grabbing the wine bottle and hiding it behind my back.

Maddie says, "Get."

She fills an ice tea glass full of water, plunks the roses in, then starts foraging through my cabinets again. She reaches for two wine glasses from the top shelf of the skinny cabinet next to the fridge. "Where's the cork puller?"

I stand frozen in the middle of the kitchen. I'm in a world of shit now—her alliance is with Paul, and not me.

"Come on," she coaxes. "You won't share your wine with me?"

She turns, starts rummaging through my drawers. "Do you guys open wine with your teeth around here? Where's the cork puller?"

"In my backpack."

"Your backpack?"

"Well, Madeline's diaper bag—we share…anyway, I was thinking about surprising Paul with a picnic tonight."

"How lovely. Do you do that often? How long is it that you've been married now?"

"Ten years. Been together for twelve." She acts like she doesn't know about my non-alcohol rule. Paul must drink with her when they're out. I've never smelled alcohol on him, but then again, he knows I can't smell.

"The corkscrew?" Susie asks, raising the bottle in the air.

"I'll get it." I put Maddie back on my threadbare Indian print bedspread, turn on her activity center and push one of the buttons. An oinking pig sounds off, Maddie claps.

"What sound does a cow make?" I yell to Maddie.

"Mooooo," Maddie calls back.

"Good girl. Very smart." I locate the corkscrew and hand it to Susie.

It's ridiculous that this woman pushes her way into my house and makes me feel like a bad teenager. I'm an adult. So I'm having a little wine at lunch. I'm entitled. "Use the other two glasses there. The wine will taste better."

She studies the label and says, "Nice selection. I didn't know you were a wine person."

"Yeah, well."

She pours two healthy glasses, hands me one and tips her

glass towards mine like a lover about to make a toast. She says, "To new friends."

"To good wine," I rejoin and we clink our glasses. My mouth waters at the thought of the wine in my hand. I take a big gulp to quench my desire.

"A loaf of bread, a jug of wine and thou." She walks past me, settles onto the couch, sips her wine. I'm incredulous, standing and watching her, but I bite my tongue.

She pats the couch beside her. "Come sit."

"Is this a seduction or something?" I ask.

She laughs and I laugh too, in spite of myself.

"Let me turn a video on for Madeline." I pick out her favorite *Sesame Street* video, the one where they sing "Fuzzy and Blue." Once you get that song in your head—it's hard to erase. I stand next to the TV, watching Madeline watch the video, avoiding eye contact with Susie.

She pats the couch again. "Come sit with me and talk."

I obey.

We drink in silence. Susie kicks her shoes off, pulls her bare feet up under her dress. "How come you don't have a boyfriend?" I ask.

"I do, well of sorts. I don't like to be pinned down."

"I've never seen him."

"Yeah, you have."

"When?"

She cuts her eyes over to Maddie. "She's so precious."

"When did I see him?" I ask again. I want her to tell me that it was the man who looked like Paul on her front porch that day. When Paul had gotten home that day, I taunted him with the news.

"Did you know Susie has a boyfriend?"

Paul pushed his plate back like he was done, only we just started eating. "Boyfriend?"

"Huh-hunh. Met him today."

"She introduced you to him? What's his name?"

"Don't you like the chicken?"

"Yeah, it's fine. How'd you meet him?"

"Very handsome."

"A blond, no doubt. Susie seems like she would go for blonds."

"Actually, he looks a lot like you. Anyway, Maddie said a new word today."

Susie's playing me, just like I did Paul that night. She wants to weave her own web of information leading to no certain conclusions on the matter of her relationship with my husband. She says, "I just play with him during the day mostly. I haven't seen much of him over the past few months."

"During the day—don't you have to work?"

"No. I'm one of those Trust Fund babies."

"Must be nice. Interesting choice of words you used about your boyfriend—'play with him'. Convenience fuck?" It seems like an awfully big coincidence that she hasn't seen him much since Jordan. But there was that guy who looked like Paul on her porch that day.

Susie puts her hands in the air stick-up style and says, "Guilty."

"Everyone needs to get laid," I say, feeling a tremor start in my toes, washing over my entire body. So it is true. Paul is fucking Susie. And here she is sitting in my house, on my couch, drinking my wine. I wished I had one of those scarab rings the Victorians used to wear. The kind that has a large jewel that hides a little compartment good for secreting poison. Just a flick of my hand and the poison would be in her glass. "Why don't you see him more often?"

"Just the way it works out. But I'm starting to get to the point where I'm lonely. It'd be nice to have someone to come home to. I never thought I'd feel like that. I always wanted my space. Well, space I got, just no one to share it with."

"What's his name?"

"Not important. He's just a convenient body with a dick." She reaches forward, gulps her wine.

My heart is racing. I feel like I want to shake her and scream, 'Say it's Paul. I already know.' If I shake her hard enough, maybe I'll snap her neck. "If we're going to be friends, Susie, I at least have to know what to call him, right?"

"Let's move on. How are you and Paul doing?"

"You're right. Let's move on."

Silence. My hands are shaking. I reach for my wine glass. Some wine spills up and over the edge. I try to steady the glass with both hands.

"Easy, Meg. What's wrong? You're shaking."

A sob as big as the Pacific Ocean tidal waves out of me. Susie grabs my glass from my hands, puts it on the coffee table and wraps herself around me. We rock back and forth, back and forth, crying together as adversaries in comfort.

chapter six

"Meg."

I'm opening and closing kitchen cabinets. I hear him, but it's like he's too far away to answer.

"Meg, are you ok?"

"Of course, why?" I can't remember what I'm looking for. God, I hate that. I stand looking at the cabinets for a clue, retracing my steps to what sent me on the search to begin with.

"You and Maddie haven't gotten dressed for the past four days. I come home from work and you're still in your pajamas. And now it's late Saturday morning and you're still in your pajamas."

"We're fine, really."

"You used to bathe and dress Maddie for dinner every night."

"Easier this way."

"Easier?"

"Sure."

"Easier to live in filth?"

"The house is clean."

"You're not."

"Where are you off to?" I ask, sidestepping his insult.

"Just going for a drive."

"To?"

"Maybe the beach."

"In that?" I ask, motioning towards his dress shirt and pants on a Saturday morning. "Can I come if I get dressed?" I sound like a five-year-old.

"I kinda want to be alone."

"Hot date?"

"You're my hot date." Paul smiles, stepping towards me. "Well, if you take a bath and wash your hair that is."

I'm so unprepared for kind words, I can't hear them, so I hang onto the sarcasm he has followed them up with. "I don't trust you anymore, Paul."

"What?"

"You heard me."

"Where is that coming from? You don't trust me? Me?"

"You think I'm blind and stupid?"

"What're you talking about?"

"The beach in dress clothes?" I run at him, pushing him with both my palms hard against his chest.

He grabs my wrists, steadies his own backwards stumble. We lurch to the side. He shakes my wrists. "Stop it, Meg."

I feel like Mike Tyson, a fighter who advances forwards, and never backward. I'm unleashed. "You fucker." I slap at him, he blocks me like we're actors in a cheap karate movie.

"Dammit. Stop. The baby. Stop."

Maddie has halted in her tracks. She looks like she's trying to gauge whether to laugh or cry.

"You think I'm stupid?" I come at him again. He picks me up and bounces me against the wall. I slide to the floor. "Fuck you."

He squats down in front of me. I'm hysterical with yelling at first, so I can't hear what he's saying. Maddie's crying too.

"Think I don't know?" I yell.

"I don't think there's anything wrong with visiting our son's grave."

"What?"

"Jordan. You've yet to go see him. Don't you care?"

"Oh, God."

"You were a good mother. I don't get it."

"That's where you're going?"

"Where'd you think?"

"You don't want to know. Maddie, come here, honey," I say.

"Get dressed. Come with me. All of us. Maddie too."

"Oh, babe," I say, just like I used to.

"Please."

"Can't. I can't."

Maddie stumbles towards me, crying, rubbing her eyes.

Paul looks down at his cuticles. I see his eyes brim as full as they can without spilling over. "Please. For me."

"I can't." I reach out to touch his cheek, but he swivels away, rises in one fluid movement.

"Come on, Maddie." He plucks her from my arms. She's still crying. Seconds later, I hear the jingle of his keys being picked up from the hall tree, the groan of the front door opening and closing and Maddie's wail receding.

I stretch across the kitchen tile. I can't cry. I'm stuck, I'm numb. I'm such an ass for accusing him. I stretch my arms out, pull myself across the floor like an inchworm. When I get to the step down into the family room, I drape my upper body over the threshold, bang my head against the tile floor. If only he'd come back. I'd get dressed. I'd put Maddie in her lilac dress. I'd sit in the passenger seat like a good wife and mother. I'd be brave enough to walk up to my son's grave, kneel down, touch the angel cuddling a lamb etching on the glossy, blue granite stone I picked out. Tell him I'm so, so sorry. But I'm a coward.

I should at least have changed Madeline from her PJs to the lilac dress. Jordan would like to see she's still wearing it. If only Paul would come back. Why doesn't he come back and give me a second chance?

I lie with my forehead pressed against the cool tile. If I hit my head on the floor hard enough, maybe I'll put Paul and myself out of our collective misery.

I wonder how hard I'd have to crash my head against the lovely Italian tile to get the job done. If I did kill myself, Paul would be the first likely suspect. If he were accused of my murder, then where would Maddie be? A kid should have at least one parent. On the other hand, if I only knock myself unconscious, I'll end up with a hell of a headache, and worse, Paul will be mad and may start to think I'm not fit to be a mother.

If I had the right force, though, I'd get the job done. If I didn't pull up short at the last minute, anticipating the impact. How is it that people drill holes in their own skulls and keep going—bad enough for the first hole, but for the next drill hole and the next? I always wondered about that. I saw a book on it when I was little and the concept horrified me so much, it got stuck in my brain—it's called self-trepanning. People do it to alleviate pressure in their brain for all manner of reasons—demon possession being one of them. The only demon living in me is my own mind.

I raise my head up, arch my neck back as far as it will flex. It's not distance enough. If I'm going to kill myself, I have to go the distance. Like to the top of the Sears Tower. Once I got to the top, I know I'd be able to jump. Any time I get around heights, like the top of Pike's Peak, tall bridges or even a balcony, I always have the compulsion to jump. Paul says that's because I really have a fear of heights. Most people think a fear of heights makes the person want to avoid heights, he says. But what it really does is makes people want to jump.

I swivel my head to the side, eyeball the kitchen clock. It's 10:35 AM and I'm still in my nightgown. What's wrong with me? I used to be up, dressed in running clothes by 6:30. By 10:30, I would have showered, had a half-hour of playtime with Jordan and Maddie in Jordan's bedroom—I like my kids to wake up softly. I would have dressed both kids and made a family breakfast. Jordan loves, loved pancakes. The downstairs would have been vacuumed and the second load of laundry would have been in the washer.

I'm going to get up. I'm absolutely committed to rising from this floor and being productive. I'll just lay here for five more minutes. I bang my head against the tile to remind myself I'm alive.

"Ouch," I say out loud, but there's no one to hear. Maybe that's how Susie feels—like she's not really living and experiencing life, since no one's around to notice or care. We haven't spoken since that day she caught me about to drink the wine, and we both ended up crying together. I've cried more in these last five months than I've cried my whole life. The scary thing is, I haven't cried nearly enough.

That day was weird and reassuring at the same time: To be able to cry and have someone cry with me. I don't think I've ever had that before, except with Paul. I look at the clock. Ok, when it's 11:00 even, I'll get up. Maybe go see Susie.

At 11:17, I roll over on my back with extreme effort. I try to will my muscles to cooperate in the joint venture of getting my body in an upright position. But my muscles won't comply. All my muscles feel stuck in the off position—not that they're relaxed, they're not mobile. It's like they belong to somebody else.

I think how lovely a glass of wine would be, but my muscles don't even respond to that. My mouth, however, starts to water. Maybe I shouldn't; I don't know when Paul will walk in. Of course, I could go to the park with my bottle of wine. Listen to me. I sound like some sterno bum, drinking wine in the park.

Maybe I should call Marci. Marci will help me. I'll call Marci in exactly two minutes. Two minutes. One minute and forty-five seconds to go.

Maybe I should go back to work. Maybe it was better when I had somewhere to go. I think of Al. There. I have somewhere to go next Saturday night. Who needs a job? But there's seven days to get through between then and now. And now. And now.

This morning, Paul acted totally innocent of the idea that he would be cheating. What if I'm telling myself a story that isn't true? What if I put down my paranoia and believe him?

But he never did say where he was the night I met Al. He kept acting like he hadn't heard me. The next morning at breakfast, when I wouldn't relent and brought the question back up for the fourth time, he said, "I told you. I had to take some clients out." But he never told me anything about clients.

I wonder if Paul has made it to the cemetery. Well, mausoleum. There are not a lot of cemeteries in South Florida, property values being what they are. But we got a space out on the grass. Had to pay a premium. It would have been creepy to think of Jordan boxed into a cement casket apartment high-rise. Jordan was scared of the dark. After the funeral, Paul said he wished we had rigged Jordan's casket with a light. How can you not love a guy forever when he thinks like that?

Maybe I should catch up with Paul. Maybe he's wishing for me to go to the cemetery as hard as I'm wishing for him to come back home and get me. I should go. Thinking about it, though, gives me the cold shivers. I'm not brave enough to face my bad acts.

Madeline's happy face pops into my head. I wonder if she'll have kids. I hope she has more than one. Not because you need a spare kid on hand so you have one left to raise, but rather because it's nice for the kids to have each other. Protection from the world and their parents when it's needed.

Twenty-two more minutes have passed. I'm not sure if Marci can help me. After all, she doesn't know the real root of my sadness. I wish I had a friend. I've always been happy as a loner, but now, I wish I had another man or woman in my life who would understand me and help me.

I hear the garage door open at 12:29. I scramble-rock onto my knees, then grab the doorframe to pull myself up. I'm woozy and see black for a second. I stagger towards the kitchen counter, take a coffee mug out of the cabinet, recover my nightgown from where it has bunched up in my ass. By the time Paul walks through the door with Maddie in his arms, I'm casually pouring my first cup of coffee that's at least four hours old, acting like it's fresh.

"Hi, baby," I say, addressing Madeline and not Paul.

"Mama, Mama," she says, reaching out for me.

"Still not dressed?" Paul yells incredulously. He snatches Maddie's hands from their outstretched position, spins on his heels and walks back out the garage door.

"Do NOT take her in the front yard, Paul," I yell. I take a sip of stale coffee, spit it out in the sink. Fuck it all, I should have just opened the bottle of wine, told Paul I changed our household rules from banning alcohol to celebrating it.

I sidle up to the front curtain. I can hear Paul's voice, but I can't see him.

"...not very good..." I hear Paul say.

"...counseling...maybe..." Susie's voice says back.

Dammit, does Susie just hang around her front door every moment, waiting for the chance to spring on Paul?

I pounce open the front door. As I round the corner, I see Maddie on the driveway between them. Her interest is caught by a bird on the driveway near the street. Paul is jacking his jaws with Susie, discussing what a nut case I am, oblivious to the danger Madeline is in. He's not even holding her hand or looking at her. Maddie starts running down the driveway towards the bird. The bird flies up in the air, lands closer to the street. She stops and then starts running towards it again.

I sprint towards her. "Dammit, Paul!" The blacktop scorches my bare feet, gravel digs into my heels. I run faster.

"What are you doing? She's just playing."

I swipe Maddie up into my arms no less than two yards from the road. A car drives by. "Slow down!" I yell. I kiss her fat cheek.

"Bird," she says.

Paul says, "Meg, get in the house."

"You could have killed her. I told you not to bring her into the front yard."

"Meg."

Susie avoids my eyes, looks at the ground. Some friend.

"Bird, Mama. Bird."

"Are you a complete idiot?" I yell.

"Meg. Your nightgown is see-through. Please go in the house."

"Big fucking deal. My daughter is alive." I stalk towards the house, cradling Maddie's head against my jerky movements, purposefully brushing between them. Susie takes a step back. Over my shoulder, I say, "Now you two can discuss how much counseling I need."

I hear Paul say, "I'm sorry."

My ass has never felt larger or jigglier before. I step softer on tiptoes, try to slide into the house and into wifely obscurity.

chapter seven

"Bird, mama," Madeline says. She gently pats my cheek as we walk up the stairs. I pause at the hallway window, finger the curtain to the side. Paul and Susie are still standing on the driveway. They're laughing. Maddie could have just gotten killed and they're laughing. God, I hate them both. Paul looks up at the window. I give him the finger. Why doesn't he come inside and comfort me?

"Bird, mama, bird," Maddie says more insistently.

"Yes, sweetie, bird. What sound does a bird make?" I shift Maddie to my left hip, turn away from the window.

Maddie responds by making the sound of a seagull, when it's walking the beach and cooing—not when it's flying. It took several months for Paul and I to decipher what bird sound she was making. The next time we went to the beach was at dusk. When the seagulls gathered around the blanket, Maddie bounced up and down, making her bird noise and the seagulls talked back to her in the same voice. It's a smart girl we have.

"Do it again," I prod.

She does it louder and faster, her little cheeks vibrating with the sound. I laugh, setting her down on her bedroom floor. I kneel down next to her, spring from laughing to crying.

"Mama sad."

This makes me cry louder. I stretch onto my side, shake my head yes.

"Mama sad." She squats down, pats my back.

I cry even harder and louder. How is it that a baby knows

what I need when my husband doesn't? I tap the floor in front of me. Maddie cuddles into the cranny between my breasts and legs. I kiss her forehead, pet her hair.

I wake when Madeline stirs. We're covered with the christening blanket I keep on a small quilt stand in her room. I was so sound asleep I didn't hear Paul come in. The blanket is delicate white silk with a flower pattern woven into the cloth and wispy fringe on the ends. It's the same blanket we used for Jordan's christening. I thought it would be nice to start a family tradition. I didn't think the family tradition of mothers killing their sons would be passed from my mother to me. God, I hope Maddie doesn't have the same curse.

I rub Maddie's back and she stirs again. She's sweaty with sleep; little ringlets have formed at the base of her neck. "Goozie girl," I whisper in her ear. Then I make up a song about goozie girl in her goozie world of sleep. I sing stanza after stanza with whatever nonsense that comes into my head.

Paul appears in the doorway. I stop singing, crane my head back to see him, then feel shy to meet his eyes.

"Go on," he says.

I tuck back around Maddie, rubbing her back. She sighs. I start singing again. Paul joins in with a stanza on goozie goes on a galaxy getaway. He takes a step into the room. My heart pounds. How is it that the father of my two children can feel so much like a stranger? How did we get so far afield?

Maddie opens her eyes for a split second, rolls over on her back, stretches her arms and legs crucifix-style. Our poor martyred daughter.

I stretch my neck back to look at Paul as he's singing, smile a sad smile, look back at Maddie. He finishes his song. I pat the floor on the other side of Maddie, hold my breath and wait.

He kneels first, staring at us. Taking us in with his eyes. I shut my eyes, pat the floor again. I feel and hear him settling in. He takes my hand, kisses it. "Look at me," he says.

I open my eyes, look into his. I can see a montage of images as I look in his eyes—our first kiss, our first coupling on the beach, Jordan's delivery, Jordan's delivery, Jordan's delivery, buying this house. It's like I'm reading his mind at the moment before death finds him.

I rise on my elbow at the same time he does. We share our first kiss in three months over Maddie's sleeping body. It's tender and forceful, salty. Tears have run into our joined lips. I'm not sure whose they are. I never want to break away. My nose is so stuffed up with the crying earlier, I can't breathe. But I don't want to pull away from his tongue exploring my lips, mouth and tongue. Smothered by a kiss, I'll be. There's worse ways to die.

Maddie sighs in a way I know she's up. We break apart. Paul keeps his hand on my neck, strokes my cheek with his thumb, rubs my tears into my skin. Maddie is shifting her sleepy eyes from side to side, looking from Paul to me and back again. A tear drops onto her face below her eye and she laughs, so we laugh. These are the mathematics of our house: Madeline laughs times love to the tenth power equals we laugh.

I brush the tears from Paul's face, then my own. Madeline pops up, clapping her hands. She is the maestro of our marriage.

Paul says, "Why don't you go shower and I'll watch Madeline?"

I'm sure he means it to be helpful, but I feel indicted and stung all over again. I'm not a beautiful woman being kissed by her loving husband. I'm just some suburban slob who has to be told when to shower.

I lower my eyes away from his. "Ok." As I stand up, my

knees crack. Everything is falling apart: my family, my career, my marriage and now my body.

I start the shower. Pulling my nightgown over my head, I catch a glimpse of my body in the mirror, shrouded in gossamer cloth. I run my hand across my stomach. It bulges slightly, but not bad for a woman who has had two children. No stretch marks. At least I have good skin. I turn around, trying to get a look at my ass by looking over my left, then my right shoulder. It's definitely not as firm as it used to be. And look at my thighs at the top. No wonder Paul doesn't touch me anymore. I twist this way and that, finding more imperfections until the mirror steams over.

My hair is full of shampoo when the water pressure momentarily decreases. I know Paul is filling the tub for Maddie's bath. I rinse off in a hurry. I want to bathe her together and then put her in her lilac dress. I don't dare walk into the kid's bathroom naked. It's a room filled with natural light. I don't want him to see how my body is falling apart. I grab the first thing in my drawer I can find.

By the time I open our bedroom door, they are crossing the hall into Maddie's bedroom. I trot down the hall. "Here Paul," I call. "I want to pick out her outfit."

"Sweatpants?"

"No, her little lilac dress."

"No, I mean, you're in sweatpants. Are you going to get dressed today in real clothes or not?"

I shrug off his question, hand him the lilac dress.

Paul tries to pull the dress over Maddie's head, but her head gets stuck.

"You have to pull the collar open harder," I say.

"I know how to dress my daughter."

He pulls it apart and I hear the fabric give a little. As he's pulling her arm through the left sleeve, the seam busts open.

"You just have to stretch it. Here."

"So you said. Meg, this dress is too small for her."

"Here, let me. She wears this dress all the time."

Paul blocks Maddie from me with his body. "Will you stop? Surely she has some other clothes to wear. Look, it's even too short."

"But she looks so pretty in this and her chunky legs are so cute."

"It's not cute when she's busting apart at the seams. We have money. She doesn't have to go around looking like some waif."

"Just let her wear it."

"Why are you so insistent?"

"I'm not."

"Yeah, you are," he laugh-sneers and shakes his head.

"Jordan picked it out for her," I mumble.

"Who?"

"Jordan. Your son? You remember him."

He grimaces. I'm sorry I said it, but it's out there and I can't take it back.

"Yeah. I remember him. I visited him at the cemetery without you this morning." Paul starts yanking the dress back off.

"No!" I yell, pulling it back down.

He pulls the dress up and I pull down. Maddie is in the middle of us like a floppy doll, being pulled this way and that. She yells, "No, no, no."

"Stop. You're hurting her," Paul yells.

I stand down.

Paul starts to undress Maddie again. I stand and watch, my arms at my sides. Maddie's arm gets stuck in the sleeve. He rips the seam open, pulls the dress over her head, flings it towards the wastebasket.

I grab the dress out of the air. "No respect for my feelings. You're such an asshole." I hold the dress to my breast, like it's a new baby.

"Watch your filthy mouth in front of the baby."

"Asshole."

"It's just a dress, Meg."

"No, it's something to hold onto. Jordan picked it out."

"You can't move through life holding onto trophy textiles."

"What's that mean?"

"It means you're still carrying around the bedspread your dad bought, Kay's skirt and now the dress Jordan picked out. How many other things are there that I don't know about? Should we buy a storage garage? You're supposed to hold onto memories in your head and by talking about them. Not by hoarding clothing."

"You never talk about Jordan," I say. "Where are your memories then? Come to think of it, I seem to remember someone who has a T-shirt with Jordan's blood smeared on it. Let's talk about that. Like you're not a textile monger yourself."

"Down, Dada." Maddie bounces up and down on her changing table. Paul lifts her down.

"So now you're not going to dress her?"

"She can run around in her diaper for a moment. You're changing the subject."

"No. You're changing the subject. When was the last time you talked about Jordan?"

"I talk about him all the time."

Maddie has grabbed her favorite doll and is making a break for the door. "No, baby. Madeline, stay in here with us," I say. "Not to me you don't. You don't ever talk about Jordan. To who then?"

"People at work, Susie…"

I stare at him.

He places his hands on my shoulders. "Meg, I want you to go to counseling."

"What? Why?"

"Because you're not yourself and I'm concerned."

"You're not yourself. When was the last time you made love to me? Do you even know?" Three months, five days and about seven hours, I think. "Or do you do that with people at work and Susie too?"

"We used to have such great conversations," he says, dodging the question.

"You used to rub my back when we got into bed at night."

"Well, you used to be excited by the world and what was going on. You're too focused inside—I can't get to you. Maybe if you went back to work, made some friends."

"Focusing on my family and not working is a fine objective."

"Correction. You're focused on Maddie."

"And the problem with that is?"

"I'm part of this family too."

"You're jealous of your own daughter? That's nuts. Maybe you should go to counseling."

"Maybe I should."

chapter eight

Paul and I stay away from each other for the next week. I hate the silent treatment, but I'm not inclined to talk. He doesn't make a connection with me either. I wonder if he has contacted a therapist. My life revolves around the cancer support group. They don't seem to mind me showing up in the sweats I slept in. If I had to get dressed, I wouldn't have enough energy to go. It's nice to commune with people who are in as much pain as I am. Still, going to the cancer support group isn't the same thing as going for one-on-one therapy and admitting you can't help yourself. I admire Paul's willingness to go.

He starts coming home later and later. I go to bed earlier and earlier. That way, I don't have to feel the sting of his back turned towards me in bed.

Part of every day, I orbit my neighborhood, slowing down cars. I'm thinking of expanding my territory—branch out into other neighborhoods with a busy traffic pattern and a high incidence of accidents. I know I could help lower the accident rate. I'm really a very loving, helpful person. I mean, in spite of the fact I killed my son. I banish a flash haunting of Jordan's bloody head out of my mind.

I go to City Hall, ask for traffic and accident statistics. The girl looks at me like I have a cow head and just said, "Moo." I ask for her manager, but he isn't in. I go back three days later. They refer me to a city planner who also isn't in. I leave when they ask for my name and address; take a circuitous route home to ensure no one follows me. I'll just have to scan the newspaper for clues and facts on neighborhoods needing a traffic monitor.

When an SUV comes barreling down the road, full of kids and no intention of stopping, I lay on the horn, pulling out into the intersection of a four-way stop—enough to play chicken, but not enough to do bodily harm to Maddie or me. The woman driver slams on her brakes past the stop sign, throws both hands up in the air, then gives me the double-barreled finger like I'm the one in the wrong. I smile sweetly, making a slow down sign out my window, then blow her a kiss and continue on my way. I hope those kids make it home safe. The hothead mother too. She peels off. I consider looping the block to slow her down again, but then she brakes and slows down.

On Saturday morning, I vow I will let air vibrate across the vocal chords in my larynx in an effort to say something meaningful to Paul. I wake up before him at 6:30, tiptoe out of the room; change into the running clothes I have left on top of the washer.

I stow my house key in the little pocket on the band of my shorts before starting out. The morning sun hasn't heated the world up yet. I can smell and hear that someone is cutting their lawn. I forgot to lay out my running watch. I like to compete against myself for my best time. No matter, it feels good to do something physical. I'm only able to run two and a half miles. It's been months since I've run and I'm afraid my legs will be sore tomorrow. It's amazing how fast your body and your life can get out of shape.

When I get home, Paul is at the stove, frying bacon. I've vowed that I will act like everything is normal. Things can't get back to normal unless I act normal. If I fake it long enough, maybe things will be normal. I walk up behind him like I'm the woman I was six months ago, kiss his neck.

I feel his skin get all prickly. A good sign. I kiss him again, grazing my lips against his neck. He shrugs me off. That's ok, I like a sexual challenge. I plant myself behind him, rub my hands down his sides to the length of his thighs.

"What are you doing?" he asks.

"Breathing you in. New shampoo?" The running has opened my sinuses. I'll check his shower to see if he's using a new shampoo. I didn't buy it. I run my hand down his ass, between his legs to the front, brush his balls.

"Stop. The baby."

"It's good for Madeline to see her parents show affection."

"But you're groping me. Kids don't need to see that."

"You know, they say there comes a time when every kid will see their parents by accident in the carnal act."

"You want me to do you here on the floor?" He pokes the bacon around the pan.

"That would be nice." I kiss his neck again.

He bounces his head down to his chest in resignation. "I wouldn't be able to get it up."

My hands go limp to my sides.

Paul turns around. "Hey. I'm sorry. That was mean."

"It was," I say, walking out of the kitchen.

In the shower, I cry so hard I become weak-kneed and have to squat down. I let the water beat down on me, just like Paul's words. I hope the drain will wash my horrible life away.

I'm lying on the bed, partially draped with a wet towel. Paul walks in with Madeline in his arms. I roll over away from them onto my side, try to cover more of my nakedness.

"Careful, Maddie will see her mother naked and get the wrong idea." I hope he can't see how out of shape my thighs look. I tug the towel down, but then my nipple pops out. He doesn't want me anymore anyway. If he doesn't like the way I look, that's just too bad. His problem, not mine. Well, ok, my problem too, since I'm the one going to sleep alone every night of the week.

Paul sits Maddie in the middle of the bed next to me, seats himself on the other side of her. I touch my face to feel if my eyes are swollen. I don't want Paul to know I was crying.

"Hi, love bug. Did you have a good breakfast?" I ask.

She nods her head yes.

Paul says, "Tell Mama what we got her."

"Pretty," Maddie says coyly.

"Pretty what?" prods Paul.

"Rose."

"Right. Where is it?" he asks.

Maddie points to the door. Paul gets up and goes into the hall. He comes back in the room with a slender, square vase filled with one huge red Don Juan rose from his garden and a black-eyed Susan. Black-eyed Susans are my favorite. Maddie claps her hands.

"Where did you get the black-eyed Susan?"

He doesn't answer the question. Just smiles at me.

I sit up, put my hands out for the vase, plant my face close enough to check the fragrance, even though I won't be able to smell anything now because of my sinuses and all the crying I did in the shower. I picture and relive the smell of childhood fields of daisies and black-eyed Susans.

"Oh, Paul. They're great. Where did you get the black-eyed Susan?" I ask a second time.

"I have a connection."

His response trips off my paranoia, but I decide to move on.

"Pretty," Madeline says, pointing her finger at the flowers until she touches a petal. She smiles big, looking from Paul to me and back again.

"Feel," I say, taking her hand and rubbing it on the rose petal. "Did you cut all the thorns off the rose?" I ask Paul.

"Of course."

I want to tell Paul how huge and lovely his roses are this year, but I'm afraid he'll tell me about all the helpful tips Susie has taught him.

Paul takes the corner of the towel, covers my exposed crotch. Lets his hand sit under the towel, his fingertips just barely touching me. The whisper of his fingertips radiates heat waves up to my throat. I look at him, roll my eyes closed and smile. When I open my eyes, he is still smiling at me.

I take Maddie's finger and brush it across the brown center of the black-eyed Susan, then show her the yellow pollen on her fingers.

She wipes it on the bedspread. "Eeew, Mama."

Paul and I laugh, which makes her say, "Eeew, Mama," again and again.

Paul wiggles his finger closer to my crotch, spreading my lips.

"Is it time for Madeline's nap yet?" I ask.

He withdraws his hand like I've burned him. I'm so stupid. I should have just gone with it. Let him be the aggressor. Why is it I even have to think about playing that game? He's my husband, for Christ's sake. I guess he was telling the truth when he said he wouldn't be able to get it up. People often let the truth slip out, then take it back.

"You never did know how to play hard to get," Paul says.

"Didn't know I had to."

"A challenge every now and then is nice."

"Never bothered you before."

"A challenge would have been nice then too."

"Teach me then," I say, taking his resistant hand, still not playing hard to get, and placing it back underneath the towel. I can only be who I am. I search his jeans for a clue of a hard-on.

Paul leaves his flaccid hand where I have placed it. Maddie plucks rose petals, smushing them between her baby fingers.

"No, no," I say. "Pretty flowers. Don't hurt them." I swing the vase to my other hand. Maddie crawls around Paul and me to get to them again.

"Tell me why you want to sleep with me," Paul asks.

Ok, we're staying on topic. "It won't sound very hard to get," I say.

"S'ok."

"Starters? I'm horny."

"And?"

"It releases endorphins."

"Yeah, but you already went running for that. What else?"

My stomach jumps, but I say what I'm thinking anyway. "I miss being touched by someone other than Maddie."

"Just anyone?"

"No. You. I want you. I want things to be the way they used to."

"And?"

"And I miss feeling close."

"Don't need to screw for that." He raises his eyebrows.

"It helps."

"It always comes back to sex for you?"

"No. You're looking at it from a micro level and I'm looking at it from a macro level."

"The economics of sex?"

We laugh. "Exactly. Put on your worldview hat." I open my legs slightly.

"I miss you. Miss laughing and talking with you," Paul says. He looks at me with the love in his eyes I used to see every day.

I put the vase down on the nightstand without looking. Maddie starts to make an "Aaah, aaah, aaah" noise, which means she wants the flowers back.

Paul wraps his arms around me. He squeezes me in a firm, warm hug that feels like he's trying to leave the impression of his heart on me. It feels wonderful.

The doorbell rings. We each pull back, like we've been caught in the act of something forbidden. Paul moves to get up.

"Don't answer it," I beg.

The doorbell rings again. Paul stands up, adjusts his hard-on to the side. I pat the bed. "Forget it. Whatever it is, it isn't important."

The doorbell rings a third time. Paul walks out of the room. "Besides," I call, "they're being incredibly rude."

I hear Paul answer the door. I hear Susie's voice answer back his hello. Holy Mother of God, must she come between us every time we try to get close? I swear, she must be either psychic or have our bedroom bugged.

I roll over, look at my vase of sweet flowers. Maddie has plucked off all the petals; only stems and leaves remain.

"Oh, goozie. What happened?" I ask Maddie.

She points to the petals on the bedspread. I herd all the petals together, cup them up in my hands. I say, "Wheee," letting them flutter down all over Maddie's head. She laughs her baby belly laugh, blinking her eyes as the petals touch her face.

"More," she says.

I collect the petals again.

"More. More."

We go through the routine four more times.

"Let's get dressed, love bug." I throw my towel over Maddie's head. She does the peek-a-boo routine with me.

In between "Where's Maddies," I try to hear the conversation downstairs. I think they are in the kitchen, but I can't make out what they are saying. I'm careful to dress myself in a pair of casual slacks and a nice top. I don't want to be accused of slovenliness two weekends in a row.

"More," Madeline says, going back to the petals.

When I pick her up, she starts to cry. I hand her a petal. She throws it on the ground, points to the bed. "More. More."

"We have to get dressed."

As I walk down the hall, I hear the front door open. They are standing in the doorway, but their voices are still muffled like they're whispering. Hell, it's my house. I should just go down and throw her out.

Paul joins me in Maddie's room, just as I'm secreting her lilac dress back in the corner of her third drawer. I'm going to repair all the busted seams next week.

Paul kisses my cheek and I palm his face for a second. Maybe we can get the mood back again.

"Want to go to the park with us today?" I ask.

"Perfect."

"Great." I pick out a pair of overalls and a tank top for Maddie. "Will you check her diaper?"

"Sure," says Paul, "give me the poopy detail."

"Poo-poo," Maddie says.

"It should just be wet," I say.

"You're right, just wet. Hand me those wet thingys."

I pass them, unsnap the overalls.

"Pooey," Paul says as he opens and shuts her diaper. This game used to make Jordan get up and run around the room squealing. Maddie surrenders herself to the attention and laughter. "How about if we cook out tonight?" Paul asks.

"Wonderful. Chicken or steaks? I'll go to the store."

"Steak would be nice. Get three," he says.

"Three? Maddie can eat off ours."

"Susie's going to join us."

"Poo-poo," Madeline yells, kicking her feet and waving her arms.

Her overalls slip from my hands to the floor.

Paul secures her diaper in place.

I bend to retrieve the overalls. As I straighten back up, Paul's eyes are locked on mine. "Can't we just have a family dinner?" I ask.

"Daddy poo-poos," Madeline says, then laughs, trying to shift the attention back on her.

"Yes, he does," I say. "Daddy poo-poos and Susie poo-poos too."

"Come on, stop it. I thought it would be nice," Paul says.

"I'd rather it just be us."

"You should get to know her better. She's nice. You could use a friend."

"I don't need a friend," I say.

"C'mon."

"Will you tell her another time?"

"I can't. I already invited her. She's lonely."

"I'm lonely too, Paul. Here all day by myself."

"Then go back to work."

I throw the overalls across the room—away from Maddie. Paul lets me storm out of the room.

Fuck it. There's no sense trying. We should just cut our losses and get on with our miserable lives. I wonder if Paul will fight me for custody. He'd probably win. All he'd have to tell the judge is that I killed our son. Trying to prove every day to myself that I'm a good mother won't help in the face of hard evidence. It will all come down to the facts.

"Did you hit your son?" the judge will ask.

"Yes," I will answer.

"Did he die as a result of his sustained injuries inflicted by you?"

"Yes." Brain snapshots of Jordan with his swollen head and tubes coming out of his mouth and sides flick past. I squeeze my eyes shut tight to banish the visions.

"Custody is granted to the plaintiff, Paul Thomas O'Hara.

Defendant Meg Gabriella O'Hara will have two hours of supervised time a week."

I stalk back to Maddie's room. Paul is snapping the last button on her overalls.

"Paul, please. We need some time alone."

"I already invited her."

"Tell her I made dinner reservations to surprise you."

"You'll see. We'll have a nice dinner. I'll cook."

I spin back around. I grab my old Coach bag off the top shelf in my closet. Paul pauses in our doorway, then goes downstairs with Maddie. I don't look at him. I tiptoe downstairs, get our Zoë backpack from the bottom of the hall tree, take it back upstairs. I retrieve my wallet, lipstick and cell phone, shove them into my purse. I leave the unzipped backpack on our bed among the broken red and yellow petals.

I trudge into the family room.

"Look," Maddie says. She's pointing to a picture in her book.

"What is that?" I ask.

"Luna."

"Luna. Good. You're so smart." I kiss her cheek.

"Luna."

"I think it's best if I go out for a while. This way, you can spend some time with Maddie."

Paul's glare holds me captive for a minute. I break away.

"Wait." I hear Paul say as I pick my keys off the hall tree. But it's too late; my feet and my will are already pointed towards the door.

chapter nine

I pull into the airport short-term parking. Fuck it. If Paul wants his precious car, he's just going to have to put an APB out for it. Probably would report his car stolen before reporting me missing.

Throwing the keys under the mat, I hit the automatic door lock. I catch the door just before it closes, snatch the keys back. Better to keep my options open. Hustling over to the concourse with all the other pedestrians, I act in a hurry to catch my flight.

In the ticket line, I feel naked with no luggage at my side.

"How may I provide you with excellent service?" The blond boy behind the counter asks, a little post-sex effect, breathless.

"I'm here to buy a ticket," I say.

"What's your destination?" He flips his hair to the side.

"Anywhere," I answer.

"Can you narrow that down a little? The world's a big place."

"Where do you like?" I ask, leaning on the counter.

He glances at the long line of customers waiting. There must be a flight getting ready to take off.

"Key West is nice." He strokes the keyboard with the tips of his fingers, anticipating my instructions.

"I was thinking about somewhere outside of Florida."

"California?"

"Somewhere more exotic," I suggest.

"Greece?" he offers.

"Tell me more."

He says, "I don't really have anything more to tell you."

"You've never been there? Don't you get to travel at a discount?"

He looks to the co-worker on his right and rolls his eyes, nodding in my direction. I know if I turned my back, he'd make the crazy swirl gesture with his finger.

People in line are shifting from foot to foot, looking at their watches. "Lady, are you gonna buy a ticket or what?" asks a female voice behind me.

"Where are you going?" I turn, hoping for a suitable destination.

"Nowhere if you don't move your ass."

I picture Maddie crying for me, wondering where I've gone. Even though it would be nice to leave my life behind, become a woman with a new life—one with no accidents anywhere in my past, I can't leave Maddie. "Ok, ok," I say, patting the counter twice, "Thanks for your help. I'm not crazy, just a little desperate."

"Sorry," I say, to the line of people waiting. But they don't care. People don't listen. I could have said, "I'm going to fuck your husband," and I still would have gotten the same reaction—nothing. That's what most people have to offer one another—nothing.

Shit, now what am I going to do? I can't go home. I picture myself, the way I ran out of the house, careening away from my SUV. It's important for Paul to use the SUV rather than the Mercedes if he takes Madeline somewhere. Even though I know all about the laudable German engineering, the SUV is bigger—has more metal to sustain an impact. Probably a false sense of security on my part. Like a wedding band. Security against ever having to be out there again. But they slip from your hand so easily when it gets cold.

Veering away from the SUV, I stalked into the garage thief-style, manned the Mercedes. I didn't want Paul coming out. My hands trembled as I located Paul's car key on my key ring. I backed out so swiftly the tires made a screeching noise. Pulling forward on the road, I saw Paul standing in the inner garage door with Madeline in his arms, his free hand raised in the air. I flipped his visor down, punching the garage door shut. I could see his torso, then only his legs as I pulled away. The garage door, like an etch-a-sketch—erasing my life, body part by body part.

Maybe I should stall for time while I decide what to do next by giving Paul's car a good once over. I'm sure there's clues about Paul's life squirreled away in the center console, glovebox or the trunk. I can't look, though. That would be a breach of trust and privacy.

I check my cell phone. If he's called, maybe I'll suck up my pride and go home. The call indicator light blinks double green for no calls. My hopeful heart skips a beat.

Fuck it, I'll go home and set things the way I want them. I have to keep reminding myself what sheer will can accomplish. I'm going to tell Susie she can't come over. I'm going to make Paul take us to the park. He'll be mad at first, but he'll have a good time. Later tonight after Maddie goes to bed, I'm going to force him to kiss me, make love to me in a roll-all-over-the-floor, mad passionate way. Then he'll remember how good things used to be and love me again. He'll forget for a few minutes that I've killed our son. A few minutes respite would be nice.

But he hasn't even called me. Shopping. Shopping would be nice. I wander around the concourse, browsing. It makes me feel good to be around people who are hurrying off to unknown places. A couple passes, I picture them in Italy, making love on a coastal shoreline. I place a red-haired woman in a business suit wheeling a computer bag at a conference where she's the keynote speaker. A man running is hurrying home from a business trip to his wife of thirty years.

I duck into a swimwear store, rummage through a rack of bathingsuits. I'm going to start going to the beach again with Maddie. We'll have fun. I'll start by going today. A day alone would actually be nice.

"What are you doing looking at one pieces?"

I turn, it must be the owner of the shop. A fat guy with a gray fringe on top. I involuntarily start singing "Surrey with the Fringe on Top". "Oh, I was just looking."

"Yes, but with a body like yours, you should be in a bikini. Let me show you."

I look down at my body to make sure he's talking about me. He leads me over to a row of bikinis, the kind with the underwire bras. I must look like a woman that's had kids and needs the extra support. He holds up a series of suits just under my face, checking the colors and the patterns. He hands me five different ones.

"Try these. You'll find this yellow and pink one will go with your coloring and the cut of the bottoms will make your hips look smaller than a one piece."

"You're saying I have big hips?"

"You have lovely full hips. Just try the suit on. You'll see."

I'm a little miffed at his declaration about my big hips, but I obey. I push the suit he has said will look the best to the back of the pile.

He stands outside the dressing room. "How does the yellow and pink one look?"

"Haven't gotten to it yet," I say.

"Well, come on out and let me see the one you have on."

"That's ok."

"That way, I'll be able to see your shape better and I'll pick some more for you."

"Really, that's ok."

"Don't be shy now."

"Do you mind?"

He stands by the door for a moment more, then moves off. This man's boldness makes me shaky. It's easy to see how women get victimized. Women don't make a fuss—they just try to end the situation as quickly as possible.

I strip the third suit off, flinging it over the hook. I was hanging each of the suits back up, but forget it. Give him and his little perverted mind something to keep busy with. He'll probably sniff the bottoms. I fumble with the yellow and pink one. I haven't liked any of them so far. Let's just get this over with.

Dammit all if he isn't right. I haven't looked this good in a bathingsuit since I don't know when. I turn this way and that in the mirror. The top is perfect and feels comfortable. The bottoms come up high enough to hide the baby pouch of my stomach. He's right, it does make my hips look shapely. I tuck my underwear in under the bottoms, so I can get the full effect. The silky fabric flatters my butt. I wish my thighs didn't look so out of shape. Nothing a one-piece suit can do about that either. Might as well buy the bikini. Maybe Paul will like it. I look at the price tag. I'm surprised it's so expensive—I guess you pay a premium for airport shopping. No matter, I'm worth it.

Opening the door a smidgen, I say, "Do you have a matching cover-up?"

"For which suit?" he calls back.

"The yellow and pink one," I mumble.

"I told you." He grabs a short dress cover-up off a rack. "Let me see."

I hang my hand out the dressingroom door. "The cover-up, please."

He hangs it on my index finger and laughs.

I shed the bottoms, pull my underwear off, then climb back into the bottoms. It's the first time I've ever not washed a bathingsuit before wearing it. I pull the price tag off both articles and throw on the cover-up. It looks cute. I fold my slacks and blouse, tuck them under my arm; cram my underwear into my purse.

"Looks like someone's going to the beach," he says when I walk out of the dressing room. "You must not be from here."

"I'm not," I say. "Do you have any dresses that are more dressy?"

He shakes his finger at me. "I've got one that would look great on you." He rummages through a few racks and hands me a long stretchy dress with a jacket. "Try it on."

"I don't have to. It's my size and I can see you know what you're doing."

"Been in the business for twenty-seven years, I ought to."

"I need two beach towels and some sunscreen too. Can you leave the dress on the hanger and put these on another one?" I pass him my slacks and shirt.

"No problem." He hands me my bag and walks towards the dressing room. I picture his face buried in the green and blue bathingsuit bottoms.

Walking down the concourse, I notice my casual beach attire melds in with all the local people picking up lovers, friends and family. Food would be nice. A day of indulgence. I cruise the restaurants, I stop short at the bar where I first met Al, look at the date on my watch.

My stomach jumps. Today's the day he's coming home. I'd only have to kill one hour to get another look at him. The scales of picturing myself on the beach and picturing myself sitting across from Al tip back and forth—Paul's blindfolded face is in the middle. Taking a seat at the bar, I commit to ordering a soda. I check my cell phone. Still no call from Paul.

"Hi, honey," the female bartender says. "What can I get for you?"

"I'll have a glass of red wine." You can't sit at a bar and not drink a real drink. She passes me the wine list. I point to the most expensive brand they have.

A woman is holding court at a table of six saying, "When he kicks the bucket, I'm gone. Good-bye Steve, hello Portugal." She gestures to a man I assume is her husband. Everyone at the table is laughing, except him.

I wonder why she's waiting for death. Worse, she's waiting for the death of someone else to start living her life. But then I realize, I've kind of been doing the same thing—thinking that death would release me into a better state than living. You might as well live. Dorothy Parker was right about that.

Four men at the bar get up. Three men sit down, size me up, order their drinks, size me up. I'm an actuarial anomaly— women don't usually sit at the bar by themselves, unless they're looking for something long and fat with a big head, that is. But then, there's another actuarial anomaly for you—a big dick. Hard to find.

I know what I'm talking about. I misspent my youth sizing them up. Most either have a good shaft, but a small head or a fat head and too skinny or short a shaft. Or a good-sized shaft and head, but small balls or worse, big balls. Big balls are only good as a metaphor. Suffice it to say, it's hard to get proportions right. But then, men get to size up a woman's proportions just by looking at her breasts and hips. By the time a woman sizes up a man's proportions, it's too late.

It's ridiculous that I'm here. He probably doesn't even remember meeting me two weeks ago. Oh well, at least I'm not home alone waiting for my husband.

Grabbing my shopping bag, I slide into the bathroom then shimmy into my new dress. It fits perfectly. Clings to my figure. The spring green color goes great with my eyes.

Several heads turn as I take my seat. I look at my watch. Stupid to think he'd remember. I resign myself, face forward, sip-deplete my reflection in the wine glass. That's ok, the beach is still an option.

I feel like Al is here. Turning, I spot him in the doorway. My stomach jumps. I stare at him, willing him to see me. I'm rooted to my seat; keep my gaze going until he finds me. I smile. He smiles. A warm twitch starts in my pants, I adjust my wedding ring, reminding myself I'm not available. I figure on twenty Hail Marys for my gynecological reaction to Al and fifty Our Fathers for even being here drinking wine and waiting for a man who isn't my husband. Who knows, maybe I have the mathematics of religion all screwed up like everything else in my life.

I haven't gone to confession to ask for my penance for killing Jordan. God, just two more seconds of time leaned in my direction and I would have seen his orange ball, seen him running into the street, had time to brake and swerve. I picture the ambulance pulling up to our house, Paul pushing me from the back of the ambulance, telling me to stay home with Maddie. I shake my head, blink my eyes to bring myself back to the present.

Al maneuvers his roll luggage like a ballet dancer, pirouetting amongst tables and drunken would-be lovers. He backs into the barstool. It's a slippery slope—I should have never agreed to meet a man who has such a nice ass. Paul has a nice ass too. I replace the picture of Al gliding between tables with Paul's face. If I stay focused on Paul, nothing will happen.

"You're here. You remembered," he says.

I'm totally enchanted. A nice ass, face and a little insecure. What else could a married woman ask for? "I remembered."

We take each other in until he looks away. He seems nervous. I'm not sure why. It can't be because of me.

"It's nice to see you, Emily," he says.

Oh, God. I'd forgotten I told him my name was Emily. "You're a nervous flier?" I ask. I can't get pulled in by his charm.

"No. Why do you ask?"

"Oh, you just seem nervous is all."

"I am," he says. I watch his chest heave up and down as he takes a hyperventilating breath. He shifts in his chair. "I wasn't sure you'd be here."

I look at him. Size up his intent. I'm not used to simple honesty. If that's what this is. "It's me. Here in the flesh."

"I'm glad." He takes my hand—the one without a wedding band. I let him. I shut my eyes, picturing Paul and Madeline. I'm a wife, a mother. I flash to Jordan in his hospital bed. Such a little body swallowed up by all those tubes, machines, a plain bed with hospital corners smeared with blood.

"Are you ok?" he asks.

"Huh?"

"Are you ok? You were somewhere else for a second."

"I'm sorry." I clasp my wedding band hand on top of his ringless hand.

"Where's your baby? What's her name?" he asks.

"Madeline. Maddie for short." I say, answering the question that doesn't require a lie. If he asks again, I'll tell him I left her up north with relatives. Better yet, I'll tell him I came back early.

"Pretty name."

"Yes. After my grandmother. Did you ski? Was there any powder?"

"Skied every day. It was great."

"Late in the season, isn't it?"

"Nah, we have about another month," he says.

"So you'll go again?"

"Of course. Nothing like spring skiing. If you come with me the next time, you can wear your bikini."

"I just bought a new one today at a store down the way."

"I bet you look fantastic in it." He lightly strokes the side of my face. His touch is spine tingling. "So you were killing time waiting for my plane to come in."

I nod, look harder into his eyes, wondering what his intention is. If he wanted to get laid, he could get any woman in the airport.

"Good, I like when things are mutual."

"Do you have a ride?" I ask.

"I always just grab a cab."

"I have a car here."

"What are you saying?" he asks.

"How about dinner?" I try out. It's been twelve years since I asked anybody out. What the heck am I doing? I have to pull out before I go too far. For now, I'm just having a little harmless fun. Probably the same thing Paul tells himself about Susie.

"If you feel uncomfortable with me coming to your house, I can meet you somewhere a little later on," I say, not pulling out at all.

"Not a chance. I've got you now, you might change your mind."

"You're not dating anyone?"

His eyes flick to my wedding ring. "No. I'm not dating. You?"

I twirl the ring on my finger. "No. I'm not exactly dating anymore either. Have you ever been married?"

"Once." He looks at the floor.

"How recent?"

"About eighteen years ago. We were young. It didn't last long."

"Children?" I ask.

"No. She never wanted any."

"You?"

"I would have if she wanted them," he says.

"Are you sorry now?"

"There's still time. Maybe I'll meet a woman who already has kids and fall in love." He salutes me with a glass of chardonnay and a wink. "Do you want more children, Emily?"

I startle at the question. "Ahh, no. Madeline is my world right now. I want to devote all my time to her."

"That's nice. You must be a good mother."

"I hope so," I say. It's so wonderful to be thought of as a good mother and not a mother who killed her son. I could get used to hanging out with Al, leave all my bad acts behind. "Let's go," I say.

"Does this mean the interview portion of our date is done?" he asks.

"Not hardly."

"Where to now?"

"Early dinner? Maybe dancing. Are you too tired from traveling?" I ask.

"Not at all."

"Cause we can meet again another night." I should get home in time to feed Maddie and tuck her in.

"I told you. I've got you right now. I'm not letting you go."

God. Why can't Paul say that to me? Why is it that you can always get what you need from people you don't want?

"I have another piece of luggage to pick up from baggage claim. Where's your luggage?"

"I already put it in the car," I lie. Shit, I've got to get the car out of the parking garage, otherwise he'll see I've only been here an hour. One lie does beget another. I wonder how Paul keeps all his lies straight. "I'll meet you outside. I'm driving a black Mercedes. I'll pull up to the curb outside of baggage claim."

He calls for the check. I feel funny, but I let him pay. I watch to see what kind of tipper he is. Nice. I swig the last of my wine while he grabs his carry-on bag. My mother used to say, "Waste makes want," every time she'd shake the last drop out of her gin bottle. Now I know what she was talking about.

We walk towards baggage claim. He puts his hand on the small of my back to direct me around people, wheels his carry-on with the other hand.

When we get to the top of the escalator, I say, "It'll take me a few minutes to loop the airport. Wait for me outside downstairs?"

He makes like he's going to kiss me, but I skitter away. I don't dare turn around to see if he's following me with his eyes. I wonder if he'll be pissed because I wouldn't kiss him. Maybe he'll slide out and catch a cab. So be it. I shouldn't be here anyway.

chapter ten

I feel a slight buzz from the glass of wine on an empty stomach. As if we Americans even begin to understand what an empty stomach is. The scene from Frank McCourt's novel *Angela's Ashes* haunts me—the one where the school kids clamor to eat the teacher's apple peels maliciously thrown in the garbage among pencil scrapings. Everyone lives with some tragedy. There's nothing that makes me so special just because I had a shitty childhood and killed my son. If I keep pulling myself up by the bootstraps, I know I'll make it. No more self-pity for me. That's the old Meg. Now I'm Emily.

Al is out on the curb. When he sees Paul's car, he pretends to hitch a ride. I help him load his luggage into the back seat, so he doesn't see that I really don't have any luggage in the trunk.

"Do you want to swing over to the beach and take a walk before eating dinner?" he asks.

"Don't you want to go back to your house and freshen up?" I ask.

"Nah, let's keep moving."

"I don't mind. I know you just got back into town and probably want to check on your house and all."

"Once you know me, you'll find I'm the kind of guy that just goes with the moment."

"Good way to live," I say.

He pats my leg. I jab the accelerator, negotiate the traffic out of the airport and onto the freeway. All twelve cylinders are pretty stinking nice right now. I shark-eye Al, he's looking out the window like he's trying to re-acclimate himself to the scenery.

"You know there's a beach in Fort Lauderdale?" he asks.

"Yeah, I've heard of it. It's *Where the Boys Are*."

"Your boy's right here."

I look over at him. "So you are. I thought we would go down to Hollywood. Is that ok?" I ask.

"Suit yourself, I'm just along for your rocket ride."

"That's where you're wrong. It's me that's along for your ride," I say.

"We'll see." He squeezes my thigh again.

Even though I'm ashamed to be enjoying the company of another man, it's nice to make contact. "How fast are you going anyway?" He looks over at the speedometer, says, "Nothing wrong with ninety miles an hour on a major thoroughfare."

Laughing, I pat the dashboard instead of his leg. A snapshot of Paul's happy little face the night he was online bidding for this car flashes in my mind. When he looked up from his laptop to tell me about the Mercedes he wanted to purchase off eBay, his cloud nine face lit up the room. It took days of bidding, but he got it. He flew out to Texas to see the car before any money exchanged hands and arranged to have it shipped home. He didn't want to put the miles on it by driving it back.

The first time we drove in it, he said, "You think I'm being stupidly extravagant for buying this car."

"What do you mean?"

"You don't respect my decision. You think it's frivolous."

"I personally wouldn't pay this much for a car," I said.

"But you did. It's your money too."

"Yes, but if it gives you pleasure, I want you to have it," I said, stroking the dashboard, making an orgasm moan voice.

"I'm being serious," Paul said.

"You work hard, enjoy it."

"But you wouldn't buy it for yourself."

"No, I wouldn't," I said, brushing his hair back with my fingers. "I'm sure I'm extravagant in other ways."

"I can't think of any. We wouldn't have the savings we do if it weren't for you."

"Stop. Just be happy," I ordered.

He accelerated as his response. I went down on him to make sure he would relax and enjoy his new car.

There's a Mozart concert on the beach in Hollywood. We drive around for a half-hour looking for a parking space. There's a few spaces left in a paid lot, but it's a gravel lot and the cars are so packed in there, I don't want to risk damaging Paul's car. If we didn't have a Mercedes, I wouldn't have to worry about where to park. What kind of people have we become? They did a study that showed "the new rich" drove BMWs and Mercedes, while "the old rich" drove modest, sometimes junker cars. The old rich having grown out of the need for conspicuous consumption. I guess we would qualify as the new rich. I better think about getting back to work soon so we can keep our new rich mantle.

Al says, "How about if we just take a leisurely drive back up A1A and go to a restaurant closer to home? I'm starting to get hungry."

"I am too."

As we drive, he points out the beauty of the sunset in the west and the tranquility of the rolling waves sliding onto the beach. When we get closer, he gives me directions to the restaurant. He's considerate, at least three blocks ahead of every turn, he tells me what our next move will be. I wonder if he gives gentle directions in bed too.

We valet park. The maître'd greets him in Italian, he answers back. Not just one or two words. He has a regular conversation. I love the sound of it; how his facial expressions and gestures are different than when he speaks English. I'm going to have to go ring my panties out in the bathroom if he keeps this up.

He turns towards me, "Emily, this is Giovanni."

I put my hand out. "Nice to meet you."

Giovanni kisses my hand. "Charmed," he says.

"Of course," I say. If I'm going to be Emily, I can act any way I want. As long as I'm not myself tonight, I'm going to be cocky.

Giovanni guides us to the bar. Points to us when the bartender looks in our direction and calls for a bottle of Barbaresco.

"So you come in here a lot?" I ask.

"It's close to home. You'll have to excuse me, Emily," Al says. "I didn't mean to be rude by speaking Italian in front of you."

"I enjoyed it. Did you spend time in Italy?"

"Long story," he says, waving me away.

The bartender opens the wine with a flourish. "To new friends," he toasts, once the bartender has walked away.

"To discovering things Italian," I say.

We clink our glasses, take a sip, smile, take another sip.

"What's Al short for? Albert?"

"Alfredo."

"Better than Albert and so very Italian."

"I am what I am." He excuses himself to go to the bathroom.

A couple and their thirteen- or fourteen-year-old son come in. We exchange greetings.

"What're you having?" the bartender asks the couple.

The man jumps in with his order first. "I'll have Red Label and ginger ale." He has an English accent. That's South Florida for you, everyone's from somewhere else, running here to leave their shitty lives behind. Problem is, your life follows you.

"And for you?" the bartender asks, turning to the woman.

"Campari."

"We're out."

"Of Campari?" the woman asks.

"Yes."

"An Italian restaurant is out of Campari?"

"Afraid so, sorry."

"Jesus, I guess I'll have Chivas on the rocks. Have you any Chivas?"

"Right away."

The kid is sitting there, a *persona non grata*. I can tell his invisibility is a regular event. Even the bartender didn't acknowledge him. What I wouldn't do for Jordan to be sitting next to me. I'd never ignore him. People don't have their priorities straight. I want to tell the woman to enjoy her son while she has him, but I don't want to explain what I really mean.

I can tell the husband is agitated about something. He keeps watching the bartender.

"Do you need something?" I ask.

"Yes. The barkeep."

I wave the bartender over. The Englishman says to the bartender, "Do you mind if I pour my own ginger ale?"

"That's good," I say, "ask for what you want."

"It's the taste of the alcohol I need tonight. I'm afraid he's going to ruin it with too much ginger ale."

I raise my glass to him. The bartender gives him a small glass of ginger ale with no ice to complement his Red Label. He pours a dollop in and takes a gulp.

The wife says, "Here, look at this, no one has asked Ian what he wants."

"I don't want anything," the teen says into his shirt.

"A coke?" the mother asks.

"No," Ian says.

"Water?"

"No."

"Well, you have to drink something."

"I'm not drinking tonight, Mom."

"What does that mean?" the mother asks. She swings her head around in the kid's direction, furrows her eyebrows.

"What do you think it means? It means you and Dad can drink, I'm not drinking tonight." He looks at her in such an accusatory way, I actually put my own wine glass back on the bar. That's how I must have looked when squaring off with my mother over drinking.

The woman blurts, "Don't look at me aghast as if I'm stupid."

The teen looks down and says, "Ok."

Al slithers back onto his barstool. Poor Ian slides back into anonymity.

"Miss me?" Al asks, leaning into me, nudging me with his shoulder. A waft of cologne comes my way. The contact made between our two bodies has dislodged scent molecules. He must have spruced up in the bathroom. Used the cologne from one of those bathroom valets. Usually cologne bothers me. Paul doesn't wear any cologne because he knows it bothers my sinuses. Al has picked a nice cologne with a sandalwood base. The cologne tickles my nose. I pinch my nose to stop the sneeze that's forming. Once I start sneezing, I have a hard time stopping a continuous loop of sneezing, blowing my nose, sneezing, blowing my nose.

"Ok," Al says, "I guess you didn't miss me."

"No," I say. "I was just drinking in your body perfume. You smell great."

"Body perfume, huh?" He grabs the underside of my barstool, pulling me over to him. "I smell even better up close."

"Indeed."

He nuzzles my neck. I feel my body involuntarily go rigid.

He pulls away. I never was a cheater. I'm just not cut out for it. Other women I knew growing up and in college made a game of the dating roulette. One for each night of the week. I always picked just one person and stuck with them until my interest ran out, even if it was only for one night; then I'd move onto the next man. A serial monogamist is what I am. Maybe it's time to see how the other half—specifically my other half—lives.

"What do you usually order here?" I ask, trying to reel him back in in a safe way.

"Food here is great. I'll order for you."

"I'm kind of picky." Maybe he's one of those old world Italians—comes across like he's liberated, but what he really wants is a submissive, barefoot and pregnant woman at home and another wild woman for his bed away from home. I'm not sure anymore what role I'd fit into best. I used to be the latter, but now maybe the last twelve years has turned me into the former. God, that's depressing.

"Where do you go?" he asks.

"For what?"

"You seem to float off somewhere. Where do you go when that happens? Do you not want to be here?"

"No. I mean, yes. I mean, I'm actually not sure."

He laughs. "You really know how to make a guy feel secure."

"I'm sorry. Maybe I should just go."

"No. I want you here."

"Why?"

"I don't know. You seem different from most women I meet."

"You don't even know me."

"I'm good at reading people."

The maître'd interrupts, says, "Come with me, Al, Madame. I'll have your bottle of wine brought to the table."

When the waiter comes, Al tries to order me some sort of fish dish, but I correct the order for osso bucco.

When the waiter walks away, Al says, "A woman with a mind of her own."

"Is that a problem for you?"

"No. I like it, like you."

"Hmmm," I say, raising my glass of wine to him.

I wonder why Paul hasn't called me, wonder what he's doing.

Someone's nuzzling my neck. I tilt my head up and away, give better access.

"You ready to go home?"

"Yes," I say, but when I open my eyes, it's Al and not Paul standing beside me. "Oh, I mean, I should be getting home to my house."

He pulls out my chair for me. "Not a chance. You promised to take me dancing."

Out at the valet, he guides me into the passenger seat, slides behind the wheel. I'm definitely drunk. I worry he might be as drunk as I am, crash Paul's car. Since I'm new to drinking, the drinking and driving routine is not something I have down yet. I've never driven when I've felt this drunk. The odds are better for Al to drive.

"You're a tiny thing," he says, moving the driver's seat back. "Where to?"

"There's a couple of jazz bars down by Las Olas Boulevard," I answer.

"Jazz music, huh? All right then."

He drives, while I flick on the stereo. Paul has a Stevie Ray Vaughan CD in. We used to love dancing at blues and jazz clubs. He isn't the best dancer I ever danced with, but he was always my favorite. He had an easy style and a willingness that made it fun. Plus, he would engage me with his eyes—like there was no one else in the room. He didn't care if there were fifty or zero people on the dance floor. If there was a song he wanted to move to, he'd take my hand and we'd be out there on the floor. He used to call the way I bop around "the freaky girl dance."

I miss him. The old him. A twinge of guilt hits me right between the legs and the heart. Before going any further tonight with Al, I should really assess what I want in my life. I picture a bar graph of attribute comparisons for Paul and Al. There's too many unknowns for Al, but that's a large part of what makes him so appealing. We're equally unknown to each other. I could have a fresh start with him.

He parks in a paved paid lot with full-size parking spaces. He runs around the car to open my door for me, pockets Paul's car keys.

I put my hand out, "Not a chance. Put the keys right here."

He starts to run, calling over his shoulder, "What's the matter, Emily, you don't trust me?"

I'm in sandals and can't run very fast. He slows down for me to catch him, then trips me and takes me down to the ground on the only spot of grass I see for blocks. I wonder if we're rolling in dog poop. He straddles me, tickles me as a prelude to his kiss. I resist at first, but then his tongue is in my mouth, so warm and gentle.

I kiss him back. A kiss is a cheat. A kiss is a cheat. I pull away, turn my head to the side.

I'm a cheater now too.

He bites my neck. I'm yearning to be touched. A low guttural moan slips from my lips without me knowing about it in advance. He takes my chin between his thumb and forefinger, kisses me again, leans down into me with his body. I can feel the heat of his hard-on.

I hear a group of people walking towards us. I push him, try to sit up. What if I know someone?

"Hey, get a fucking hotel room," a male voice calls out.

"Very original," I yell back. Al clamps his hand over my mouth. I bite it.

"Ouch. Keep it up and you're going to get spanked," he says.

I chomp at his hand again. He makes like he's going to spank me, but then he takes my hand and helps me up.

I put my free hand out. "The keys, please."

He takes them from his pocket, hands them over. "Not a very trusting person, are you?"

"I just like to know I can get myself home."

"What if I drove my car tonight?"

"I'd make sure I had enough cab money with me."

"Damn, you're harsh."

"Not harsh, just practical. My mother taught me to always carry cab fare. She called it her 'mad money.'"

"Maybe I'll get to meet her and talk to her about that sometime."

"Not a chance."

"Another one of your trust issues?"

"No, she's dead."

"Oh, sorry."

"Yeah, so am I."

He side hugs me as his answer. I could get to love a guy who knows when to be quiet.

We walk over to the first jazz bar we find. The band is playing "Little Sister". It's one of Paul's favorite songs to dance to. Al leads me out onto the dance floor. I sit my purse down in the corner where I can keep my eye on it. I join Al, start my freaky girl dance. Ok, he can move. The more he moves, the sexier he looks, the wetter my pants get.

The song ends. We crowd into a spot at the bar. I wish I

didn't have to lug my purse around. Al takes it from me, sets it on the bar.

"You're a great dancer," he says. "What're you having?"

"Just Sprite. I've already had too much to drink tonight."

"Very conservative." When the bartender comes, he says, "A Sprite and a Patron straight up, no salt."

"Chilled or room temp on the Patron?" the bartender asks.

"Room temp. Thanks for asking."

The bartender produces a Sprite and a Patron in a rocks glass. "Go ahead and start a tab," Al says, passing her a credit card.

"What's Patron?" I ask.

"Tequila. Try a sip."

I hesitate, then take a sip. "Very smooth," I say, passing him back his glass. I've never tasted hard liquor before. Of course, with all the drinking my mother did, sometimes I could taste it just by the overwhelming smell in her small bedroom—the open bottle, liquor spilled onto her sheets and rug from the glass in her passed-out hand.

The Patron heats me up from my throat down to my stomach. Between the sensation he's giving me in my pants and the Patron, my whole body is on fire.

"You want one?" he asks.

I shake my head no.

He sips his drink. I kiss him. He grabs a handful of my hair, pulls me closer. I grab a handful of his ass back. We start grinding at the bar. The band plays, "Moondance". "Let's dance," I say.

I'm having a wonderful time. We dance and kiss through five more songs. I quit the dance floor when they start up "Love Struck Baby", but Al pulls me back, dances close with me, even though it's a fast song; sings the words in my ear like he means them. The song ends. I wish the words were true and that I were free to believe them. Al kisses me, then excuses himself to the bathroom. I go back to the bar, grab some napkins; wipe my face and neck off.

The woman standing at the bar next to me says, "I hope the kids are all right."

It's like I've been shot. Boom. I'm back in my life again. Paul. Shit. I am in so much trouble. I look inside my purse, see the red light on my cell phone indicating someone called. Paul is the only one who ever calls me. He finally called me. He does care. I've got to go. I take a swig of Al's Patron, mouth the glass where his lips touched seconds before.

I slip around bodies on my way to the door without looking back. I'm afraid to see Al's surprised and hurt face. He seems like such a good man, this isn't fair to him. I feel like Cinderella trying to beat the clock before midnight. If Al knew how shabby my real life actually is, he wouldn't want me anyway. Instead of a wicked stepmother and three stepsisters, I'm tortured by a dead mother, father, brother and son. If only I could really be Emily turned Cinderella; rewrite my life—be somebody else with a life story happier than mine.

Once I hit the street, I run-walk so Al can't catch up. He probably thinks I'm in the bathroom. Tripping out of one of my sandals, I double back and retrieve it. Kicking the other sandal off, I stuff them both into my purse. I skid into Paul's Mercedes, power the seat forward, slink away from the curb. I've got a good buzz going. But sweating some of the alcohol off from dancing should make it ok to drive. I hope the Mercedes doesn't turn into a pumpkin.

chapter eleven

Order of magnitude. Which is another phrase for juicy rationalization. So I kissed him. Big deal. It's not like I let him stick his dick in my mouth or worse, my pussy. I guess some women would say it's worse to let a guy stick his dick in your mouth than fuck you. Everyone's got their sex rules. Nothing like a well-formed dick in your mouth though. I'd stop eating chocolate for the right one.

Shit! Where do I turn? I drive down a dead end circling a duck pond. I don't want to hit any of the ducks, but I sure would appreciate it if they'd move faster. The scene from *A Clockwork Orange* flashes in my head. The one where the droogs hit the ducks on the way to rape a woman in her own house. Now that woman had a hell of a dildo. I wonder what her sex rules were. Different after the rape, I'm sure. I swerve around the ducks, holding down my impatience. I'm way overdue.

Ok, break it down. It's midnight. I've been gone all day. My husband doesn't know where I am. I'm not sure what he did, but I'm pretty sure he spent the day with his lover. I, on the other no less guilty hand, met a man at the airport, then proceeded out to dinner and dancing with him. Sounds like a date to me. I rolled around on the ground with him, melded my hips with his in a slow grind at the bar. Let him bite my neck until I growled. I'm a bad person. I'm a cheater. Order of magnitude. Paul has been sleeping with Susie for almost a year now. What if Paul really isn't a cheater? What if I'm turning into both my parents' bad traits—a drunk like my mother and a cheater like my father?

"Shut up, shut up," I yell, smacking my right cheek. I roll the window down for some fresh air; a moist heat air blanket assaults me. I'm having a hard time concentrating on the road, drunken vibrations run through my body. Pick a car that appears to be driving in a reasonably straight line. I lock in behind a nondescript white sedan. If I imitate their trajectory on the road, I can get myself home. A DUI would really complicate matters.

The white car buzzes through a yellow light. I get caught at the red light. If I were two seconds more up their ass, I'd have made the yellow light. Now I'm here out in front by myself. No one to follow. I spot a patrol car to the right in my periphery vision. Shit, shit. I don't dare look over there. Gotta be calm. There was a TV show that said cops look at a person's driving pattern for signs. Something like driving too slow and hugging the right line meant you were drunk; while driving too fast and weaving over the left line meant you were under the influence of psychotropic drugs. Or maybe it was the other way around. Either way, unless I can maintain the middle of the road demeanor, I'm cooked. Kind of like my marriage. I think it's a fair assumption that I deviated from my middle of the road demeanor tonight. I'm not proud of myself. I'm not proud at all.

I pull away from the light slowly. The cop turns onto the street behind me. My stomach jumps. I look in my rearview mirror to see if he's watching me. I can't tell. One block passes. I slow down a little—but not too much, encouraging him to pass me. Two blocks pass. Let's just get this done and over with. I'm guilty. I'm a cheater, a drunken driver, a bad mother. Let them just throw me in jail. I pull into the next parking lot I see, negotiate a turn into a space without too much trouble. Look in my rearview mirror. The cop car is gone. The parking lot is empty. My throat is empty, save my heart.

It's not like I have a lot of things in my cavernous purse. My hands are shaking so bad I can't locate the cell phone. I want to hear Paul's message—get some clues about how to act when I get home. I'm so glad he called. He really does care.

Breathe, breathe. I put my hands on either side of my head, steadying myself and my thoughts. I plunge back into my purse, locate the cell. The display reads "1 Missed Call," but the voice mail indicator is blank. The caller ID displays a number that's not our home number or Paul's cell. Maybe it's Susie's. Maybe he called me from her house to see how much time they had for a little action before I got home. As if they haven't had action enough already. I haven't gotten laid in three months and twelve days. At least I got kissed tonight. I'd forgotten how exhilarating it is to be with someone new. Even so, I wish it were Paul I was dancing with and kissing.

Maybe it's a wrong number. I never get wrong numbers though. The first three digits are the same as ours. I throw the cell phone into the back seat, put my head down on the steering wheel. If I go home and he's not there, I'm going to be really mad. Madder than mad. Go ballistic mad. Nuclear mad. *Hiroshima Mon Amour* mad. I'll call him. Too bad if I wake him up.

Leaning over the seat, I spot Al's luggage. Shit, shit, shit. I'm such a shit. I can't believe I left that man stranded and took his luggage on top of it. Could I be any bigger an ass? He probably thinks I'm some kind of luggage thief. I run my hands over the zipper of the big piece to see if it's locked. Just one of those cheapy locks. I could have that off in no time.

I wonder what he's got in there. Maybe he's really a drug runner. Maybe somebody will hunt me down for his luggage. What if they hurt Maddie? Just dump it out here in the parking lot. Leave his luggage and my guilty conscience behind.

I can't sit here all night. My buzz is fading, replaced by an adrenalin rush. Gotta keep moving. I'll think on the road.

Once on I-95, I pick the middle lane. That way, I'm not going too slow, but I'm not the fastest car on the road either. Middle of the road. That's what my life is going to be from now on. MOR—middle of the road. Now there's a message. That's what the middle-of-the-road kind of life would be like—always leave you looking for more. I'll never make it living in moderation. I'm much happier bouncing on and off the edges of extremes. That way, you can really feel yourself living. Gotta understand where the edges are, use them as a yardstick. Extremely happy and extremely depressed—my life as a kid. Extremely happy and extremely depressed—my marriage in two halves. The epilogue is divorce.

Actually, the epilogue is death. Statistics show death occurs to humans ten out of ten times. It's just a matter of when. In two more years, I will have outlived my brother, father and mother. My mother lived the longest. Made it to forty-two before her liver turned on her.

Summertime after twelfth grade was when she died. The apartment we had came furnished. I just boxed up the few things my mom had—personal effects is what the hospital called her watch and purse. She had been taken there after collapsing on the floor of some hole-in-the-wall bar with alcohol poisoning. For college, my guidance counselor ended up qualifying me for some pauper orphan scholarship. Every semester, standing in line for hours with my hands out saying, "I'll have more, sir." The dorm-resident assistant said my mother's boxes would be safe in the basement. But when I went down to get them at the end of the year, her boxes were gone. My childhood was lost in the basement storage of a dorm.

Wish I had had the presence of mind to keep my parents' wedding album with me. I loved the black and white photos—

my parents moving like perfectly coifed action figures. On their way down the aisle, arms swinging out towards the camera, wedding rings on hands, beatific smiles; into the car, rice at their backs; leaning over each other out the car door; the just married sign strung to the black Cadillac fins retreating. If only my father had kept his dick in his pants, I would have had a perfect, middle of the road life. Probably wouldn't have picked a man who would cheat on me, in keeping with patterns repeating themselves.

Moment of truth here. The Sample Road exit is looming large. What am I going to do? If Paul and Susie are up, I won't be able to drag Al's luggage to a safe hiding place. I don't even know where a safe hiding place is. I can't very well climb up into the attic this time of night. It's not like it's a bottle of wine I can hide in the fridge. If I leave it outside, Paul may do yard work tomorrow and spot it. Or it could rain and Al's things will be ruined. I've done enough mean things to Al already. Shit, I've done enough mean things to Paul, myself and my marriage.

What would Emily do? The bus station. Where the hell is the bus station? They have lockers I can stow the luggage in. At least that's what all those '70s cop shows taught me. I know there's one in Pompano. I just don't know exactly where. I can't drive in circles all night. I have to get home. If it weren't so late, I'd call Marci. Ask for help. But then what would I tell her? I'm running away for the day with some stranger's luggage? Obviously, I need more help than one night of counseling can offer.

Pausing at the turn onto my street, I'm still not sure what to do. If I drive by and Paul is outside talking to Susie, he'll spot me and wonder why I don't pull into the driveway. Dammit. If Al had just let me take him back to his house before going out, I wouldn't be in this predicament. Emily would never blame other people for her bad fortune.

I try to think like the Emily Al thinks he knows. Turning left instead of right, I negotiate my way back to Federal Highway. The luggage isn't the only issue. I'm drunk. I smell like smoke. I have the remnants of Al's kiss spit in my mouth. How men can kiss and fuck other women, then bounce home to their wives is beyond me. Maybe it's just because this is the first time I've kissed someone else since I started dating Paul. Maybe it gets easier as it goes on.

I turn onto Hillsboro Boulevard, head over to the beach. There's a bunch of motels down there. Any motel will do—it's just to freshen up a bit. I drive by the Fairy Tale Motel. I used to date someone who dated the daughter of the owners. Once she heard he was considering marrying me, she knocked on my boyfriend's window in the middle of the night, trying to get him back. Even though I can't remember her name, I still don't want to give her parents any of my money. Funny how things that were so important, you can't remember the details given enough time and distance. Maybe tonight will be like that for me. Just a passing thing and not a defining moment.

I pull into one of those chain motels. They have a bigger parking lot where I won't have to park Paul's car out on the street. I don't want anyone we know to drive by and see his car there. They'd probably think he was cheating on me. I'm not sure which is worse, people thinking Paul's cheating on me or me cheating on him. I sure don't want people thinking I'm a victim.

The check-in goes smoothly until I'm five bucks short of the room charge. I don't want to charge it. Even though I do the bills, Paul might see it.

"I'm short."

"You can charge it."

"No I can't. Do you have an ATM here?"

"No." The kid stares at me like I know what to do next.

"All right. I guess I'll go somewhere else."

"But I've already got you in the computer. It's a pain to back people out once they're in."

"Like the roach motel. Once you get in, you don't get out?"

"Something like that. But you didn't hear about our bug problem from me."

"You got any five dollar off specials? Help us both out."

"Yeah. Now that I think about it, they did have a coupon in the paper."

He tells me how to get to my room.

"I'm going to get my stuff from my car."

"Is that your Mercedes out there?"

"Yep."

"Phat ride. No wonder your credit card's maxed."

I don't speak. I hear Mom's voice in my head saying, "Silence is the hardest argument to refute." I retrieve Al's luggage from the car, struggle onto the elevator. I could have made two trips. When the elevator doors open on the fifth floor, a thirty-year funk of ocean water, mildew and suntan lotion assaults me.

They still have keyed entries here. Al's luggage falls over as I fight with the lock. I flop his carry-on piece and my purse in the doorway, then wheel the big piece into the room. God, it stinks in here. There's one powerful smell in here if it can get through to my sinuses. I kick my purse and the carry-on into the room. I shouldn't even let my purse sit on this floor. The carpet looks like it's at least ten years old. Harboring all manner of germs, no doubt. I flick on the bathroom light. Man, I look rough. I wash my face with the sliver of cheap hand soap. The water and soap sting my bloodshot eyes.

I take the comforter off the bed, throw it in the corner, smell the sheets. I'm just going to lay here for a minute, gather myself before I have to face Paul.

Face Paul. Paul's face. I can see him smiling at me. He's holding his hands out, calling me to come home. I step towards him. He turns, puts his hand out to the side. A woman's hand clasps his. They walk away. I bolt upright. The room is dark. I reach over for Paul. The bed is empty. I fumble for my nightstand light. There's an old clock radio on the nightstand. It's lit up on the numbers 3:32. How am I ever going to explain this day away to Paul?

Placing my hand on the luggage, I spot Al's name and address tag. Could I be any more dense? Amazing how a little alcohol can cloud the brain. All I had to do last night was drop it off on his front porch. I look at the address. At least he didn't lie. He does live in Fort Lauderdale down by the restaurant.

Ok, I'll drop the luggage off, then go home. My dress stinks of smoke. Pulling on the shirt and pants I wore when I left the house yesterday, I consider leaving the dress, but I like the way it looks on me. I stuff it in my purse and spot my underwear in the corner of the room. They are so wet, Paul will be able to smell me a block away. He will think I did have sex if I wear those home. I hope I make it home before he wakes up. I hope he forgives me for being such a hot head.

TWA—Terraces, Ways and Avenues run north and south; Streets, Drives and Courts run east and west. That's the way Fort Lauderdale was planned and built. No winding country roads here. Only square quadrants topped by square houses. How's that song go? Something about little boxes all looking just the same.

Al's porch light is on. The garage door is shut, so I can't check out his ride. I feel bad. Maybe I should knock on the door, turn the hijacked luggage over, become lip-locked one more time before returning to my married life. At least feel his package with my hand instead of my clothed pelvis. Give me something to jerk off to. A door has been opened now. It's just whether or not I want to step through.

"That's enough, Meg, Emily, whoever you are," I say out loud.

I leave my car door open, so it doesn't make a sound alerting Al to my presence. My resolve is weak. One more kiss from him and I might move in.

The big piece of luggage makes a loud bump as I drag it up the step. I lay it on its side so it's not as conspicuous from the road.

My heart pounds as I retreat into marital safety.

chapter twelve

Somebody's hitting my shoulder with spring-loaded fingers.

"Get up, damn you."

My top and bottom eyelashes are woven together. My eyes roll open, then shut, catching a glimpse of Paul's red face. Pounding, pounding, my head is pounding. I should have drunk water before I crept to sleep last night, but I didn't want to make any noise. I roll over on the couch.

"Meg, I'm not kidding. You asshole."

"Look who's got a dirty mouth now," I mumble.

He grabs my arm, pulls me off the couch.

My head grazes the edge of the coffee table. "What the fuck are you doing?" My head is ringing. I remain on the ground. A tactical decision. If I stand, it will only escalate the fight. If I stand, I'll take a jab back at him.

"Where the hell were you all day yesterday?" he yells.

"Where the hell were you?" I yell back.

"Here."

"Right. That's the problem," I say, sitting up.

"That I stayed home?" Paul looks at me with the hugest scowl I've ever seen.

"Right. Home with Susie. In our house."

"You're mad at me because I stayed home with our daughter?"

"With Susie."

"With our daughter."

"You're skirting the issue, Paul. You stayed home with Maddie, yes. But you also stayed home with Susie."

"Meg, you're nuts. Get some help."

"Don't make this into one of those 'the woman's nuts' things. That's not going to fly. You stayed home with Susie."

"I did not."

"She at least came for dinner."

"I told her not to," he says.

"Let me get this straight. When I asked for a day as a family, you said no. But then I leave and you tell her not to come?"

"Yes."

"You're the one who's nuts. You better get some help."

"It's the truth."

"Explain," I say.

"I was mad."

"So when you're mad, you do what I ask?"

"It's not like that." Paul's voice has a pleading edge to it that I don't know how to read. Is he pleading because he's guilty and he wants to stop talking about it or is he pleading because he wants me to believe him? There's a thin line between the truth and a lie. I must need glasses to read the line properly.

"Oh, so how is it?" I spread my arms wide. "I'd love it if you'd once and for all tell me how it really is."

"I love you," Paul says.

"What?"

"I love you. I can't stand this contention any more. I don't know how to find my way back to you."

I put my hands down. "I'm right in front of you."

"No, you're not."

I look down at my body, clasp my hands over my heart, then move them out to my breasts. "I feel real to me."

He laughs. "There you are." He squats down, hugging me. I hug back.

"You didn't call me," I say. Half of me still feels wounded. The other half wants him to fess up to the strange phone number on my cell last night.

"You didn't call me."

"I didn't," I say. "I'm sorry."

"I'm sorry too. Where'd you go? Maddie and I drove around looking for you."

"The miracle of technology would have found me faster," I say, avoiding the subject. Good God, what if I'm the cheater and he's the innocent?

"Really, where'd you go?" His voice goes down a register. I know it hurts him to ask me again. But I'm happy to tickle his insecurity up a notch. It's nice to see him wearing my uncertainty for once. "Meg?"

I shake my head. "Yes?"

He pulls away from me. "Why are you avoiding the question?"

"What question?"

"Where the FUCK did you go yesterday?" He yells it so loud, Maddie screams upstairs.

"Now look what you've done." I pull away from him and crawl on my knees towards the stairs. He grabs my naked hips, pulling me back onto my ass.

"Leave her. ANSWER ME!"

Maddie's up to a full-tilt scream now. As I rise with swifter intention, he grabs my arm. I look at his hand, raise my eyebrow. "What? You're a wife beater now?"

He squeezes my arm.

My voice comes out low, between clenched teeth. "Let go right now or you'll be sorry."

His claw-hand goes flaccid.

I look back over my shoulder. He's staring at me like I'm some intruder in his house. "I drove around, then went to the beach. There was a Mozart concert on the beach down in Hollywood. Why don't you call and verify it?"

Running up the stairs, I can feel Paul not following me. It's been forever since I've seen Maddie. I didn't dare go upstairs and check in on her last night—well, this morning. I must have gotten all of about three hours of sleep.

I dress Maddie to stall for time—give Paul a chance to get a hold of himself. I frame and reframe my story to Paul about my whereabouts all day yesterday. Maddie and I bounce downstairs, refreshed, armed with half truths.

"Where's Daddy?" I call out.

"Dada," Maddie mimics.

"Right, Daddy." We walk from the kitchen to the den, to the livingroom. "Paul?"

I open the front door. Maddie cups her hand to the side of her mouth, yells, "Dada."

Paul's car is gone. He better be getting donuts. I hope his sophisticated car doesn't have some sort of geographical device capable of retracing my steps.

We wait for Paul, playing *Sesame Street* videos; singing and coloring in her books outside the picture boundary lines. I don't want my daughter to know about boundaries at this young age.

If it's going to be tit for tat, I can play that game. Madeline and I climb the stairs one by one. I go into my closet, pull Al's business card from the bathrobe pocket hiding place.

I press *67 before dialing the home phone number Al has scribbled on the back of his business card. I don't want him calling me back sometime when Paul's home. I get a recording. He has call block on the people who have call block. Technology for technology. It's a funny war we wage these days. I hang up. I'll just have to call him from a pay phone or I could wait to call him at work on Monday. But if

Paul's going to be off gallivanting around today, I don't want to be stuck home wondering.

To clear Al's phone number from the redial function, I dial Paul's cell number, let it ring once, then hang up. I hope it interrupts whatever it is he's doing. Throwing the mobile phone on the living-room couch, a piece of cloth stuffed in the corner catches my eye. I pick it up. It's the dress I wore last night. I can't believe he was snooping through my purse. I would never do that with his stuff. No wonder he hightailed it out of here. I pick the dress up, it stinks like smoke. The dress is ruined now—it has a bad association to the day I struck out on my own. Now Paul will never think it looks good on me. I bury it in the laundry basket alongside the bathingsuit and towels I stuck there last night.

I need to find out whether or not he's with Susie. Maddie toddles in to the bathroom with me, I sit her in her spinning chair, give her a toy to play with. Jump in and out of the shower so fast, I'm not even sure I got wet. I shimmy into Paul's favorite dress. If he does come home today, I want to look good.

Maddie and I bustle over to Susie's house. My stomach jumps as I knock on the door. I hate invading people's space when I'm not invited. No answer, except Susie's barking dog. I ring the doorbell. No answer. Fuck it all. She is with Paul. I bang on the door so hard that if she is home sleeping, she isn't now. No answer from Susie, her dog paw-pounds her front picture window. I give her door a swift kick. The door knocker bounces up and down as the final knock. We stalk back home.

Maddie says, "Doggie. Doggie."

"You're right, goozie. Susie is an absolute dog."

A half-hour, an hour. Emily would never wait around the house for a man like this.

"Let's buzz," Maddie yells.

"What? Say it again."

"Let's buzz."

"Let's buzz?" Now I'm the one mimicking Maddie.

She shakes her head yes. "Yeah."

"Who taught you that?" That's not the sort of phrase Paul or I use. I don't want to start cross-examining my own daughter to find out what her father does when I'm not around and who he does it with.

"Buzz," she says.

"Ok." My kid is right. We need a change of scenery. I'm taking charge and going to the beach. A day with Maddie, with the sun and waves serenading us would be nice.

The idea of a closure ritual at the beach pops into my head. I used to do closure rituals all the time as a teenager with my mom. I got the idea from a book. If my mom took a certain man's not calling particularly hard, I'd take whatever personal item he had left in the house—usually a pair of underwear—and burn a piece of it in the kitchen sink. As the swatch of underwear burned, I'd make her list ten things she liked about herself, then I'd list ten things I liked about her. It always seemed to buoy her back up.

Breathless, I run upstairs, telescope my arm to the back of my closet for Madeline's lilac dress—the one Jordan picked out. It goes in the beach bag with scissors, paste, towels, sunscreen, a blanket and munchies. A bottle of wine goes in and comes back out.

I have to start picking the life I want to live. I'm going to pretend to be Emily after today's ritual. A woman who has one child and is a good mother. A good mother. A woman whose marriage can be saved. We've both had our indiscretions. I'm taking control. It's time for me to live again.

At the beach, Maddie and I slather sunscreen on each other. Maddie laughs when I dot her nose and cheeks with it, then show her her reflection in a mirror.

"She's so cute," the woman on the blanket next to us calls over.

"Thanks."

A man with an ugly face and the biggest dick I've ever seen, packaged in a red Speedo, walks by. I can't help but stare. When I raise my eyes to meet his, he's smiling proud.

The woman laughs, then practically swallows half her Pepsi bottle blowjob style.

"Have you ever?" I ask.

"You'd have to put a bag over his head first," she says.

We laugh. "You're right," I say. "But it might be worth it."

The bag of potato chips calls to me. I cram the entire contents of the bag into my mouth like it's a feedbag I've hooked up to my face. I don't even share with Maddie. Three months and thirteen days. Three months and thirteen days. I can't let another day go by without getting laid.

Maddie pulls her lilac dress out and tries to put it on over her bathingsuit. She starts crying when she can't get her head through.

"Here, goozie." I take the dress away from her, which makes her momentarily cry louder. "Your brother Jordan picked this dress out for you." I say, cutting a heart-shaped piece of fabric out from where her heart would be if she had the dress on. Maddie takes the heart from my shaking hands. "He loved you. He used to feed you your bottle. Do you remember?"

At the edge of the dunes, I spot some big sea-grape leaves. Maddie watches as I cut a triangle piece of fabric from the back and another from the side. The dress is almost all gone, metamorphosizing into a new purpose. I tell her about my love for Jordan as I dip her little hand into the paste and rub it all over the sea-grape leaf. "Do this," I instruct.

Maddie gets so excited, she flings paste all over the blanket. Enough of it gets on the leaf and I paste the heart-shaped piece of fabric on top. Then I take two twigs and use a sea-oat stalk—even though it's illegal to pick them—to lash the two twigs together in a cross. Maddie's hands, directed by mine, press a triangle from the lilac and yellow flower dress to each side of the cross. I take the scissors and make a hatch mark in the cloth-fortified sea-grape leaf and stick the makeshift sail into it. With a pen, I make the three Reiki symbols for power, mental/emotional healing and enlightenment/peace onto the cloth-covered leaf. Then I write, "We love you and miss you, Jordan." Maddie scribbles her own note. It's little circles all looped together that look like an infinity of wedding bands.

Holding the tiny sailboat in my hands, I say, "Jordan wants us to be happy. With this boat, we set our sins out into the ocean. Oceans have no memory. In return, we ask that God brings peace, harmony and happiness into our lives." I kiss the boat and hold it above my head.

"Yes," screams Maddie. "I want hold."

"No, honey, this is us letting go."

She shakes her head yes again. "I want hold."

I pass the boat to her, let her play with it. She turns it this way and that. I pick her up, carrying her towards the water. We sit down, letting the water lap our feet. Maddie splashes, looking for a reaction from me. I splash the water too. We laugh. She sets the little boat down. A wave knocks it sideways, carrying it in towards the beach, then out seaward. Maddie claps her hands, then runs into the water after it.

I swoop down, swing her into the air. "Boat," she yells, kicking her feet for emphasis.

"Let it go," I say.

chapter thirteen

As Maddie and I are walking up to the front door, Paul and Susie pull into the driveway. The moon roof is open, music is blasting, all the windows are rolled down. I can't believe he drove through the neighborhood like that. Letting all our neighbors see them together like he's got nothing to hide.

Maddie's yelling, "Dada, dada."

Stomping over to Paul's window, I say, "Nice of you to come home."

"So anyway, Susie," Paul says, ignoring me.

I look over at the seat and floorboard on Susie's side. There's sand all over the place. Not a grain on Paul's side of the car. Even after my trip to the beach with a baby, there's no sand in my car. I know to be careful about that kind of shit. It's the little annoyances in life that break people up. I'm sure he cringed the whole time. Susie getting in the car, treating it like it was a sand box. If there's anything that will give Paul a limp dick in a hurry, it's a messy woman.

I walk back towards the house. Maddie is still calling for her father laughing in the car with Susie, her hands outstretched towards him. Maybe she thinks her arms will tether her father to us.

I hear the car doors shut behind us. Susie slams the door on her side. Paul says, "Hey, be gentle with her. You don't have to use that much force."

I know if I turn around, Paul will be stroking the car and

not Susie as he's talking. In as much time as he thinks will be courteous, he will be out here vacuuming the car.

"Thanks for the beach, Paul," Susie purrs.

I spin around. "The beach, huh? Where are your suits?"

"Nude beach," says Paul.

"Very funny, honey. I know you'd never expose your lily white to the sun. You'd be afraid it would burn off."

Susie laughs.

"Oh, Susie," I say. I pass Maddie to Paul, walk around the car so I can set my bead on her. "Some guy came over to your house."

Her eyes light up in a skittish way. "Who?"

"Some guy in a white Lexus," I lie, remembering the car of the man who looked like Paul that one day.

"Really?"

"He knocked on the door and everything. I told him I didn't know when you'd be home."

"You talked to him?"

I nod, looking over at Paul. He looks like he just got cut in on at a dance, his partner now twirling away with somebody else.

"What else did he say?" she asks.

"Oh, this and that. Nothing important," I say.

"Did he..." she stops herself.

"He looked really disappointed you weren't home, if that's what you were going to ask."

I turn, smiling to myself, walk back in the house alone. I know Paul and Maddie will be along in a moment. Susie will blow him off. She's wiggling all over the place with anticipation. She wants to get home, sniff her front porch for clues, see if he marked her territory as his, check her messages, worry about whether or not to call him. She'll be busy all day now. Finally, I'll get to spend a family day without interruption. I hope Paul's got his head out of his ass now that he can see it's not really him Susie wants.

I'm in the kitchen starting Maddie's lunch when Paul walks into the house two minutes later. The vision of the little sea-grape ship sailing out into the ocean calms me. I have to remember what sheer will can accomplish. I am going to pull my family together. Divorce doesn't have to be an answer for me. It's ok that I'm furious with Paul right now, but that doesn't mean I have to walk away.

"I'm sorry," Paul says, walking up behind me, invading my thoughts and personal space.

"Sorry," Maddie says.

I turn from the stove. "You don't have anything to be sorry for, love bug," I say, kissing Maddie on the cheek.

"Kisses," she says.

"Right. Kisses." I turn back to the stove.

"Got any kisses for me?" Paul asks.

I can hear Maddie giving Paul a big smoochie-kiss.

"Kisses," Paul laughs.

"Kisses," she says.

"Mommy gives Daddy kisses," he says.

"Mommy doesn't," I say. I stab Maddie's chicken around the pan, cut the pieces up smaller.

"Mommy does," he says.

He leans her in towards me, saying, "Give your mommy kisses."

Maddie squeals, gives me a kiss.

I say, "Thank you, honey."

"Daddy's turn," Paul says.

"I think your turn lives next door. Oh, I'm sorry. She's on the phone with her boyfriend. How awful for you."

Paul's hand drops from my waist. "Don't be a bitch," he whispers in my ear.

I spin around on him, pointing at him with the fork. "You better stop calling me names. It's disrespectful."

"You're right. I'm glad you noticed. It is disrespectful."

I grab a plate out of the cabinet. "Does Maddie want some chicken?"

"Yes," she says.

"I'll stop if you stop," Paul suggests.

"Ok, you little a-hole."

"Feel better?"

"Much," I say.

Paul sits Maddie in her high chair.

I set her chicken and carrots in front of her. "Get her a fork? They're in the dishwasher. It's clean."

Paul obeys. Passes the fork into Maddie's waiting hand. "Baby?"

I look around me, place my hands on my chest, then point to Maddie.

"You," Paul says.

"Me?"

"You. Me. Upstairs right now," he commands.

"We can't leave her in her high chair." I hope his erection will hold out.

"You're right."

"You want to shower while I feed her?" I ask.

"Don't need to."

"Thought you went to the beach."

"We did."

"And where else?" God, I hate that I need to know—just like Paul hated having to ask me repeatedly this morning where I was last night.

"Breakfast."

I can feel my wet-on drying up. "So Susie's the woman you break your bread with these days? The Susie weekend—dinner, breakfast, what more could a man ask for? Got a condom in your back pocket or did you already use it?"

"I told you. We didn't have dinner last night."

"So you say." He always sidesteps my real question.

Paul grabs my face as I swivel away, turns it towards him. "Hey. I want you to believe me." His eyes are moving back and forth, searching my eyes, telling me to believe him. It reminds me of the way my mother's eyes looked when she would barge into my room on a tirade, determined to finish an argument I had left four hours earlier. An argument usually centered on her drinking. Like I was the vigilant parent and she the child.

"I want to believe you," I say. It's the most honest answer I can give.

He kisses the right side of my neck. I know he means business now. The right side of my neck in particular really gets me going. It's a direct connection right down to the kitty. That's what Paul says. He says my heart is wired to my neck, which is wired to my pussy. He says it's a circuitous path to both my heart and my pussy, but a trip worth making. I'm hard wired, but I wish I could rewire my heart. I've got love and sex all mixed up. No wonder I feel so distant from Paul. No sex for three months and thirteen days. Who would feel loved with that much time passing when they climb into bed with the same man every night?

Paul waves at me from the hallway, rounds the stairs. I hear him taking them two by two. My libido just got another jump start.

"Ok, baby girl. Let's eat." I try not to shovel food in her mouth. I don't want to choke her, but then again, I don't want Paul's mood to pass. I hadn't realized I was such an opportunist. The only reason why he's pumped up, so to speak, is because he's spent the whole morning with Susie. It's disgusting, really. Like I need her to be my warm-up act.

"Stop it," I say out loud, startling Maddie. "Oh, sweetie. You're a good girl," I correct.

"More," she says.

"You like?" I ask.

"Huh-huhn," she nods her head up and down.

"You're Mommy's good girl." I kiss her head.

I fork the last piece of chicken into her mouth. "All gone."

Maddie pulls her bib off while I run a washcloth under water. I gently wipe off her face and hands.

We go to her room, passing the shut door of Paul's and my bedroom along the way. I picture him in there jerking off as his foreplay. He better wait for me. I don't want him coming first like the last time.

I pick a short picture book. We settle into the glider rocking chair in her room. She sits on my lap, sippy cup of milk in her hand. The book's repetitive rhyming words spill from my mouth. I wonder if Paul can feel my desire tugging at him from her room.

Maddie's head rests against my chest. She's so sweet. The culmination of Paul's and my love. Just like Jordan. How can I ever turn away from Paul when he gave me such gifts?

I wonder if there is a heaven. If Jordan can see Paul and me struggling through our marriage. That would be a disappointment. Maybe Paul, Jordan, Madeline and I will all come back in the next lifetime together. Get our relationships right. Maybe Jordan sacrificed his life because Paul and I needed to learn how to work through difficult times. God. If that's true, I'm failing my son in a new and different way.

I kiss Maddie, lay her in the crib, rub her back and cover her with her little bear comforter.

I crack our bedroom door open a space, put my eye up

to the slit like a voyeur. Paul is on the bed, naked. He looks great.

He cocks his head to the side, grabs a pillow from the bed, covers himself. "Is somebody there?" he asks in a scared girl's voice.

He knows I love the virginal bride routine. I breathe heavy at the door.

"Don't hurt me," he says.

"I won't," I say, entering the room. I stay by the door. Now that we're in the moment, I'm scared, like I've never experienced Paul before.

He rises from the bed, hard-on a divining rod pointed at me and vibrating. I'm the water source he's been searching for. He spreads his palms out on either side, grins like a little boy. "See anything you like?"

I shake my head yes, smile sadly. I feel like I'm going to cry.

"Are you ok?" He advances, wrapping me in his arms, pulling me close, poking me with his hard-on.

"Oh, my," I laugh. The laughter makes my eyes well up, a solitary tear escapes.

He scoops me up, kisses my cheek, lies me on the bed. He climbs up and over me, nestles himself next to me, pets my hair. "You look really pretty in this dress," he says.

"Thanks. Your favorite. That's why I put it on today."

"Mind if I take it off now?"

We laugh. He sits on his haunches. I sit up, raise my arms, he pulls the dress over my head. The dress grazes my cheek, wipes my tear away.

I didn't bother with underwear today, but I have a bra on. I hope he takes my bra off.

He places his hands on my shoulders. "Remember me?" he asks.

"I do."

"Right," he says. "I do. Till death do us part. Do you think we can try harder to make this work?"

"I do."

"Will you go to counseling with me?" he asks.

"Can I think about it?"

"Always the commitment problem with you." He smiles. "Let me know when you're ready and I'll make the appointment."

"I'm ready now," I say, closing my hand around his penis.

He reaches back, unsnaps my bra, takes my breasts in his hands and mouth. Hands, neck, feet, mouth, balls—we're in a maelstrom of body parts, swirling, joining, parting and trembling. He sits with his back against the headboard, guides me down on top of him, modulates my hips with my breathing and not his. He's gentle with our movements, rough with my neck, soft with my lips, biting my tongue. It's perfect. I come unexpectedly. I feel so overwhelmed with pleasure and love and wanting more. A sob gusts out of me. Paul flips me on my back, staying inside me.

"Hey, hey, baby," he says, wiping my tears away, kissing my face. "I love you so much."

This makes me cry even more. It's not that I'm sad. I'm overwhelmed with emotion. I've never had this happen before. He moves like he's going to get off me.

"Don't stop," I say. "It feels incredible." I still can't shut my tears off. I grab his ass, start to move his hips, gyrate with him.

He kisses my tears. I quicken my movements, he responds. I bite his nipple, palm the sides of his ass so I can feel his muscles work. We're moving faster and faster, our breath coming quicker and quicker. A moan starts from my solar plexus, moves up my body and out my mouth. Paul moans with me, we shudder together—joining and retreating and joining again.

It's that same dream again—the one with my father and my

brother Jake. Only now, I jump through the hoop of my wedding band when Jake offers it up to me, his small arms stretching and lengthening until he's holding it twenty feet above his head. The neon light of both their eyes lights my way. I easily fly through the gold band. My father cheers and turns towards another woman that isn't my mom. She turns her eyes towards me and little laser beams of ruby light shoot out at me.

In the distance, I see an object. My body begins hurtling towards it. There's a whooshing sound in my ear as I get closer and closer. I squint to make out the object. I look for a purchase to plant my feet on, I want to resist, but I'm in a vacuum vortex—flying straight towards what I know will kill me. Collision, collision. I can hear glass and metal ripping. The sound goes on forever into eternity. God, it's so real. I look down at my body in the dream to see what damage the object has done.

Paul is standing up, looking out our bedroom window. I'm drunk with sleep and the nightmare. My heart is pounding in my ears. I look down at my body to see if I'm hurt or not. "What's the matter?"

"An accident," he says.

"What?"

"There's an accident on our front lawn." Paul falls to the floor crying. I grab my dress, sprint down the stairs and out the front door.

chapter fourteen

"Can you hear me? Sir?" I ask. "I'm going to help you."

The man in the car moans.

I sprint around to what used to be the passenger seat of the car. I take a deep breath, poised with baseball bat at the ready. Smash. Another deep breath. Smash. The window glass crackles into a million pieces of light. The teenagers on the lawn with their beepers going off are alternately giggling and yelling for me to stop. I can tell which one is the driver, because he is sitting with his head in his hands. I can tell the driver wishes the dimming of the day weren't so dim. I look up at our bedroom window, see Paul's figure. I hope he's called 911. I fill my lungs, swing again as hard as I can. The window gives way. I poke it with the bat, crush it to the side and out.

The man is moaning louder—in a pattern like a song. Ah, ah, ah, ah. Each "ah" goes up one octave like he's practicing his scales. Then he starts over at middle C, rises in tone again. I turn to the teens on the lawn. They're drunk, stumbling around. Just a few scratches are all I can see. Just a few thousand moments ago, they poured out of their car window like a bunch of ants on a pheromone trail, one following the other.

"Get me the floor mat from your car," I order.

"What?"

"Floor mat. Your car. Go." I point with my bat at the kid who seems the most lucid. "Now."

He scrambles. I point again to the kid with a cell phone instead of a beeper on his belt. "You there with the phone. Call 911."

He sits and looks at me.

"This man dies and it's vehicular homicide. Now. 911." My voice doesn't even sound like it belongs to me; it's deep and commanding. He dials.

Neighbors are gathering from their houses now. Tentatively, like there's a UFO on my yard. No one comes forward to help. My eyes are focusing kaleidoscope-style—stop on the pattern of the teens. Stop on the pattern of the man in the car—lots of red in that one. Reel around to the neighbors—left, right, nobody forward. Maybe they don't want to help because I'm involved. Maybe they don't want to be associated with another accident. Too bad, they're already involved and inaction is an action. They'll each have their own conscience to live with when they lay their heads down for the night.

I swipe the proffered floor mat from the teen holding it at arm's length. Am I albatross marked? Can no one get close enough to me to help? I toss the mat over the window opening, covering the broken glass. Not my preferred entry into the car, but both doors are misshapen and stuck. I'm not even sure what kind of car this used to be. Maybe a Lexus.

I go up and in the window. My dress flips up and in with me. I know I have just totally mooned and more all my neighbors and the five teens in the yard. They have just seen everything I own in triple vision.

"Damn, man. Did you see that?" says one of the teens in a man-acting little boy voice.

Maybe this is what they mean when they say the folly of youth—the ability to be totally ignorant of the situation and the far-reaching ramifications. One by one, I notice the teens leaving. Each one does a little nervous dance, then spins out down a side yard. The driver is the last to pirouette into the night. Their crumpled car sits in the swale of my yard—alone, like a jilted lover.

I gotta help this man. It's my chance. If I can save him, maybe God will forgive me.

"Sir, can you hear me?" I ask again.

There's a whooshing sound when he breathes I couldn't hear from outside the car. Maybe he has asthma. I hope his lungs aren't punctured. He's got blood on his face, arms and chest. Seems like he's riding the steering wheel from his middle—the airbag looks like a spent condom hanging down between his legs. What should I do? Time matters here. I can't move him. What if his neck is broken? Don't want to paralyze him. But I can't sit and do nothing. I see his blood, see Maddie in her crib. I'm scared to touch him.

"Mary, Mother of God, please protect us in our hour of need," I say, wiping his face with the hem of Paul's favorite dress, summoning the help and protection of Jordan, Jake, Dad and Mom; air lock my mouth around his, pinch his nose. I breathe in rhythm for him. Whoosh and bubble blood.

Shit, God please help me to know what to do. CPR is out. Even if I could move him into the right position, I can't push on his chest. I try short pants of breath into his mouth. With each exchange of breath, I'm making bubbly blood pulse from his chest. His blood mists the side of my face.

"God, God, please help," I yell. There's an echo out on the lawn. I look through the shattered windshield, see a thousand Susies falling to her knees, grabbing her hair. Sirens serenade her in the background.

I'm ineffective. God doesn't think I'm worthy to use as his instrument. I cuddle next to the man. At least if he's going to die, he should have a warm hand caressing his hair. The distance between the sirens and us is a lifetime.

Why isn't anyone else trying to help? I don't think he's going to make it from what I'm looking at. He can't possibly make it. Jordan didn't look that hurt and he didn't make it.

"It's ok. It's ok." I repeat, lying again and again. But I want it to be true. I wonder if Jordan could feel me next to him that day. Feel my energy reaching out and around Paul's body. Paul separated me from Jordan at the moment he needed me most. They both needed me most. But I guess it was also the moment when Paul needed Jordan the most. There's a million connections tethering us to earth. I wonder where this man's mother is.

"For the love of God," I invoke. "Please, please save him." I'm thinking about Jordan, but the tactility of running my fingers through the man's hair, spreading his blood around as if it were hair gel brings me back. I'm cooing nonsense to him. His breathing still has a whoosh, but sounds more relaxed now.

"That's good, relax," I say, kissing his cheek, stroking his hair. Kindness is paid at such a small price. It takes five lifetimes for the red beam of the sirens to reach my lawn.

A face appears at the window. "Ma'am, can you climb out so I can get in there?"

I look up through tears. There's a trillion million faces at every window. Paramedics. Never neighbors. I kiss him on the cheek quick. One more time, I lie to him that everything will be all right, then scramble back through the window. The seam of my bloody dress rips. I can feel and hear it giving way as I spread first one leg, then the other, straddling the floor mat up and over the window. An exposed shard of glass cuts my inner thigh.

The man's moaning reaches back to its earlier crescendo of octaves. Maybe I was a help. I make to crawl back into the window, but a cop restrains me. "It'll be ok, ma'am." Like me, he promises what he should not.

"Neck brace," the paramedic inside the car yells, extending his arm through the window.

In time, a contraption that must be the Jaws of Life starts

snipping away at what I hope isn't a tin-can grave. Watching the paramedics work is mesmerizing. The words of encouragement they offer are different than mine. Words like, "What's your name? You married? Kids? Good—think of your wife and daughter and you'll be home soon."

Susie has reached a full-tilt scream now. I run from the restraining cop's arms towards her. Paul is at our bedroom window—a mannequin frozen in place.

"Susie, it's ok," I say, kneeling down next to her. There's a lot of people assuring each other everything is ok, everything is normal. Except it isn't. She's rocking back and forth. Now it's my turn to wrap my arms around her, rock in rhythm. "Shhh," I say. It's good to be of comfort to people. It's stupid to say I feel of service, but that's what I'm thinking. I feel so needed. God, please let me be of service, I think. But then I realize I've said it out loud. Susie's screams have calmed to a whisper.

I stroke her hair, just like I was stroking the man's until I realize both my hands are bloody, the dress she's crying into is bloody. "Susie?" I say, pulling back. "Susie, you shouldn't touch me—I'm bloody." I wonder how many little cuts on my body his blood has seeped into. I hate that I even think that.

She holds on tighter. Her voice is muffled, but I hear her say, "It's ok." God, I hope she's right.

The paramedics are finally pulling the man out of the car. They hand-hammock him to a stretcher. I hear his "Ah" song rising and falling on the octave scale again. Susie scampers to her feet, climbs into the back of the ambulance with him. I think she must be having her own flashback to Jordan or something. A paramedic grabs her, about to expel her.

"No," she yells. "For God's sake, I'm his girlfriend. Let me be with him."

I see the paramedics exchange eyebrows. A cop shuts the back of the ambulance door, raps on it twice. I'm lying on the grass on my back now, watching the ambulance pull away upside down, siren crying. I hope Susie makes out better than I did the last time an ambulance visited our driveway. Godspeed, I think. God has been summoned tonight here on my lawn more often than in a Catholic service. I hope he's available.

I'm exhausted. It feels so nice to just be still. I pivot my head towards our bedroom window. It's empty—just an ordinary window fringed by floral curtains. Oh God, Paul. I've been so concerned about everyone else in the fray, I've forgotten about my own husband. I'm a bad wife. I don't have my priorities straight. What the hell is wrong with me?

A cop is approaching me. I look around. Neighbors are straggling into their houses. Rolling over on my stomach, I launch from grass blocks, hurdle over my front door threshold. I can hear the cop calling after me as I leap through the door. He knows where I live, he can come back another time. Let the neighbors do something useful, tell the cop what happened. Madeline is crying. I look down at my body, hands, dress—all blood-smeared, automatically pull my hand back from the railing, soar up the stairs two at a time.

"Paul, Madeline," I cry out. "I'm coming."

She is in Paul's arms. They are waltzing about her room, cheek to cheek; their commingled sobs acting as metronome.

"Paul," I say gently, starting into the room. I can see he's in a daze.

"Blood," he says.

"Yes, blood," I say. I don't dare touch him or Madeline. I feel dirty, soiled, contagious. What if I'm wearing death in the form of blood all over my hands, mouth, lips, arms and legs? I shouldn't have given that man mouth to mouth. I put my family at risk. I have cuts on my hands, hang nails, my tongue is still raw underneath from Al's kisses, ripped back open today by Paul's kisses. I've been monogamous my whole marriage. Now inside one weekend, I've laid my lips on two other men. It was worse, though, for me to touch the man in the accident. But I did it with a pure heart—to be of service, to help. Would God really punish me for helping? And if he did, would it be my atonement for breaking my marriage vows with a kiss? A kiss in exchange for illness and death. Seems harsh. I know I really am the one to blame for Jordan, Jake, Dad and ultimately my mother's death. I can't fool myself anymore with stories about unfortunate circumstance. I should be treated like a leper. I'm not worthy of people's love and trust. If only I hadn't wanted that cursed blanket. My kids would have had grandparents, an uncle...

I step closer to Paul and Madeline.

"Don't touch," Paul says.

I put my hands in the air criminal style.

Maddie reaches out, says, "Mama boo-boo."

"No baby, mama's fine. Mama's not hurt." I can't even kiss her to assure her. To Paul, I say, "I'm going to shower. Are you ok?"

"Fine." He doesn't say it mean. It comes out like he's caught in a dream.

I back from the room. I want to watch them for as long as I can. Remember what they look like when they both really need me, even if I can't help at the moment.

I choose Paul's and my bathroom, because it has a small shower stall in addition to the spa tub. I bathe Maddie in her bathtub every night. Not that Paul and I are more dispensable than Madeline, it's just that she's an innocent with a whole life ahead of her. A life I pray will be happy.

Stepping into the shower stall, I strip my dress off. Paul's favorite dress is ruined. I use the inside of my elbow to pull the water on—a spot not marked by another man's blood. I've got to touch something sooner or later. I pick up the bar of Ivory soap, scrub my body back to baby-fresh innocence, sing the hymn,

"Pure as Snow". This wasn't my fault. I could be worrying about nothing. But to not consider it, I could put Maddie and Paul at risk for the same outcome as hitting Jordan.

I wonder what Susie meant when she said it was ok when I said I was bloody. Maybe they've had AIDS tests. But still—he was a cheater. If he cheated on his wife with Susie, maybe he was cheating on Susie too. That happens. Some men can't stop at one affair. Some need to prove to themselves again and again that they can get whoever they want. I bet the wife doesn't even know about Susie. Sad how you can be married, have children together and not really know what's in your partner's thoughts and heart.

I wash my hair with the same soap. Standing under the showerhead, I will my body healthy; banish away the thought of any virus entering. I imagine the pictures of phages from eleventh-grade microbiology class—little rockets ready to destroy cells by injecting their virus. I open the shower door, pluck the towel from the rack with just my thumb and forefinger. Throwing the towel on the shower floor after rubbing myself dry, I step out of the shower one dry foot at a time. I grab a hand towel, open my bureau, slap socks on my feet and throw a second pair into the bathroom. Pad downstairs for a bottle of Clorox. I get in the shower again with a washcloth, take my socks off. Wash my body with Clorox. Now I can feel little cuts on my hands and legs burning from the bleach. I sneeze and sneeze, but keep scrubbing, pouring bleach all over my body a second time. I know it's paranoid and probably won't help, but I can't stop myself. After rinsing myself and the shower stall with super hot water, then with cold, I get out. I stuff my dress—Paul's favorite dress—into a plastic trash bag, followed by my first and second bath towels, the washcloth, hand towel, socks and bar of soap. I shake bleach all over the shower until there's nothing left. Wipe my hands on a second hand towel, throw that in the bag and tie it shut. I feel so dirty. And all for helping a stranger stay alive. I hope he's alive.

The smell of bleach is so strong, it's giving me a world-class headache. I open the window in the bathroom, then open our front bedroom window, stand where Paul was standing, watching, waiting. I know he was powerless to help. Instead of blaming him for his powerlessness, it makes my heart open up towards him. We're both so fragile in different ways. I notice the ambulance has left deep tire marks on our pristine front lawn.

chapter fifteen

Paul is on me first thing in the morning. His eyes are squeezed shut, even though the room is dark. It's not me and my body he's trying to shut out. It's his thoughts. I wonder if he sees similar images to mine or if he has his own recurring nightmares.

I've never seen anyone with a head as swollen as Jordan's. At least I don't remember mine or my mom's head being that swollen. Then again, I think I was out of it for about two weeks after my parents' accident. Once I did come to—actually, I think they must have backed off the drugs enough to let me come to—they wouldn't let me out of the hospital bed anyway. No standing, no passing mirrors. No glimpses of the plastic surgery to come. No finding out my brother and father were dead.

He's stabbing me with his penis. Which would be wonderful if I were ready. I try to catch up, but all I keep thinking is that he has a biological urge in the face of chaos to keep his gene pool alive. I keep seeing what I imagine are the pictures in his head. I'm like a barometer, sensing the pressure the people around me are experiencing. Trying to roll on top of him, he pins my arms and hands together above my head, moves inside me deeper and faster.

"It hurts," I say. But Paul isn't in the room to hear. I go limp. Wait and wait and wait, wondering when the last time was he lasted this long.

I try to roll on top again. He squeezes my wrists until the

small bones inside rub together. I try to move, but he has me pinned. I'm panicked, I'm mad, I feel sorry for him. I think about the blood from the night before.

I want to get excited, but I can't. After no lovemaking for three months and thirteen days, getting it twice in a twenty-four hour period feels like a monsoon.

I might as well get it done and over with. At this point, he could pound away on me for the next three months and thirteen days and I still wouldn't be able to come. Maybe if he wasn't pinning me down, I'd feel better about the whole affair. I grind my hips with his. Slowly at first, then fast. He quickens.

"Move," I command. I'd slap his ass if my hands were free. But they're not. I'm trapped in the marital bed, pretending. I breathe fast in his ear, moan loud. Ok, he's hitting the home stretch, galloping for the finish—orgasm prize at hand. He changes leads, like a dressage horse, smooth and imperceptibly. But the shift is just enough to swing in my direction. I grind and breathe faster.

His orgasm starts at the base of his penis, growls out his mouth. The sensation almost tips me over. All I need is two more seconds. His body is writhing in tortured pleasure without me. He pulse grips my wrists—harder and softer, harder and softer, collapses on top of me. Kisses my neck softly, even though he still has my wrists in a death grip. I can't breathe. I try expanding my lungs, but they don't have the strength to breathe or bounce him off me.

Paul squeezes my wrists one more time. My lungs feel as if they're imploding—dying on a carbon-monoxide cocktail.

"Can't breathe," I say. He lets go of my wrists. My freed hands urgently tap both his shoulders. He rolls off. I swoon to my side, gill-gasp for air.

He kisses my back. "That was great."

"Hmmm," I say. My stomach jumps. We are not on the same

page at all. I wonder how Al makes love. I picture him slow and gentle, waiting for me to come first. That's the greatest thing about undiscovered love—you get to fill in all the gaps, write the story to your advantage.

But then I picture Paul waltzing Maddie around her room last night, trying to comfort them both. How can I ever leave him? He's such a good father. He used to be a good husband. I have to be patient—grow him back to the husband I lost. It's like he's a beautiful amaryllis bulb, lying dormant. Waiting to bloom and bring me pleasure again. A perennial. Not an annual that's only here for a season. I have to tend to him, grow him wild to his full splendor again. Bigger transformations have occurred in the world, why not our happiness and days at the park with Maddie? Why not a family in love?

The sound of Maddie rustling in her crib comes through the baby monitor.

"I'll get her," Paul says.

I roll over a whole revolution further, expanding the distance between us. He places his hand on the swell of my hip, lets it drop down across my ass.

Once he leaves the room, I feel the urge to cry. But crying is such a luxury. A drink is a lesser luxury, but right now would be equally as nice as crying. I hate having to control myself on weekends when Paul is home. Crying or a drink, not a healthy way to start a Sunday morning.

I get up to go to the bathroom. Paul's rubbed me sore. A shower will soothe me. I'm careful to dress fashionably. Paul is in a pair of flannel shorts at the stove, scrambling up some eggs. I picture our juices drying on the inside of his shorts.

"Happy?" I ask.

He nods, gives a sorrowful smile.

"I'm sure everything is fine," I offer. "All the kids ran off one by one. They weren't hurt."

"Why us?"

"They say God gives you what you can handle." It sounds ridiculous, someone as close to self-destruction and blatant paranoia as me saying those words. Well, the cornerstone of every twelve-step program is the realization on the part of the indoctrinee that they need help. I better go to the cancer support group tomorrow to help sort this out. But then Marci could find out where I live if the story hits the paper. I don't want her showing up on my doorstep some night to offer counseling to Paul.

"God gives you what you can handle? Is that what I heard you say?" There's a look of disgust, incredulity and amusement on Paul's face.

"It is what I said." I smile.

"Well, clichés make the world go round."

"I thought love makes the world go round."

"No, it's money that makes the world go round." He rubs his fingers together. "You watched the wrong movie."

"Hey, big spender," I say.

"Spend a little time with me," he sings, then bumps his ass against my side.

"Isn't that supposed to be my line?"

"Babe, if I had believed in traditional male-female roles, I would never have married you."

"You certainly were the gothic missionary man this morning."

"Every once in a while, a Viking has got to take back his birthright."

"Raping and pillaging. Those are fine family values to bring Maddie up by."

He grabs me, bites my neck, pats my pussy. "I'm sorry, how's she feel?" I notice he looks to see where Maddie is. He doesn't have to worry, she's rapt at the Sunday morning TV altar.

"Fine, a little sore."

"I owe you one."

"Don't worry, I'll collect."

He pats my ass, then says, "I should go over to Susie's. See how she's doing."

"I'm dressed, I'll go," I say.

"But…"

"Hey, every once in a while, a woman's gotta take back what's hers. I'll be right back," I say, already moving for the door before he can argue. Pausing at the front door, I survey the lawn damage. The car must have spun all over our yard before coming to a stop in front of Paul's rose bushes. There's green spray paint on the road where they tracked the trajectory of each vehicle. I could hear the tow truck once Paul and I were in bed—each of us immobile. I'll have to go buy sod tomorrow to repair the yard. It's not fair to make Paul spend his day off running errands when I have every day off. Well, from work that is. I have to remember that a stay-at-home-mother counts for more than what people want to give her credit for. I wish I had made that choice for Jordan—for myself. Maybe I could have taught him about the dangers of the road better and how bright orange balls can always be replaced, whereas little boys cannot. I feel a light pat on my head, like someone comforting me. I turn. No one is behind me. Weird.

Susie's door is slightly ajar. I check the time before knocking. It's 8:43. I think Susie's a night person, but if her door is ajar she must be up. I ring the bell. No answer—not even a bark from her dog. Holding the doorknob so the door doesn't fling open, I knock hard, then stick my face through the doorway. Susie's dog walks up to me with her tail between her legs.

"Susie?" A weird feeling washes over me. What if she's in there—wrists slit, bleeding out into a warm water bath? "Hi sweetie," I say, crouching down to pet the dog.

"Susie?" Maybe I should go home and get Paul. But I don't want Maddie to see anything bad. She's seen enough. I have to start being braver. A drink would be perfect at a time like this. I'll just beeline it to Susie's fridge, see what she's serving before I look around the house. But if something is in the fridge worth finding, I won't be able not to take a swig. She could just be sleeping on the couch for all I know. Worse, she could be in need of finding and there I'll be lounging in liquor on her kitchen floor.

I step inside. One foot follows the other like I'm an awkward gymnast on a balance beam, waiting to fall off. "Susie?"

I feel funny. I've never been in her house before. Moving from room to room with the dog following, I avoid the kitchen by glancing around it from the safe distance of the doorway. The fridge calls out to me, asking me to open it, promising riches in wine and beer, maybe some chilled tequila. That sip of Patron I had with Al was great. I run upstairs, open the hallway bathroom door, nothing in the tub. Every door upstairs is shut. Who keeps every door in their house shut? Her house is fairly neat. Not up to Paul's standard, but not messy enough to repel him.

In the master bedroom, I approach her night table. I once saw a professional burglar on TV saying that people keep what's most important to them in their nightstands. In my nightstand, I keep cancelled checks and Astroglide—it's like KY jelly, only liquidier. Feels just like a woman's wetness. Maybe Susie has love notes from Paul in her nightstand. I sweep the room with my eyes. A picture on her dresser catches my attention. I tiptoe over to it, but keep my hands to myself. It wouldn't be right to touch anything. I don't belong here. The picture must be of Susie and her father at her high school graduation. Lucky girl. Crossing the room, I call out again, fling open the bathroom door. Nothing, no one. Not a spot of blood or a stretch of rope with a body dangling off it anywhere in the house that I can see. She must still be at the hospital.

I let the dog out for a bio break, then shut, but don't lock the front door. Susie might not have her keys with her. She probably didn't anticipate that it would be her boyfriend being pulled from the wreckage when she ran from the house last night.

Paul's coming down the stairs with Maddie when I get home. They're both dressed in matching jeans and red T-shirts. Very cute.

"Everything all right?" he asks.

"Door was left standing open and she's not home," I say. "She must still be at the hospital. She went in the ambulance last night."

"She'll find her way home." He walks into the family room.

Maddie is chattering nonsense in between intelligible words. She wants to watch her *Veggie Tales* video. Paul plays it for her. She claps her hands, gets her miniature plastic chair and stations herself back in front of the TV for the second time this morning.

"We should go to the hospital," I say.

"I'm not going to the hospital." His voice is flat.

Why doesn't Paul want to go? Maybe he doesn't want to wish his competition well. I, for one, am going to get down on my knees and say a prayer for a speedy recovery at his bedside. As long as Susie has a boyfriend—even if he belongs to someone else—then she can't be too serious about my husband.

"Paul, if Susie's been as supportive as you say she has been about Jordan, why wouldn't you want to be supportive back?"

"I just can't go."

"It's your chance to return the favor."

"I can't. Why can't we just call the hospital?"

"I don't know his name. I heard him mumble his name to the paramedics last night, but I couldn't make it out. Besides,

I think one of us should go. I'll go then." Part of me feels sorry for Susie. I don't think she has any family in town. She was so hysterical last night. She shouldn't have to be alone. No one should have to be alone when they're facing something like this. Even if he's not really hers. A loaner boyfriend—he's like a library book, passed from one woman to another.

I wonder if his wife knows about Susie. I hope she doesn't find out. Maybe the accident will be the thing to glue his family back together. It's easier to glue things back together after an accident if no one dies. Then everyone is thankful to be together. At least, that's the way I imagine it would be. I've never been involved in an accident where everyone walked away. But I know that's how I'd feel. Happy and appreciative to have my life just as it is.

"Meg. How can you go to the hospital again and not the graveyard?"

"Because somebody at the hospital may need me. There's no one at the graveyard that needs my help anymore."

Paul moves his head back like I've just bludgeoned him with a roundhouse kick.

"Jordan knows I love and miss him. I don't need to visit a graveyard to commune with him."

Paul looks at me like a little, vulnerable boy. "Do we have to talk about this today? I don't feel like being sad."

"No, we don't. I'm sorry." I rub his back. It's interesting how different we both ride our emotional scars. I can't go to the graveyard and he can't go to the hospital.

Maddie toddles in. "Want some." She points at an eight-ounce bottle of water on the counter.

I pass her the whole unopened bottle. She hefts it and makes a little noise like it's heavy. She puts it on the floor and tries to open it.

"Mommy help," she says.

"Of course," I say. I pour most of the water out into a tall glass. I don't want to give her the whole bottle to spill. She starts screaming.

"You're right," says Paul. "I should go to the hospital."

"I'll go with you." I pass Maddie the bottle and she stops crying, starts smiling instantly. When was the last time something as simple as a bottle of water made me happy?

"No, you stay here with Maddie," says Paul.

"I'm coming, Paul. We'll go as a family to offer our support."

He nods his agreement.

chapter sixteen

Dressed all in black for the second time this year, I slide into the back of the church. People's eyes canvas me, trying to place me as a puzzle piece in Cameron's life. Smiling at them sadly, I bow my head, kneel and make the sign of the cross before entering the last pew. I wouldn't have pictured Susie with a Cameron. But then again, three years ago when we moved into our house, I wouldn't have pictured Paul with a Susie. I feel nervous to be here in God's home. I haven't spoken to God in a church since Jordan's funeral.

I scan around for her. People meet my eyes; a few turn in their seats. I hope no one thinks I'm his girlfriend. It would be bad to cause a scene in a church. Even more, I'd hate to take the rap for Susie's deeds. I hope people don't ask who I am. I don't want to admit that I'm the woman who tried to save him and failed.

Maybe Susie will be in Cameron's wife's kitchen serving up the casserole offerings like she did in my kitchen after Jordan's funeral. I wonder if she'll be her perky self playing with Cameron's daughter. I wonder if she's ever met his daughter before. When I tried asking Susie questions, she kept repeating that it didn't matter any more.

I feel sorry for Susie when I think of the state Paul and I found her in, wandering outside the hospital like a homeless person— no shoes, purse, hair a mess, blood on her blouse, hardly able to tell us that he'd passed away just two hours before. As we neared the hospital, Paul was about to crawl out of his skin. I've never seen him engaged in so much kinetic movement without him driving for an orgasm or doing something athletic. Maddie was chattering away in the backseat. Even with all the noise and movement in the car, I was focused enough to spot Susie.

Once Cameron's wife was called, Susie wasn't able to be at his side. She heard that he died from a nurse who came into the patient waiting room to tell her. But she already knew. She said she could hear the crying of the wife and daughter from down the hall. She confessed to us that she sneaked into his room after everyone was gone to say goodbye. She said his body was cold, his skin bluish-black. I can picture her slipping onto the hospital bed, lying beside him one last time. Jordan was small enough to hold. The nurse and Paul had to pry my fingers off him. The IV got pulled from his little arm during the struggle. If Jordan were alive, I would have bruised him with the grip I had on him. But his heart had given up pumping his blood. I'll never be able to get over Jordan. The most I can hope for is to not feel guilty every second of the day. Guilt just once a day might be manageable.

The whole scene must have been quite the gossip generator. First Susie coming out of the ambulance, then the wife and kid, then Susie again as rigor mortis set in.

What a sad, lonely life she must lead. Getting in bed alone every night while her partners get in bed with their wives. I wish I didn't feel so bad for her. I have no business empathizing with the woman who is taking my husband away from me piece by piece. Now that Cameron's gone, she'll make even quicker work of Paul.

Susie never shows up to the funeral. At least she has a thread of common decency. She must have thought it was ok to come to my house after Jordan's funeral, since she is the next-door neighbor. And, of course, because she was there at the moment of impact.

I follow Cameron's funeral procession to the graveyard, wait in my car. Then I track the cars back to the widow's house. I circle the neighborhood, find a good vantage point. Cameron certainly provided for his family. They have a house, a two-story, on the Intracoastal. I hope he has good insurance. My father didn't. But that was a lifetime ago.

The hearse pulls up. I wonder what has taken them so long to get here. Usually, I thought, the widow is the first to leave the cemetery. That is, if she hasn't thrown herself into the open grave. The driver comes round and opens the hearse door for the widow and her daughter. The paper said the widow's name is Paige and the daughter's name is Kira. It's amazing how much information you can get from an obituary. His job, family status, survivors, number of family members predeceasing him.

The daughter is nine years old. She nestles herself to her mother's side. Paige wafts down to her knees, holds Kira shoulder to shoulder right there on the walkway in front of the house. My mother would never have done that. They cry until some Polly Purebred woman rushes from the house and places her hands on Paige's shoulders. Why is everyone so afraid of emotions that they have to put a stop to it at first sign? Why can't people just let others express their grief?

I have to stop myself from running over and tackling the emotion sniper. At the other woman's touch, Paige stands up, straightens her dress, wipes the tears from Kira's face and smiles at her. Kira automatically smiles back.

I watch the house for more signs of grief, wanting to see how another family gets through it. Surely they can teach me something about living on while those you love have died. I watch until I'm full of sadness. Wandering inside their house appeals to me, but I don't want anyone asking me any questions. I better get home to Paul and Maddie. Paul was mad at me for going to the funeral in the first place. Maybe I should have asked Susie if she wanted me to go with her so she wouldn't be alone. Shit, maybe Paul is busy giving her comfort. Maybe that's why she was a no-show.

I spring my keys forward in the ignition. I come out on a bar that's on the Intracoastal. It's close to my house. What could one little drink hurt? If Paul says anything, I'll say someone handed me a glass of wine and the sadness of the moment made me take a sip. A few sips.

I don't valet park. I don't want the ticket to be left in my car and I know I'll forget to take it off the dashboard. The best way to avoid questions is to avoid situations that will beg the question.

Because I'm new to bars, never mind going to bars by myself, I always get tunnel vision when I first walk in. I take the first seat I see. I'm sorry I've sat here. The man next to me is sucking away at his cigarette like it's a damn nipple. He eyeballs me like I'm a big hors d'oeuvre. When I sense him about to talk to me, I make a break for it. Circling the bar, I seat myself next to a group of people who look like they've been drinking for a while. They should be safe to sit next to. Two couples and a pair of extra women. No one will hit on me now. I'm not here to pick up a man after all, I'm just here for a drink.

The bartender tosses a napkin on the bar in front of me. "Whatcha havin?"

"What do you have for red wine?"

"Cabernet and merlot."

"No, I mean what brands of red wine do you have?"

He lists three outright cheap wines and two mediocre wines. I choose one of the mediocre. I whisk the full glass from his hands before he has a chance to put it on the napkin. It's been two days since I've had a drink. The first sip curdles my mouth, warms my throat. Calms me in a way my thoughts never do.

Apparently, the two women are a couple. The guys make

dyke jokes and ask them questions like, "Who handles the finances?"

The dark-haired woman says, "I do, of course."

I've been watching her. She has a big mouth. If someone tells a joke, she has to tell a raunchier one. If someone talks loud, she talks over them. She would wear me out with her incessant talking. Her partner, the blonde, lowers her eyes. She has a sweet face. She's talking to one of the guys about the marathon she's training for. She says in two weeks she'll join them for a drink, but for now, she's drinking 7-Up. They try to badger her into a drink to no avail. Good for her.

The rest of the group is cutting their teeth on margaritas. When the bartender comes for the next round though, they graduate to shots of Wild Turkey. When it comes time to pay, the big mouth makes a huge production over paying. She brandishes a wad of bills from her fishermen's shorts. The two men in the group stand down, put their egos back in their own pockets. She wears her hundred dollar bill on the outside of her money roll. She inspects the bill, then calls the bartender over for a full accounting. They are dickering over what's considered a well drink and what's considered a premium drink. The blonde ducks her head down to the rim of her 7-Up.

I better get home. I signal for the bill, throw the bartender an extra fiver to make up for the paltry tip I imagine he got from the big mouth. Rounding the bar, a hand lands on my shoulder. I turn, my momentum pushing me forward still; catching a glimpse of Al in my periphery. My stomach jumps.

He calls out, "Hey, Emily, stop."

It takes several steps for me to put on my brakes. I should just keep going, but I can't. I'm happy to see him. Good thing I paid cash. Otherwise, the bartender would have my real name.

"Al?"

"What's the matter, you don't recognize me without my luggage?"

"Oh, the luggage. Did you get it from your front porch?"

"I did. After I had to take a cab home."

"I'm sorry."

"I forgive you." He stands up, kisses me right on the lips. "Nice to see you." He pulls the barstool out next to him. "Have a seat."

I look towards the door. "Oh, I shouldn't. I mean, I have to be getting home." I sit down.

"How about a quick shot? Two 1800 tequilas, no, make it Petrone," he says.

"No, hey. I'm driving and my little girl is waiting for me."

"One shot won't hurt."

"Yes, it will. I've got to go." I slide off the stool, slither for the door.

He catches up with me just as I'm getting into the SUV. "Not as flashy as the Mercedes, but it suits you."

I put my palms out. "I'm a mother."

"If I get in the car seat, will you give me a ride?"

"No. Your butt is too big, you'll break it."

Al turns and looks over his shoulder at his ass. "I thought it was little and cute."

"I'm sure that's what all the girls tell you."

He places both hands on my shoulders. "I've been hoping I'd run into you. I would have come up to you sooner, but I thought you were meeting your husband here."

"So you've been stalking me in my own neighborhood?"

"Maybe."

"Hmm. I'll have to remember to tell the next man I meet that I live in Fort Lauderdale instead of Lighthouse Point."

"I'm your next man, Emily." He swoops in on me; bites my neck, kisses me and kisses me. I let him. My whole body feels alive and hopeful. Untangling my arms and legs from around him, I slip backwards into the car. God willing, no one we know has seen me.

"I have to go. Sorry."

"Call me?"

"I can't." I look in my rearview mirror. His wave droops as I pull away. I feel sad that I may have hurt him. I don't know why he feels so compelled to pursue me. Maybe he has some sort of emotional glitch that draws him to unavailable women.

I pop a mint in my mouth, chew it up, then pop a second one in my mouth and suck on it; check my rearview mirror to make sure Al hasn't followed me. I loop a few blocks in the wrong direction. Once I'm sure he's not following me, I turn down our street. From down the road, I can see someone has put something on my lawn right on top of the new sod.

"Holy Mother of God," I say, crossing myself as I pull into our driveway. Someone has placed a two-foot white cross on our lawn. It's the sort of cross that people are given to marking the scenes of accidents with these days. If Cameron had a lot of friends, our yard could end up looking like a shrine, with flowers and personal mementos circling the miniature cross.

I kneel down in front of it. There are red roses at the base. On the cross is written, "We miss you, Cameron."

I jump up and run for the house like a ghost is chasing me. "Paul. Paul," I call out.

"We're in here," he calls from the kitchen.

I dash into the kitchen, skidding to a stop at what I see. Maddie, Paul and Susie are eating one of Paul's famous omelets. There's a wad of used tissues in between Paul and Susie. I wonder who has used the most.

"What are you doing?" I ask. I'm so stupid. I'm worried all morning about Cameron's family while my own family is getting chipped away at.

"Mama, food," Maddie bangs her fork against her plate. I wrap my hand around her head to her chin, kiss her cheek. She offers me a piece of masticated eggs, I open my mouth.

"Yummy," I say.

"Brunch. Grab a plate. I saved you some," Paul says.

So this is how it's going to be. Like Susie is part of our extended family now. All my empathetic feelings dissolve. I touch my neck where Al's kiss has dried.

"Did you give permission for them to put the cross on our yard?" I ask.

"Stop it. I think the church service must have you seeing visions." Paul and Susie laugh. Maddie laughs too.

"Paul. The cross is on our yard where the accident was." I shift my eyes over to Susie. "Maybe Cameron's wife put it there."

Susie stands up, shouting, "She has no right. This is my neighborhood."

Paul marches out, Susie at his heels. I follow.

Paul yells, "Who do they think they are? Putting this shit in our yard without asking permission." He yanks the cross up and out in one fluid movement, sails it into the neighbor's garbage can across the street. He kicks the roses into the street, walks all over them, jumps up and down on them before kicking them over by the same garbage can.

"Stop, Paul. It can stay."

"It can stay? You want to come home to a cross on our yard every day?"

"It doesn't hurt anything. Maybe it makes them feel better," I say, realizing that it makes me feel better to have a cross on the yard where Jordan died too.

"We didn't put a cross here for Jordan. I'm sure not going to allow one for some asshole."

"You didn't even know him." I look over at Susie. Her

mouth is hanging open, wordless. I walk across the street to retrieve the cross.

Paul says, "I forbid you to put the cross back on our yard."

I turn towards him. "Let's talk. Susie, will you excuse us?"

Susie stays planted where she is.

"Susie?" I repeat.

"Leave her alone. There's nothing to talk about. Shit, we left Maddie alone in her highchair." Paul turns, runs back into the house calling for Maddie.

Susie and I square off for a stare-down.

A few minutes later, the garage door opens. Paul walks out into the driveway with Maddie in his arms. "Here, take her." He passes Maddie to me like she's a five-pound bag of potatoes.

"Hey, be nice," I say.

"I'll see you later."

"Wait. I want to talk with you."

"Not now." He makes a stop sign in the air as he walks back into the garage. He straddles the Harley he hasn't ridden since before Jordan died; taps the electronic ignition. It fires full to life on the second try. He kicks the stand back, revs the throttle, toes it into gear and weaves off around Maddie and me. I hope he's not leaving with a death wish in his heart.

Susie runs after him, calling, "Wait. Take me."

He turns his head at her voice, but keeps going. I stand there incredulous. She turns and looks at me, I cock my head to the side. I can feel my whole brow is wrinkled.

I walk up to Susie. "What did you just say?"

"I'm sorry, I wasn't thinking," Susie smiles at me.

"You weren't thinking? That's right, you weren't thinking that he's my husband. Get your own husband and quit trying to steal everyone else's."

"Meg, I don't want you to think..."

"I'm sure you don't." I approach, stay just outside striking distance. "Susie, listen, I know you've had a rough week and I'm sorry for that, but dammit, if I catch you coming around Paul again when I'm not home, I'll…"

"You'll what? You're not the boss of Paul. He can do whatever he pleases."

"If that's how you want to play it, then fine. Get the hell off my property and don't let me catch you coming back."

She stands her ground, stares at me. "Paul says I can come over any time I want if I need him."

"Move, Goddamn you." I run at her. Maddie laughs, she thinks it's a game.

Susie starts, pops up in the air and runs into her yard arching her back, like she thinks I'm going to grab her by her clothes. "Meg, if I wanted Paul, he'd already be mine."

"He doesn't want you," I yell.

"You have no idea what's been going on here. Besides, if you hadn't lied and told me Cameron was here that day, I never would have called him and asked him to come over. I had stopped seeing him. He's dead because of you."

"If you hadn't been gardening with your shorts stuck all the way up your ass, Paul would have been watching Jordan and he'd still be alive."

"Don't you dare blame that on me or Paul. That was your fault, same as Cameron. How many other skeletons do you have in your closet, huh? If I were Paul, I'd be afraid to let you keep Maddie. You'll probably kill her any day now too."

"You're an evil bitch."

There's no sense going round and round with her. I retreat into my house with Maddie waving over my shoulder.

As I shut the garage door, I hear her yelling, "You're not fit to be a mother."

chapter seventeen

I startle awake at the part of my reccurring dream where I'm being sucked into a vortex before the collision happens. My heart is drumming out dark piano notes. I turn my head towards Paul for comfort. He usually rubs my back when I have a nightmare. His side of the bed is empty. The most movement I can muster is a roll over onto my back. It must be the dream-terror G-forces keeping me in place.

I try placing myself back into my dream to create the ending I want. Paul's absence is nagging me.

I tiptoe downstairs. I'm relieved when I turn the corner and hear the TV on. Paul is reclining naked in the easy chair. He's watching *Biography* on A & E.

"I had that bad dream again." I go over to his chair and make to snuggle up next to him.

He puts all his feet and hands in the air, points to the couch. "Over there."

God, he's so hurtful. Every time he could easily reel me in with a word or a gesture, he pushes me away instead. I'm sick of it. I want something different in my life. I wonder if Al is a master of the silent treatment too.

"Silly of me to expect a little comfort from my husband."

"Knock it off. Go sit."

I remain standing in front of him, blocking the TV. My arms hug myself the way I wish Paul would.

"Hi. My name's Meg. Remember me?"

"Yeah, I remember."

"What do you remember?" I hope he'll think of something pleasant and soften.

"I remember I wish I could forget."

I blink. "When did you get to be such a prick?"

"There's that mouth of yours again."

I click the TV off.

He stands, swipe-grabs at the remote in my hand. I whisk it back and out of his reach.

"I said I was watching that." He comes at me. "Meg, please why can't you just leave me alone?"

"Is that what you want?" I keep passing the remote from hand to hand. He waves around my naked body, grasping and not getting. He's usually much more coordinated and he could easily overpower me. I look over at his chair. There's a plastic bag filled with spent beer cans.

"Please, just go."

I hand him the remote. "From the room or the house?"

"Both."

"I'm sorry I asked."

"You push too much."

"That's only because I want you to comfort me."

"I can't."

"Paul, if I could take back killing Jordan, I would. Let's not lose everything."

"I can't."

"Can't what?"

"You. This." He gestures around the room.

"Ok, ok. I'll leave the room, but I'm not ever going to leave the house. You're the one who's going to have to leave."

"Fine."

Just like that. He'll let me go just like that. Like I'm a dollar bill that slips through his hands without notice. I can't believe it. I walk from the room. "Good night then."

"Good night."

I turn around and go back to him when I reach the bottom of the stairs. He's still standing in the middle of the room where I left him. "We can make it if we both try. I know we can." I despise the begging tone I hear in my voice.

"I don't want it any more."

I can't breathe. "What do you want?"

"I don't know," he shouts. "Stop asking me questions." He lowers his tone, "Just…just go back to bed."

"It's Susie."

"What?"

"It's Susie, isn't it?"

"Leave Susie alone. You're always attacking her. What's wrong with you?"

"You want Susie. I just want to hear you say it."

"What are you talking about?"

"Don't treat me like I'm stupid. I see you. You don't have any problem comforting her over her dead, married boyfriend."

"Meg, stop it."

"You're my husband. Why don't you comfort me?"

"I have."

"Then comfort me now. I need you."

"I can't."

My eyes are starting to brim with tears. I keep blinking to hold them back. "Do you want a divorce?"

"I don't know."

"What do you know then?" I'm spinning. Why do I ask questions I don't want to know the answers to?

He looks past me, doesn't answer.

"Did you ever go see a therapist?" I ask.

"Yes."

"Man or woman?"

"Woman."

"What does she say?"

"She says I'm not supposed to discuss what we talk about with you."

"Great. You're going to a therapist that's a control freak. That's just what we need, another controlling voice in this house."

"She said you'd be mad."

"Oh, she's part psychic too. How nice for you."

"Your little barbs are so unproductive."

"How are we supposed to work things out if you won't talk through them with me?"

"I don't know."

"Stop saying that," I holler.

"What?" he asks.

"I don't know."

"I don't either."

"Who's on first?" I laugh.

"What?" He scowls.

"Never mind. Can we go together?"

"I think I need to go by myself for now," he says.

"But you said before you wanted us to go together."

"I changed my mind."

"Paul. I'm going to ask you a question. Promise me you'll answer with the truth."

"Ask your question."

"Do you promise?"

"No. I don't know what you're gonna ask."

"So honesty isn't your starting point?"

"Don't be argumentative. You want to know something, ask it."

I swat away a tear on my cheek. He looks the other way, then flicks the TV back on.

He momentarily shuts his eyes. "What's your question?" He switches channels, stopping at an image of a skull and other bones on an examining table.

"Never mind."

"What?"

"You want another beer?"

He looks back at the plastic bag. "Sorry." He grins a little. "I know you don't like alcohol in the house."

"It's ok."

"Was that your question?"

"No."

"What then?"

"Are you in love with her?"

"The therapist?"

"No. Susie."

"I feel sorry for her."

"But are you in love with her?"

"Of course not." He looks at the floor.

I bend down into his line of vision. "Are you sleeping with her?"

"No. I'm talking to you."

"You know what I mean. Don't be difficult."

"And you shouldn't have to ask." He picks at a hangnail.

"I'm asking."

He breathes out hard and shrugs his shoulders.

I repeat, "I'm asking. Tell me the truth. If it's no, just say no. If it's yes, let's for once be honest and get it out in the open. I won't ever ask again."

"You're unbelievable." He walks over to his plastic bag of empties, rummages around. He cracks open what looks like the last beer of a six pack. I look at his bare ass, the way his balls move as he bends over. His body looks foreign to me. I hate the thought that he's shared it with someone else.

"Paul."

He swigs a gallon gulp from the can. "Meg. This conversation is over."

"Just…"

"It's over."

"You're right." I turn, walk defeated from the room. If he loves me and not her, he'll come after me. I pause at the base of the stairs. I hear him settling back into his easy chair.

chapter eighteen

Paul uproots the new miniature white cross on our yard. For two weeks now, every morning he stomps one into the garbage. On days when Susie emerges from her house, Paul pretends like he's going up for a lay-up shot, slam dunking the cross into the garbage can. She cheers from the sideline of her lawn. She can't stand that Cameron's wife and daughter are now invading her territory—just like she invaded theirs when he was alive. Susie doesn't cross over the boundary into our yard. At least not when I'm outside.

When Paul misses his shot this morning, I say, "Paul, that's not a very Catholic thing to do."

"What?" He spins around on me.

"Throwing crosses out."

He lunges for the cross, breaks it over his knee with a thwacking noise and tosses it into the trashcan. "Yeah, well, neither is cheating on your wife."

"Are you talking about you or Cameron?"

"I thought we were talking about both the bad Catholic men's behavior," he says. Paul and Susie both laugh.

"You're being obtuse."

"And you're being argumentative, as usual." They both laugh again.

I storm into the house.

Susie yells, "Where's that see-through nightgown of yours? I miss watching you jiggle around in that."

"Fuck you, Susie," I yell back. I don't see how Paul lets her talk to me like that. I'd go out there and clock her one, but I know Paul will intervene before I throw my punch. He's on her side now, not mine. I look down at my wedding ring. A strand of metal with a dollop of diamonds on top. Something that came from the ground and can just as easily be buried back into the ground again.

That's it. I'm definitely calling Al today. I have to get a life of my own again. The thought of having somebody who wants to be with me has a calming effect. I'll worry about being in love later. I can picture Al's sexy face, the way he kisses my neck.

Cameron's wife's tenacity in the face of our unneighborly behavior is something to admire. Although, you would think she'd ask permission to stake a cross on someone's yard day after day. Poor thing, she's probably not thinking clearly.

I walk Paige's neighborhood now. I like to keep my eye on her. See how she's making out. I wait until Paul leaves for work. No sense giving him and Susie a chance to be alone together in my house.

"Go walk?" Maddie asks as I'm loading her in her car seat. She knows now that we take a walk almost every day.

"Yes, sweetie."

She claps her hands.

I drive the short distance to Paige and Kira's neighborhood, stowing my car at a park around the corner from their house. Then I put Madeline in her stroller and off we go. I'm sure the people I pass who try engaging me in new mommy conversations think I've recently moved to the neighborhood. A baby in a stroller is a good cover. Maddie and I have been spying on them since the day of the funeral.

Today, I can see Kira diving into the pool. It must be a teacher workday. When she surfaces, Paige claps and calls out, "That was a nine. Great form. Hardly a splash."

Wow. It must be wonderful having a mother like that. I hope I'm like that with Maddie. I think I am. I think of myself as an encouraging person. But it's hard to see yourself as others do. I try to make sure I do and say to my kids—well, just Maddie now—all the things I never heard from my own mother.

Maybe that's what's wrong with me. All these years I thought I was missing a father, when really I was missing a father and a mother. Maybe my whole problem could be solved if I could just find someone to parent me. Obviously, Paul doesn't want to nurture me. And, really, it's not his job. He's my husband. Well, for now. I think of Marci from the cancer support group. I miss her. Her brand of overkill nurturing might be the very thing I need.

Or maybe I should go for rebirthing therapy. I saw a business card up at a new-age store Maddie and I went to the other day. I was thinking about getting a tarot-card reading, but I chickened out. I was afraid to know the future, even if it is someone's made-up version.

Being a psychic is kind of like being a novelist. You get the seed of an idea and grow it. If things turn out different in your real life than what the psychic divines, they'll just tell you that it's a beautiful thing, how free will is powerful enough to change the course of fate. I wonder what a rebirthing session consists of. My problem is that I need rebirthing, rechilding and readolescenting. I'll take the responsibility for screwing up my adulthood. Maybe I should give some consideration to hiring a voodoo priestess who will put a curse on Susie so her appeal to my husband wanes. Why rely on rebirthing and nurturing a healthy mind and spirit when you can rely on the dark forces in the world? Maybe that's where I've gone wrong. I've put too much credence in God's ability to help me. Or perhaps not enough. I wish someone would help me find the answers. I'm getting so tired.

Slipping into Paige's garage, I pretend knocking on the interior door in case anyone is watching. I stand there patiently, taking in the garage. Cameron was a total neat freak. All his tools are hung and labeled on a pegboard. Worse than that, he's gone and outlined the shape of each tool in black magic marker. According to the labels and shapes, the medium-sized pliers and a hex-head screwdriver are missing. They have separate recycling bins for clear glass, colored glass, foam cartons and newspapers. All are labeled. Boxes are stacked on shelves up to the ceiling. Again, all neatly labeled: Christmas angel, baby clothes, Cameron's college notebooks, etc.

I wonder if Paige realized that in spite of her seemingly neat, orderly life, her husband was busy with another woman. I watched one of those women's talk shows where they reported one of the signs of your husband cheating is an increased sex drive. Too bad Paul doesn't fall into that pattern. My heart skips a hopeful beat, then I recall one of the other signs of your husband cheating is a decreased sex drive. A decreased sex drive is also one of the signs of grief. There are too many signs in the world to read to know what's really ever going on.

Maddie reaches out for the wheel of Cameron's bike. I make a jerky movement with the stroller and hit the bike. It topples over. I freeze in place. I hear the scraping of Paige's lawn chair against the cement.

"Hello?" she calls out.

"Who are you talking to?" Kira's voice.

"I thought I heard a noise."

"I don't hear anything. Want me to check?"

"No, it's ok. Stay here with me," Paige says.

I admire the way they cooperate and communicate. I wonder if either one is thinking about Cameron's absence and how he would have been the one to check out the noise.

"Bike," Maddie yells.

"Shhh, baby," I say. I kneel next to the stroller, tap her lips with my finger and do the same to mine. She imitates me.

"Mom, watch this," Kira says. I hear her spring leap off the board and a splash.

"Perfect, Kira. Really perfect."

I want to be part of this family. I look at the bike lying on the ground. Odd, as organized as this family is, I'd have thought they would have had the bikes hanging in the air or up against the pegboard. Maybe no one wanted to draw the shape around each bike. Maybe this family is only equipped for small jobs. Or maybe Cameron was over at Susie's house the day he was supposed to hang and draw around the bikes.

When I lean down to pick up the bike, I spot a stack of one-by-two wood. The whole stack has been painted white. There's a can of white wood paint sitting on a square of newspaper with a cleaned paintbrush on top. I see now that they have made each and every cross that Paul has trashed. That breaks my heart. What dedication. I wonder how it must pain her every morning to build a new cross for the one Paul has tossed so carelessly away. Two crosses are already made, waiting for our yard. I thought maybe Paige was buying pre-made crosses. But now that I think about it, I don't know what store you'd go to buy one. I pick the bike up as quietly as possible, lean it up against the workbench.

"Mama go," Maddie commands.

"Ok," I whisper. I swipe one of the two crosses, stowing it in the bottom stroller pouch. I put a blanket on top to cover it.

We jog out of the garage and down the block. I turn at the end and double back. I want one more glimpse of their life. I cross to the other sidewalk, distancing myself. As we pass their house, I see Paige standing in the garage. Her hand is on the bike seat. Did I not put it back in exactly the same spot? Can she really discern the movement of a bike by inches? If so, she surely would have known her husband was a cheater. She waves. I wave back. Maddie follows suit.

When I get home, I take the cross from the car. This one

has written on it in little girl block handwriting, "Daddy, I Love You." Each word gets smaller and slants down. Maddie and I cross our yard hand in hand. With my shoe, I pound the cross into the ground. I'm putting it back for Cameron, but I'm also putting it in our yard for Jordan. I feel bad that I'm giving him a hand-me-down cross.

Maddie says, "Pretty Mama."

I pick her up, swinging her around in circles until she giggles. When I stop, she yells, "More, more."

I swing her again, then put her on the ground. She walks like she's drunk. I chase her towards the house, tickling her little neck. She scrunches her shoulders up and tries to run faster. I let her get away from me so she knows that sometimes if she tries hard, she'll be strong enough to win.

Putting the cross back on our front yard makes me feel like I'm getting right with the world. I decide it's time to go back to the cancer support group and set things right.

Walking into the old high school room, I realize how much I've missed the support group. There's some reliable faces missing. Hopefully, everyone is alive and fighting.

Marci rushes up to me, touches my hair, my shoulder, Maddie's face, like she's making sure we're real. "I'm glad you're here. How's our little one doing?"

Maddie hides her face behind my legs.

"Better than fine," I say.

"Her chemo must be done by now."

"We'll talk." We squeeze each other's hands at the same time. It's nice to make a connection. I approach Jackson to find out how his son's brain tumor surgery went. It's odd his son isn't here. Maddie follows me by holding onto my pant leg.

"Jackson, how is your son?"

"What?" He has such a startled look on his face, it scares me.

Marci claps her hands. "Ok, let's get started. It's so, so wonderful we're blessed to be able to gather together today."

Nods and grunts of assent like, "God is good" pass around the room.

"I want to welcome Meg and Maddie back. Meg has some good news about Maddie. She's gone through her chemo with flying colors." Marci claps.

Maddie claps with her. She smiles up at me; I kiss her forehead.

A few people laugh, fewer clap. I see on their faces a mixture of relief, anger and jealousy. I can almost hear them asking, "Why Maddie and not my kid?" They don't realize that I'm living with the reality of their fear—the loss of a child.

Marci beams like she has just given birth. "Meg, would you like to say a few words?"

"Later, if that's ok."

"Of course, when you're ready. Next, I'd like to hold a moment of prayer followed by sharing remembrances for Jackson's beloved son."

I gasp.

"You didn't know?" one of the women asks accusingly.

"God, that's awful. I didn't…I wish…"

"I say hallelujah," she says.

"He's in a better place," one of the other women says.

"Wrong. There's no better place than with your family," I say.

"What do you know? Your kid is alive and doing well."

"I know plenty, believe me."

Marci interrupts, says, "We were going to have a prayer."

Jackson whispers, "No one knows what the death of a child feels like until it's their reality." He stares at me as he speaks.

"I know," I say. It's like I'm an outsider now. I need to belong again.

He says, "What do you know? You don't need us, Madeline is fine."

The woman says, "She never even lost any hair."

"I lost my son." I draw Maddie into me, protectively cover her ears.

"Son? What son?" asks Marci.

"Jordan. Maddie's older brother."

Marci clasps her hands to her bosom. "He had cancer too?"

"I killed him."

A chorus of gasps ring out.

"I didn't mean to. CPR, prayer, none of it worked. Such a tiny body and all those worthless tubes."

"I'm sorry for your loss. But you must know you need to focus on Maddie now." Marci bends down evangelist-style in front of Maddie and me.

I realize that they will never accept me now. I blurt out, "Maddie is fine."

"Denial never helps, Meg. You should know that."

"She doesn't have cancer!"

Silence; stricken faces.

"What do you mean?"

"She doesn't have cancer," I whisper.

"Get out," Marci says.

"No, please. Let me explain. I didn't mean to lie. I went to the support group for parents who've lost children, but they kicked me out because Maddie was alive and I brought her with me."

"You lied to us. You took our good will and lied to us."

"I didn't mean to lie, I swear. I saw you in the hall and you assumed. I never corrected you. I just needed somewhere to belong."

Marci stands, grabs my arm, propels Maddie and me to the door.

"Please, please let us stay." I hug Maddie tighter as Marci moves us to the door faster.

"Please," Maddie cries.

"Get out, you liar."

The classroom door slams behind us. I feel like my tether has snapped. I'm hurtling into free fall. It's just like my recurring dream. I'm hurtling towards some crash I can't see.

I hustle home, clean the house top to bottom, just the way Paul likes it. I set the table with pink candles, make veal marsala. I want to show Paul, in spite of my actions of late, I'm a good wife. I'm a good mother.

In the morning, the burned-out candles and Paul's uneaten dinner are still on the table. I look for clues that prove he came home sometime during the night, but I can't find any.

I need a touchstone to talk to. Paul would say, "Get a therapist." Of course, now he'd amend his statement with "Get any therapist, except for the one I'm going to." That's what I'll do. I'll make an appointment with his therapist. That way I can tell my side of the story. Maybe she can help us get back together. There's got to be some way to reach Paul, bring him back into the fold of our family.

I can hear my mother's voice telling me, "Quit fighting against a wind that is blowing you down." She used to say it when we would be fighting about how much she was drinking. She meant it as a way of telling me I'd never win against her and alcohol. Maybe I'm hearing my mother's voice now, because my subconscious is telling me Paul and Susie are much too united. Patterns repeat themselves. I'm a liability in my own household all over again.

Maybe Al will be my touchstone. I get his business card from its hiding place in my bathrobe pocket.

A woman singsong answers. "Good morning. Mr Longo's office. This is Debbie. How may I assist you?"

"Is Mr Longo in?" I ask.

"Who may I say is calling?"

"Emily."

"With what company?"

"I'm a friend."

"Hold, please."

I start to say thank you, but I'm already on hold. I should hang up.

"Emily, what a surprise."

"Yeah, to both of us."

"So you've been thinking about what a great dancer I am and you want to go again?"

"Among other things," I banter back.

"Good then. Tonight?"

"Hold up there, cowboy."

"What?"

"You're moving too fast," I say. "How are you?"

He slows his voice down to moron speed. "Fine and you?"

"Living." He doesn't know what an ironic reply that is in my household.

"Would you like to meet tonight?" Still with the slow-voice rhythm.

"Talk normal. I was thinking more lunch for starters."

"Ok."

"Ok then, bye."

"Emily, wait."

I pull my hand back from hanging up the phone. "Yes?"

"Lunch when? Where?"

"Oh, sorry. How about today?" I ask.

"You want to meet at the bar where I saw you last?"

"Is that close to your work?"

"About a half-hour away."

"I'll come down by you. I don't have a work schedule to keep."

"That's very considerate." He gives me directions, then says, "Tell the receptionist you're here for me and she'll page me."

"How about if I meet you in the parking lot?"

"No, come on in and meet people."

"I'll have Madeline with me."

"Can't you get a babysitter?"

"I'm in an overprotective phase. I'm not ready to leave her with a babysitter."

"That's fine, then. Come on in and let me show you off, I mean around."

I laugh. I didn't know I was show-off material. I say, "I don't really think you want to show me off with my wedding band on."

"We'll work on that."

"I'll see you out front at 12:30 then?"

"Make it noon. I'm starving for you."

"Right." I hang up the phone.

Pulling up in the SUV, I spot him pacing by the turnaround in front of his building. He's wearing a crisp white shirt and a red and charcoal print tie with black pants. He looks good pacing and talking on a cell phone. He sees my car. I watch his lips say, "Ok, later." He flips the phone closed. I'll never know who he was talking to and I don't rightly care.

He swoops into the car, kisses me, swivels in his seat as he's buckling it, says, "Hi, Madeline."

She cuts her eyes over to me, smiles a little. That's what Paul calls her shy-guy routine.

"Maddie, say hello to Al."

"Hi," she mumbles. Pointing to her Winnie the Pooh shoes, she says, "Pooh."

"Winnie the Pooh, good," I say.

"V-pooh," she says.

Al reaches over the seat, shakes her shoe. She pulls her foot up onto her car seat.

"Hard to get, like her mother."

"Hmmm. Where are we going?" I ask.

"I guess my place is out of the question."

"Right."

"Pity. Turn left up here." He pauses, "Do you remember how to get to my house?"

"I do."

"Maybe you'll stop by sometime."

"Is that what you want?"

"Of course," he says.

"To get laid?"

"No. To spend time together. Get to know each other better."

"You're good-looking. I'm sure there's a world of women waiting to spend time with you."

"I don't have any problems finding a date, if that's what you're asking."

"Then why me?"

"You're different," he says.

"If you usually date single women, you're right. I am different."

He takes my hand in his. "Let me ask you this. Why are you here?"

I shrug.

"Things can't be all that great if you're calling me."

I feel the urge to cry. "They're not."

"You can talk to me."

"That's what I'm hoping," I say, looking over at him.

He smiles encouragingly, pats my hand.

chapter nineteen

I hear the garage door open, then close. I listen for sounds of Paul exiting his car. 6:30—it's the earliest he's been home in weeks. I'm not even going to ask him where he stayed last night.

Good thing I took the cross back up and hid it in the garage. I don't want to start the evening off with an argument. I'll put it back after Paul leaves for work in the morning. Ok, he's home, I've got dinner started. I thought only Maddie and me were eating together again, but I made enough for him just in case. The only problem is I have a bottle of wine open. Too bad, if he can drink beer in the house, a little wine won't hurt. He'll say it's ok to drink the beer, because he does it at night when no one is around. We're not really so different, Paul and me.

Five minutes go by. I listen at the garage door. There's no noise. I open the door. His head is on the steering wheel. He lifts his head, puts it momentarily back down. The car door opens, his body melts out.

I walk back into the kitchen, remove a second wine glass from the cabinet, pour him a healthy portion. "Cheers," I say, passing him the goblet of Merryvale Cabernet as he sets his briefcase down by the table.

I clink my glass against his, hold my breath.

"What are you doing?"

I see his eyes edge over to the bottle. It's three-quarters empty.

"I was hoping you'd come home tonight. I thought we could

use a romantic evening." I'm scrambling around in my head for more words that will make this night go smoothly.

"What happened to your 'no alcohol in the house' rule?" His voice sounds peevish.

"It's been broken." I withhold the words "by you drinking beer every night." I don't want to blame him. It's not his fault he doesn't know I've been drinking ever since Jordan died.

"I don't want a wife who's an alcoholic like her mother."

"What?" My stomach jumps. I can't believe he's using my past against me. I never thought he'd be this kind of person.

"I don't want to come home to you drinking every night. If you're going to do that, then go get a job to occupy your tortured mind."

"Wow. When did you get to be so righteous?"

"You need help, Meg."

So it's going to be all about my problems and not about his. I say, "And you need a tongue transplant. Who sneaks downstairs in the middle of every night and drinks a six pack? Who knows what bars you stop off at on your way home."

"Where's Maddie?" he asks.

"Up in her room."

"Alone?"

"We all play alone sometimes." If we were the old Paul and Meg, he would have made a joke.

"You're down here drinking while she could be upstairs putting her finger in an outlet?" He smells the wine for the first time.

"That's what safety plugs are for."

"Don't make light of this. You should be watching her. Do I need to get a babysitter to watch you now too?"

"You can't watch a kid every second of the day. You know that," I say.

"What's that mean?"

"Just what I said."

"Speak plainly, Meg."

"All I meant was I think we both know you can't watch a kid every second of every day. That's all."

"Susie told me you blamed her and me for Jordan. I didn't believe her." He sips the wine. His forehead wrinkles, then he makes a not bad move with his mouth. He takes a healthier swig.

"Well, I guess now you can believe your girlfriend."

He points his finger at my right eye. I can feel the intent and vibrations wave off it with each up and down movement. I'm surprised to realize I'm waiting for the finger to turn into a fist. "You need help."

"So you said."

"You're crazy," he says.

"Now you're a therapist. I didn't know you'd gone back to get a second degree."

"So you're just free and clear of any responsibility in the matter?"

"The matter? The matter, you say." I throw the dishtowel on the counter. "Since you're such a big therapist, I'd think you'd be the one to call things by their name."

"You're just talking gibberish."

"No, I'm talking about Jordan's death—not some engineering matter." I'd take a big swallow of wine, but my hands are shaking too much. I don't want to spill any and have him accuse me of being drunk.

He stares at me like I really am crazy.

I continue, "And yes, I take my share of responsibility. It was my car, my bumper and my foot on the accelerator when it should have been on the brake. But I wouldn't have needed my foot on the brake if you hadn't taken Jordan out in the front yard in the first place or if you'd been watching him once you did, instead of ogling Susie's ass. Are you happy now? Is that what you wanted to hear? Guilty. We're all fucking guilty, Paul."

"No." He gulps half his wine. "I'm not happy at all."

"Either am I," I whisper. I can't believe I've finally said what I've swallowed for nine months. It should feel freeing, but it feels worse.

Paul looks me in the eye. His mouth opens and closes. I see love and pain and hate swirling around his pupils.

"What?" I ask.

"Nothing."

"Just say it."

"Meg, you don't want to be here and I don't want you here."

I'm reeling. I expected a lot of ugly words, but not these. "I'm not leaving."

"It's never going to work. Please, just pack your bags."

"This is my house as much as yours."

"You're not working."

"How could I forget, when you remind me every night? I'm a mother. Not all mothers work."

"Is that how you've decided to mother Madeline? By corralling her up in her room so you can drink in the kitchen?"

I stick to the numeric facts. "Approximately sixty-three percent of the money in the bank and our investments came from my salary. If I weren't in charge of the finances, we wouldn't have a veritable pot to piss in. We certainly wouldn't have this house."

"That's probably true."

"Think, Paul, before you say things like that to me."

"Right back at you."

My stomach is flip-flopping. I want to ask him where we go from here, but I'm afraid to escalate things even more. Instead, I say, "Agreed." It's good for him to hear that I agree with him on something.

He says, "Where does that leave us?"

I laugh.

"Is that funny?" he asks.

"No, it's just that I was wondering the same thing, but was afraid to ask."

"So where does it leave us?" He doesn't smile.

"Counseling?" My voice goes up four full octaves. I hate myself for the pleading little-girl voice I hear squeaking out my mouth.

He shakes his head slightly no. He doesn't say anything, just stares me down.

"What is it you want, Paul?"

"To be happy."

"With me?"

"With myself."

"With yourself and me?" I tickle his side. I don't know how to bring him back any more. I've lost my magic over him.

"I have to be happy with myself first."

"Is that what the therapist tells you?"

"She does."

"What's her name?"

"Schneider."

"You call her by her last name like she's a guy on your basketball team?" I wonder how many Schneiders there are in the phonebook. I'll make my own appointment with her.

"Dr. Schneider. Hope Schneider."

"Hope," I repeat. "That's a good name for a therapist."

Maddie cries upstairs. Paul turns to go, but I slam my glass on the counter, pushing past him.

"Coming, goozie," I yell. I take the stairs two and three at a time, feeling like a ghost is pursuing me. What if she did hurt herself? Paul would never, ever forgive me—even if she just hurt herself a little. Worse, I'd never forgive myself. When I reach her room, I leap over the baby gate. I drop to my knees, scoop her up.

"What's the matter, baby?"

Paul skids up to her doorway. "What happened?"

"Nothing. I think she was bored and frustrated."

"That's ridiculous."

"That a baby can get bored? Where have you been?" I hold her hands up. "See? One, two, three…" I count off up to ten for both hands then count her toes, wiggling each one as I go. "All still intact."

Maddie laughs, puts her foot back in my hand so I'll count again.

"Burly, burly, burly, boo," I say, twirling my finger at, then poking her stomach.

I catch Paul looking wistfully at Jordan's closed door. We don't go in there any more. Well, not together. Maddie and I play in there sometimes. I pretend Jordan is there with us. She just pretends, playing with his cash register and his hobby horse.

I know Paul goes in there, because I always smooth out the comforter on Jordan's big boy bed before leaving the room. Paul always leaves behind his imprint.

Maddie pokes my stomach and says, "Boo."

"Do Daddy. Paul, come in here."

He unlatches the baby gate. I pat the floor next to us. He settles onto the floor.

I lift his shirt up, exposing his belly button. He lets me. His stomach has started to soften from drinking beer. "Look, Maddie, get Daddy."

She twirls her finger and yells "Boo" when she touches his stomach. We all laugh. Paul does it to her, she squirms on my lap and I tickle her until she belly laughs.

"Are you eating with us?" I ask.

He looks at his watch.

"Going somewhere?" I ask, before I can take it back.

"Stop it."

"You looked at your watch when I asked a simple question. I'll ask it again. Do you want to eat dinner with us?"

He stares at me. God, he hates me.

"Because, we'd like it if you would."

"I guess."

It's the best he can give right now—caveats, semi-commitments cloaked in disinterest. I can live with it or move on.

"Good, then, good," I say. "We're having lemon chicken and rice."

"Great," he says.

"Do you want to change her while I go make the salad?"

"Ok." He stands.

Passing her to him, I swing into kiss him. He pulls back. I slap his ass instead. I give it a little pinch, moving on my way. Looking back over my shoulder, I see him slightly smile in spite of himself.

A smile is something I think I can work with.

Settled in at the table, Paul asks, "What did you guys do today?"

"This and that," I respond, imagining a montage of Kira diving, Paige clapping and Al kissing me goodbye after a two and a half hour lunch swirling in my head. He must think it's weird that I haven't asked why he never came home last night.

"Al," Maddie yells.

My head snaps up at Paul. I turn to Maddie. "Good girl," I say. "Owl."

"Al," she confirms.

"We went to the library today and read a picture book about owls."

"Hoo-hoo," Paul calls, imitating an owl.

"Al," she says again.

I never imagined Maddie was old enough to become an informant.

chapter twenty

I slip in the back window, then reach out and lift Maddie in. She laughs. She thinks it's a game. I'm a little nervous. Since I first had the idea, it's taken me four days to get my nerve up to go into Paige's house. For four days, Maddie and I have played in the backyard as a way of acclimating ourselves to their surroundings. Even though they have a metal security plaque stuck in the front flowerbed, they don't have a security system. I checked through the window for noise detectors and on all the screens to make sure.

They have a six-foot wood fence and the houses on all sides are single-story houses, so the neighbors can't see over the fence. About half the block, including Paige's house, has been renovated to two-stories. That's the way it is with these old Florida neighborhoods. The houses used to be vacation homes. They didn't even originally have air conditioning. Little by little, the year-round-resident transplants, accustomed to northern multi-level homes, are building up two-story, hurricane-target homes in South Florida.

Paige always leaves this window unlocked. It's a curiosity to me. It's the only window missing a screen—double vulnerability. Not that a screen can't easily be cut through. I stand still just inside the window with Maddie in my arms, waiting to see if an alarm goes off in spite of my checking. Nothing. I take one step into the room, then another. I'm home free, so to speak.

I know their pattern. Kira leaves for school at exactly 8:00. Paige leaves at exactly 10:00. I'm not sure where she goes. I've been busy watching the house, so I haven't followed her yet. But I will one of these days. Maybe she has a boyfriend she meets for lunch. That would be nice. She always comes home at 12:30 on the dot. Schedules and organization seem to soothe this family. Maybe I should try that.

The house looks like it belongs in a design magazine.

"Oooh," Maddie exclaims, pointing to a mammoth floral arrangement on the dining table. I think it must be silk, something that big, but find it's real upon touching it. A white lily petal lets go, fluttering to the tablecloth. I stuff it in my pocket. Maddie is so excited over the flowers; I pinch a small violet off, arranging it behind her ear.

Her little hand searches for it. I hold her hand. "Wait," I say, walking on tiptoe down the hall to the mirror, like we have to be quiet or we'll be found out. "Pretty."

"Hmm-hmm," she says, nodding her head, turning it from side to side to look at the flower.

We stare at our reflection in the gilt mirror. We smile at one another. I imagine what it would be like to wake up in this immaculate household every morning. For two houses—Paige's and mine—in relatively the same neighborhood, we sure live different lives. Maybe that's why Cameron strayed over to Susie. I think of Al, then understand Cameron a little better. Maybe he couldn't stand the regimentation of it all and needed contact with someone who was more free. Maybe he had a need to be someone else too. Still, it doesn't excuse his behavior or mine either.

We waltz around the living room, taking in life-sized family pictures, a crystal decanter on a teacart and Queen Anne chairs. We twirl and twirl, our heads thrown back, faces lifted towards heaven, until the flower falls from Maddie's hair. I dip down, swiping the flower up so Maddie doesn't see it, secret it away in my left pocket with the petal.

I sashay down the hall and up the stairs to keep Maddie from getting antsy. I'm giggle-drunk with the act of trespassing. Kira's bedroom has a bold red rose comforter on the queen-sized bed. I had a twin bed all the way through college. Two walls are painted hunter green. It seems like a bedroom for a girl that's older than nine years old. Just as well. Now that Kira's father is dead, she'll need to act like she's older than nine years old. Pictures and figurines of angels decorate the room. A tiffany-style lamp with sprites playing is on her nightstand. Next to it, there's a picture of Kira and Cameron. They're cheek to cheek; green mountains are in the background. I bend down to get a closer look, searching for clues of a happy family. On her dresser is a picture of all three of them.

I don't touch anything. I only want to witness their life. I wonder if Paige is upset that the picture Kira has at her bedside is of Kira with Cameron and not with Paige. But it's natural for people to cling to what's missing. I imagine Paige placing the picture on Kira's bedside table the first day Kira went back to school after Cameron's accident.

Except for her anal tendencies, Paige seems to be a fine role model. Paige seems to be all about the business of moving on with life. Wherever she goes everyday, she hasn't missed it once. Where is the wallowing about in despair and self-pity? If she were striving to keep up appearances for Kira's sake, she still has plenty of time to collapse while Kira is at school. But no, Paige keeps going—to the grocery store, a new hairdo, new clothes; on and on she goes. I don't see one box of tissues anywhere. And this is not the type of family to make do with blowing their noses with toilet paper. If I can understand how this family lives and endures in grief, maybe then I can replicate the feeling back at my house.

Maddie struggles to get down. "Let's see Paige's bedroom," I say.

"Ok," she says, popping up and down on my hip.

I whinny like a horse, pretending to gallop down the hall. Their bedroom looks and smells different from the rest of the house. I breathe in deep so I can catch the smell. It's sandalwood. A rough-hewn, pine-stump poster bed dominates the center of the room. All the furniture is designed to look handmade. There are pictures of animals on the walls—horses, bobcats and wolves. I laugh and feel sad at once over the bad metaphor of him trying to bring wildlife into his bedroom. Obviously, Paige let Cameron have his way in decorating this room. Maybe if she had let him have his way in the more prurient bedroom matters, he wouldn't have cheated. I used to think a cheater is a cheater. And I still think that. I think some people will cheat no matter how good or happy their situation. But now I understand how circumstance can turn someone who isn't naturally a cheater into that very thing. People can only be pushed so far.

The only thing on either of the dressers is their wedding picture. From the style of their tux, gown and Paige's feathered hairdo, I'm guessing they got married in the '70s. They must have waited a long time to have Kira. I wonder if she's adopted. If you live in my head, you can make up stories all day.

I hear voices outside. My heart pumps blood double time. My feet are planted. I bounce Maddie twice, then cement-foot my way over to the window. Her drapes are open, save a gossamer blue lace curtain. I peer through the holes in the lace. Two women are talking outside. One looks up at the window. I swivel-duck to the side. God, what if they saw me climb through the back window? They would have had to be snooping over the six-foot fence. Not unheard of, but I wasn't in the backyard even one minute. Once my mind was made up to come in the house, I moved from the side gate to the window with swift intent.

I run with Maddie down the stairs and through the house. The marble hallway is slippery. I slam open the back window.

It's a tall one that we can practically step through. It must be driving Paige nuts that the screen is out of place. I lift Maddie out first. I don't want her running away from me inside the house. She starts running towards the pool.

"Madeline," I cry out in as hushed a voice as possible. I leap out the window, hitting my shin on the sill. I fall to the ground, both hands skid me to a stop. In a deep voice, I yell out loud, "Stop now." I don't care if I get arrested for breaking and entering if my little girl is safe.

Maddie stops, turns long enough for me to scramble over to her. I swoop down on her, mother claw-hands at the ready to pick her up. I kiss her cheek.

"Mama," she says, pushing my face away. I kiss her again anyway. My knees and hands are smarting from the fall. No one has rushed into the backyard. We must still be safe. I walk towards the side gate. With a jolt, I remember I've left the window open. Jogging back, I juggle Maddie onto my left hip, then close the window.

Pausing at the side gate, I can still hear the women talking. I consult my watch. It's noon. I have a half-hour to wait these women out before Paige comes home. I squat down. I don't know how long I can keep Madeline quiet.

What if those women really are waiting for the cops? I walk the perimeter of the fence. Behind the shed, there are three boards missing, just enough for us to squeeze through. I scope out the neighbor's yard. No fences.

We slide through the fence. Oh jeez, there's an old man on the side of the house. He looks like he's taking a piss, but then I spot a hose in his right hand. Why is it that men water plants with a hose at penis level? I drop to my haunches. He turns his back to us. Hopefully, we won't catch his peripheral vision.

Just as I'm about to round the corner of his house, he spots me. "Oscar, Oscar," I call out.

"May I help you?" he calls out.

I keep moving.

The hose has tethered him. He drops it and it sprays the back of his pants. "Miss, may I help you?"

I turn. "Oh, yes, have you seen a small black poodle?"

"No."

"Oscar," Maddie slurs out. It's a new word to her.

He smiles at her.

"That's ok, honey," I say, patting Maddie's back. "We'll find him." I start off again.

"Does he have a tag?"

"I'm afraid not." I hurry along, trying to put some distance between us.

"Where do you live?"

I pretend not to hear him. "Oscar, Oscar," I call, hustling down the block. As I round the corner, I look back. The old man is still stationed on his sidewalk, looking this way and that. I see him cup his hand to his mouth and hear a whistle. He's calling for Oscar.

"Whew," I say. Maddie mimics me. This was absolutely the most exciting day I've had since, well, since the night I went dancing with Al.

I feel alive.

chapter twenty-one

Maddie and I lounge around Paige's house almost every day now. I've started packing lunch and cooking it in her kitchen. She has a great kitchen, beautiful china, all stainless steel appliances and the best pots. I bring my own dishtowel, so I don't leave a wet towel behind after washing and drying her good china and pans. Yesterday, I almost left one of my blonde hairs on her dark blue bedspread when we lay down for a rest. Paige is definitely the sort to notice a long blonde hair. Both Kira and she have dark hair.

I use the jogging stroller when we come over now, in case we have to make a quick getaway. I hide it back behind the shed. All this walking has firmed my legs up a bit. I could carry Maddie and run with the stroller if I don't have time to strap her in. I don't want her falling out and hurting herself.

I love being in Paige and Kira's house. The orderliness has become refreshing to me. The other up side is that my drinking has reduced. I suppress the urge to drink in her house on the grounds it may make me do something careless. It's important not to leave clues that we've been there.

I must confess, I've become a bit of a snoop. No rummaging through their drawers—that would be a breach of privacy. Although, I did go through their medicine chest to see if there were any prescriptions for Paige. There weren't. Mainly, my snooping is in the form of following them around. Kira has a little boyfriend, she just doesn't know it yet. Paige is seeing someone for sure. He's a doctor. I'm sure they've been dating for some time—since before Cameron died. I watch them at lunch on occasion. They have a relaxed, easy style with each other—not like a new romance. Sometimes, they go to a little condo overlooking the ocean close to his office. I haven't noticed a ring on his finger. Maybe their houses are too far for a lunch fling. Nice to have the money to spend on a luxury sex nest.

I wonder how long Paige is going to wait to spring the doctor on Kira. Maybe she won't ever introduce Kira to him. Maybe she'll just keep her romantic life and her home life separate. That would be selfish of her to keep apart the people she loves the most. Maybe she's just nuts—like she's a split personality or something, living two different lives. There are lots of nutty people in the world. Maybe she likes the idea of treating the doctor like he's a whore she takes off the shelf and plays with when it suits her fancy.

No wonder she was able to go on after Cameron's death without faltering. But that's bad reasoning. It would be like someone telling me it would be easy to go on after Jordan's death because I had Madeline. No man or child can substitute for another. Really, his death must be a windfall to her. No messy divorce and a huge life-insurance settlement. What could be better? Even so, I hope she wishes the father of Kira were alive to see their daughter grow. Even if she hated him, his death is still a devastating thing for Kira.

I'm learning from Paige. I wouldn't do with my investments what I've done with my monogamous marriage. I'm learning that it's good to diversify. Why keep all your emotional stock in one man when the world and people are such unstable, unpredictable things?

I've started calling Al at the office. I want to keep him interested while I'm sorting out my feelings. I see him here and there for lunch—mostly on days when I don't feel the need to go to Paige's house. Her house gives me a sense of hope. If she can get through losing a husband, I can get through losing a son. A son and a husband are different, but grief is grief.

Maddie seems to understand she has to be careful when we're in Paige's house. Today, we're having hummus, pita and a tofu stir fry. Paige has good spices. I open the Tupperware cabinet for Maddie to play in while I cook. Maddie thinks the tofu tastes funny, but she eats everything else. I watch my time—it's 11:30 by the time we finish eating lunch.

I start washing the dishes, but I'm so tired lately. It's 11:45. We have time to lie down on Paige's bed. In fifteen minutes, I'll get up and finish the dishes.

"Ma'am. Ma'am, please get up." I'm having a dream where six sinewy muscled men are dancing around my sleeping body. They look so good; all are naked and flexing their muscles for me. One of them reaches out, touches me brusquely on the shoulder. My eyes flutter open. I see navy pants.

"Mama, hi," Maddie says.

I roll over, kiss her on the cheek. "Hi, love bug." Damn. That was a good dream. I'd like to get back to it.

"What are you doing in my house?"

I jump. It's Paige's voice shrilling at me. Oh shit.

"What are you doing home?" I exclaim, looking at my watch. It's 12:45. I slam my body into an upright position, swivel my feet to the floor. The cop bounces me back to the bed.

"Are you kidding me?" Paige says. "This is my home. Who are you?"

"Who are you?" the cop echoes.

"Meg."

"Meg who?" the cop says, taking over the questioning.

"Meg O'Hara." Maddie climbs in my lap, burying her head in my neck. I bounce her up and down.

"Let's see some identification."

"It's in our backpack in the kitchen." I make a move to stand up again, but the cop puts his hand out.

"Mr..." I search for the cop's badge, "Mr Cox..."

"Sergeant Cox. You just hold up there a minute. Henry?"

I look where he's looking. There's a second cop in the hallway. He's in a semi-lunge forward posture with his hand on his unsnapped holster.

Could he be any more melodramatic? I'm just a sleeping woman with a baby.

"Henry," Sergeant Cox snaps.

"Yes, sir?"

"Go down to the kitchen and find her backpack."

"What's it look like?"

"For God's sake, it's a backpack, figure it out."

"It has a picture of Zoe on it," I say.

"Who's Zoe?" he yells back from the doorway as if there were an imaginary line barring him from entering.

"Orange hair, *Sesame Street*."

"Officer, get her off my bed," Paige says.

"Paige, I'm Meg. Do you know who I am?"

"You're a trespasser is who you are," booms Cox.

"Sergeant? I know I shouldn't be here."

"Darn right you shouldn't. You nearly gave this lady a heart attack."

Paige says, "You've left my kitchen a mess."

Maybe she isn't quite the role model I've been looking for. I could think of a lot of other things to object to in this situation.

"I'm sorry, Paige," I say. "I'll clean it."

"Quit calling me Paige like you know me," she yells. She turns to the sergeant. "Aren't you going to arrest her?"

"Don't you know who I am?"

Sergeant Cox roughly pops me up to my feet when Henry comes back in holding my backpack at arm's length.

"Please be careful, my daughter," I say.

"You should have thought about that before you went about

breaking and entering into people's houses. What kind of mother are you?" Cox asks.

The sergeant dumps our backpack on the bed. Diapers, wet naps, tissues, a zip lock with cheese and crackers and two books fall out. Henry takes his post at the doorway again.

"Do you mind? My bed." says Paige.

"Sorry, ma'am, I just want to find her ID."

"It's in the pocket that's buckled shut," I say.

He gives me an irritated look. He removes the license, looks at the picture, looks at me, looks at the picture. "She's telling the truth, her name is Meg O'Hara. She actually lives pretty close by." He grabs me by the elbow. "Let's go."

"Book," Maddie says, reaching for her *Love You Forever* book.

"Wait a minute," I beg. "Just let me talk to her. Paige, I'm the one who tried to help Cameron the night he died. It was me who crawled through his window. It was me."

She's startled.

"I feel so, so sorry I wasn't able to save him for you and your little girl. I've been coming by and checking on you. I know it seems strange."

She lets her tears slide down her face uninterrupted.

"I lost my son in a car accident recently too."

"You did?" she asks.

"In the same spot Cameron died."

"That's awful."

I nod my head yes. I have momentum pushing me towards a full confession. "I hit him with my car by accident as I was pulling up to my house."

"Oh, my God."

"He ran into the street to get his ball. My husband couldn't react fast enough. I never saw him."

"Still, I don't understand how that gives you the right to break into my house. I have a daughter. What if she came home first?" Her voice is stern, but she approaches the bed cautiously.

"You're right. Coming in to your home like this, it's not right. I watched you after Cameron's funeral and you seemed to be getting on ok…I just wanted to understand how you kept everything going."

She smooths her skirt, looks at her French manicure. "Was Cameron conscious after the accident?"

"All right, ladies, you can tell each other all the stories you want after we're done booking Meg here. Henry, we should call in Child Services for this little girl."

He goes to touch Maddie's face, but I swing her out of his reach. She is looking from face to face, bewildered. I'm sorry I've got her into this situation. I hope she doesn't remember this when she gets older.

"Paige, please," I say.

"Let her answer," she says. "Was he conscious? Did he ask for anyone?"

"He was conscious, but he was in so much pain, he didn't say any words." The sound of his moans going up and down the octave scale comes back to me.

Paige cocks her head to the side, like she's trying to remember something.

I continue, trying to make a connection. "I broke out the car window to get to him. I gave him mouth to mouth. I thought if I could save him, then maybe God and my husband would forgive me for killing my own son."

"So you really were there. The paramedics told me a woman was with him, comforting him. Thank you for what you tried to do for Cameron."

I duck my head, pat Madeline's back. "You're welcome."

"Please sit down," she says, taking a seat on the bed. When

the sergeant doesn't let go of my elbow, she says, "I think that will be all."

"You mean you're not pressing charges?" Cox practically spits.

"I think not," Paige says.

"Perhaps you should look around. Make sure everything is in order."

"I'm sure it is. You said yourself she lives in the neighborhood. It isn't as if she's some street person. She's just—" she waves her hand around "—mixed up a bit."

"It's now or never, lady. If you're going to press charges, you have to do it now."

"Mind your manners, please. I said that will be all. Thank you for coming."

"All right then." He tosses my license on the bed next to the diapers.

As the cops are going down the hall, I hear Cox say, "Do you get these women?"

"You're shaking," Paige says. "What's your baby's name?"

I settle onto the bed next to her. "This is Madeline."

"She's adorable." She rubs my hand.

"Thanks. She looks like her father mostly," I say.

"No, I see you in her."

"I'm sorry I couldn't do more for Cameron. And I'm sorry for breaking into your house."

"Ok."

"You seem to have it so together. I watch you and you just go on. How do you do that?"

"Is there really any other choice?" she asks.

I feel myself flinching.

"Dear, you don't do anybody any favors by being wretched." She goes on, "God doesn't give out any medals for the most miserable."

"But how do you get out of bed every morning?"

"You have to show up in life, Meg."

"Yes."

"You can't put yourself to bed thinking things will be different in the morning. You have to make the world be different." She points to her head when she says it.

"I guess you're right. It's just that I can't help myself most days. I lost my son, my husband hates me, he's having an affair with the next-door neighbor..." I stop myself before saying that it's the same woman Cameron was having an affair with. She's been so nice, I don't want to hurt her. There would be nothing gained by her knowing.

"Then have an affair of your own and get on with it."

"Just like that?"

"Of course. You think affairs were made only for men?"

She's such a surprise. She's uptight and out there at the same time. I reinstate her as my role model. "You don't even get the least bit sad when you get in bed at night? Aren't you sad for Kira?"

"You've done your homework, I see."

"The newspaper is a wealth of information."

"Of course I'm sad. I may be sad for the rest of my life, but that doesn't mean I can't have fun. No sense me dying right along with Cameron."

"Wow. Are you sure you're not just enmeshed in denial?"

She laughs. "You'll get there, you'll see."

"Thanks. And thanks for letting me off today."

Maybe this is a sign. Maybe God has let me atone for Jordan after all.

chapter twenty-two

"Al, it's Emily." It's the first time I'm calling him at home.

"I know your voice," he says.

"Good. That's a start," I say.

"Have you agreed to start with me now?"

"What're you doing?" I ask.

"Getting ready for dinner. How are you?"

"Feeling energetic," I say. "I should let you go."

"Nonsense. I'd rather skip dinner and talk. You haven't called in a few days. I've been thinking about you."

"That's sweet."

"How's Madeline?"

"Busy painting."

"You don't worry about her getting paint on your rugs?" he asks.

"We have a lot of tile in the house. But even if we didn't, I wouldn't mind. Material things are made to be used."

"That's a philosophy."

"Words to live by," I say. "I don't stress myself out over possessions."

"It's so good to hear your voice. Thanks for calling," he says.

I take a big gulp of air before asking, "So do you think Maddie and I can tag along to dinner with you tonight?"

"That would be wonderful."

"You don't mind? Have a date?"

"No to both," he says. "I'm glad you asked."

It is so fucking refreshing to be wanted. I'm even more

exhilarated than when I left Paige's house the other day after dodging getting arrested. She made me promise not to come back unless I knocked on the front door. I gave her my word.

He says, "I'm sure you don't want me picking you up."

"Sorry."

"Do you want to meet?"

"I can come by you."

"What time?"

"Give us forty-five minutes."

"I'll be waiting."

"Ok, see you."

"Emily?"

"Yes?"

"Bring something to keep Madeline busy—like a video."

I laugh. "I'll see you soon," I say, hanging up the phone before he says anything else to make me lose my nerve. My nipples get hard over the thought of standing in front of each other naked. I look down at my wedding ring. I turn the diamond around so I don't have to look at its accusing glitter. Paige is right. It's good to have more than one thing going so you don't get left with nothing.

I think about having a glass of wine, but then I realize I don't need it. For the first time, I realize I have really needed the alcohol. Well, maybe just a teensy glass would be nice. The twelve-step program would say I just made my first step—acknowledging I have a problem. My mouth is ahead of me, watering for the first sip. I resist.

I picture Jordan's sweet face. He would have grown into a handsome man. He smiles at me in my head, just like he did a million times in life. I miss him. I'm ok with missing him. It's natural that I should. He'd want me to be happy.

"Come on, Bugs. We're going out."

I start out the front door, but remember the video. I pause. I think I might as well keep my options open. I rush back in and grab the first one I see. I check myself one more time in the hall tree mirror. I have a slinky dress on that I bought at the airport bathingsuit store. That old pervert who owns the store really knows how to dress me. We're on a first-name basis now.

As I'm locking the front door, Paul pulls in. I'm frozen in his headlights. Two minutes more and he would have missed me. If only I hadn't gone back in for the video.

Dammit all to hell. I could make a getaway while he's pulling into the garage. I know how slow he is at getting out of his car these days. We could be a safe block or two away by then.

I walk to the passenger door, open it. I'm through kowtowing to him. Let him chase after me now. I go about the business of snapping Madeline into her car seat. Turning from the car, Paul is in my face. There's an urgency about him. I can feel it.

"Where are you going?" he asks.

"For a drive."

"What about dinner?"

"You said you were working late," I say.

"But I'm home now."

"I can see that."

"So what about dinner?" he asks.

"Do you need a formal introduction to the stove?"

"I'm home."

"So you are, but you're too late," I say.

"Can I drive with you?"

My heart stops.

"Let's buzz," Maddie says. She makes a buzzing noise and flies her hand around her head.

"In a minute, baby," I say.

"Can I go with you?" he asks again.

"Not tonight, babe."

"Why not?"

"Because I've made other plans," I say.

"With who?"

"Paul, this is the second night you've come home for dinner in a month. You can't expect me to just wait around night after night praying for your arrival."

"With who?"

"I don't know what you do all the times you don't come home until the middle of the night. Now you can see how it feels." I shut the door.

He grabs my arm.

"Let me go," I say, swinging my arm up to detach him. He's got a bulldog jaw's grip on it. "What do you think you're doing?"

"You're not taking my daughter with you wherever you're going."

"Paul, you're hurting me."

"Where are you going?"

"None of your business."

"Come inside. We need to talk, please." There's a pleading tone in his voice.

"I think I'll pass."

"Please."

"Paul, you've been pushing me away and now you want to reel me back in. Shit, for all I know, you want to lure me inside to talk about divorce again. In any case, it's hot. Maddie is waiting."

His hand drops from my arm. As I get in the driver's seat, he opens Maddie's door, starts unbuckling her from the car seat.

"You're not taking my daughter," he bellows. "I won't have her in a car with a drunk driver. You ought to know better than that."

"Smell my breath!" I yell, running around the car. "You're the one that's been drinking, not me."

He can't get the seatbelt off the plastic clip on her chest. "Leave her, Paul."

"Daddy." Maddie holds out her arms.

He yanks the seatbelt.

"Look at you. You're the one who's drunk. You can't even perform a simple manual task."

He yanks the seatbelt harder.

Maddie cries.

"Stop. You're tugging on her. She doesn't like it."

"Where are you going?" he shouts.

"Nowhere," I yell back.

"Then you'll stay?"

God, I feel bad that he's so pitiful. It makes me want to scoop him up in my arms. "I can't," I say weakly.

"Why?"

"Truth?"

"Yes."

"Because I can't let you get your own way anymore. I'm sick of living by your rules while you don't even notice I'm alive. I'm alive, Paul. So is Maddie. So are you."

"Just come inside, please." His voice breaks, he's crying. "I don't know what to do anymore. Please come inside."

Maddie's cries go up in register.

I rub his back automatically. I turn towards Madeline and rub her head. I'm not sure who to comfort. "Hey, stop," I say to both of them. God, I hate that I said that. My mother would never let me cry over anything—not over the small stuff and certainly not over the big stuff. I wrap my arms around his waist, lay my head on his back. "I didn't mean to make you feel bad. It's just that you make me feel like shit every damn day of the week. I'm shriveling. I want to live. I can't sacrifice my whole life to pining away and dying. Jordan wouldn't want that. We have Madeline to think about. I want her to grow up in a happy household."

He straightens up, then hugs me. "I'm so, so, sorry," he says. I hug him back.

"Will you get Maddie out of this blasted carseat?" He laughs, wiping at his tears.

"I will," I say, feeling bad that I'm going to let Al down again.

"Thanks."

He waits beside the car. I lift Maddie out and kiss her, she sniffles a whimper. I pass her to him. He kisses her, puts his arm around my shoulders. We walk into the house as a family.

chapter twenty-three

Paul and I make exquisite animal love. In the morning, he tells me to go back to sleep when we hear Maddie rustling around her crib.

I wake up an hour and a half later, sleep-falter downstairs. Paul is sitting at the breakfast nook drinking a beer. I can tell he's been crying. I think maybe I slept the whole day away. I glance at the wall clock. It's 9:00 AM.

"Isn't it a little early for that?" I ask.

"Sit down." His voice sounds tired.

I look into the rec room. "Where's Maddie?"

"At Susie's," he says.

"What?"

"I just wanted to see your reaction."

"You're not funny," I say. "What's up? Last night was great and now you're being mean."

"Sit down. We need to talk."

"That's what you said last night." I rub myself against him like I'm an alley cat. "But you were pretty monosyllabic in bed." I bite his cheek.

"Stop."

I pull back. It's like he's a totally different man. "Really, where's Maddie?"

"With my sister," he says.

"What? When did she get to town?"

"Yesterday. Last night."

"Why isn't she staying with us?" I don't like his sister, but she's family. She should stay with us.

"She's on her way back home."

"With Maddie?" I start running for the front door. Paul tackles me in the living room. We hit the ground with a thud. I scramble to my knees. He pulls me back to the floor, sitting on me. His knees have my arms anchored to the ground. I try to buck him off, but he keeps repositioning his weight.

"Listen to me," he yells.

"Let me go. You didn't even consult me."

"Listen!" He shakes me.

"You fucking bastard. I'm her mother."

"Settle down."

The doorbell rings. Paul hesitates before getting off me. I bum rush him, punching him between his shoulder blades.

"Ouch. Damn you," he yells.

"Damn you."

He grabs my arm.

The front door opens tentatively. A woman in a neat business suit, purse held in front, is standing at the door. She has long, straight, shiny black hair. "Hi."

"Who are you?" I ask. Now I know how Paige felt when she found me asleep in her bed. I try twisting away from him. "Please let me go." I shrink to my knees. He picks me up by my armpits.

"Hope, this is my wife, Meg."

"Your ex-wife," I say.

"Meg, this is Dr Schneider," Paul says, going on with the introductions like this is a normal meeting.

"How do you do?" she asks.

"How do you do?" I mimic. "How does it look like I'm doing?"

"It looks like you're having a bad morning."

"Please tell him to let me go. I've got to go get my daughter."

"How about if we just all talk for a bit?"

"This is nuts. He's stolen my daughter. His sister isn't even good with kids. I need to leave."

She looks me in the eye. She has a hypnotic effect. "If you'd just let us all talk for a while, then we'll consider it."

"Please." I start to cry. Little cries at first, then so loud I can't even hear what they're saying to me.

I see Hope gesture to the couch. Paul picks me up and carries me towards it.

"Do you know who I am?" she asks.

I nod.

"Good." She's talking to me in a quiet voice. "Do you know why we removed Madeline from your household?"

I shake my head no, moaning out a cry from my uterus.

"Why don't you tell her, Paul? She deserves an explanation."

"Your friend Marci called me two days ago," he says.

"She's not my friend."

"She said you were acting strange the last time she saw you. She called me to see if Madeline was doing ok."

"She's not ok, she's with your fucking sister."

"Meg, she said you'd been taking Maddie to a cancer support group. How could you?"

"That bitch," I yell.

"Were you? Taking her to a cancer support group?" he asks.

"That sneaky bitch."

"It's not her fault you're a liar."

"Paul, let's be constructive," Hope says.

"I ended up at the cancer support group because the grieving parents group only allowed parents to have dead kids, not live ones. They threw me out for bringing Maddie in. I went into the cancer support group by mistake. They were so nice, I stayed."

Paul looks at his hands latched on my shoulders.

I turn my head towards Hope. "I needed somebody to talk to. I needed to see other people in the world in as much pain over losing their children as I am."

"That's a reasonable explanation," Hope says. "But you shouldn't have misled people about Maddie having cancer."

"I didn't lie. I just never corrected their assumptions."

Hope nods towards Paul.

"Please. Can I please get Madeline back?"

"Soon. Let's chat a bit more."

I try to sit up again. Paul tightens his grip.

"Is the strait-jacket routine really necessary?"

"We think it is," says Paul.

"When did you become 'we' with your psychiatrist?"

"Do you see how combative she can get?"

"I have every right. You kidnapped my daughter," I scream.

"And you've been going through the neighborhood breaking and entering into people's houses with my daughter."

"What are you talking about?" I know Paige wouldn't betray me the way Marci did. She has different sensibilities.

"A Sergeant Cox came to my office yesterday. Hearing from Marci the day before was bad enough, but hearing from him…"

"I can explain," I say.

"Sure. You're full of explanations," he says.

"Not everyone can be as damned stoic as you are."

"Breaking and entering?" he asks.

"I gave him mouth to mouth. I had his blood on my hands. I couldn't save him." I'm not sure if I'm talking about Jordan or Cameron. Everything is blurring on me.

Paul says, "Child Services could have taken her away."

"How does it make you feel that you couldn't save him?" Hope leans forward.

"Like shit. First my son and then Cameron. Like my

husband can't forgive me. Like I'm cursed. How would it make you feel?"

"If Maddie gets taken away," Paul says, "I'll never forgive you."

She nods at me, ignoring Paul. "You're very angry."

"So?" I ask.

"Anger is one of the acceptable stages of grief." She smiles.

"I suppose breaking and entering isn't?"

"Paul said you were quick."

"No, I'm frantic. I want my daughter back. He's drinking beer at nine in the morning and he's the better parent? I'll be good. I promise I will."

"Let's talk through this," she says.

"Why?" I ask.

"We want to understand your motivations."

"Do I get to ask questions? Paul, don't you love me enough to talk to me before spiriting my daughter away?"

He looks at me for the first time. "Dr Schneider...I...we thought an intervention was necessary."

"An intervention?" I ask.

"Meg, I kept telling you that you needed help." He runs his fingers through his hair.

"Then why didn't you take me to one of your appointments when I asked? All of this could have been avoided."

Silence.

Hope says, "Paul?"

"I don't know," he says.

"Give it a guess," I say.

"Because I didn't want to include you anymore."

"That's good, Paul," Hope prods. "Go on."

"Oh God. Then why didn't you just leave?" I ask.

"I don't know," he says.

"Do you hate me?"

He shrugs.

"Do you blame me?"

"I blame myself. I just can't stand to look at you anymore."

"I sure couldn't tell that from the way you were thrashing around the bed with me last night."

I see Hope's eyebrows go up.

"I thought it would help," he says.

"Well next time, help me by opening your mouth, not your pants."

He looks at me like I've punched him square in the face.

"I know I've done some things I shouldn't have. But I don't think I deserve this."

"What do you deserve?" she asks.

"I deserve a husband and a family. I'm a good person. I've been depressed and…and misguided. Please. I never hurt anyone. You can ask Paige. She's Cameron's wife. We're friends now."

"Paige, the woman whose house you broke into is your friend?" Paul laughs. "You are something, you are."

"Pass me the phone. I'll call her right now."

"Whether Paige is your friend or not is not really the issue here," Hope says.

"What is the issue? Can I sit up?" I struggle against Paul until he lets go enough for me to sit up. He holds onto the yoke of my nightgown.

"Meg," Hope says. "Do you think you're well enough to be a wife and a mother?"

"I don't think anyone in the world is well enough for the shit that comes their way. But that doesn't mean we get everything taken away from us by the people who are supposed to love us. Paul, I would never, ever have done something like this to you. We've spent twelve years of our lives together, two kids, this house. Doesn't any of that mean something to you?"

He shrugs.

"You're the one who has been seeing a shrink. Aren't you in touch with your feelings?"

"I wanted to protect Maddie."

"Protect her? Then for God's sake, let's go get her away from your sister. Madeline barely even knows her."

"My sister isn't that bad."

"Don't say that after all the stories you've told me. I see the way she roughs her kids up. Whose judgment is in question here? I think it's yours."

"Maddie is already on a plane," he says. "There's nothing I can do."

"I don't want her on a plane. It's dangerous. People are always sick on planes, she'll catch cold."

"It's too late."

"Can we just call the airport and see if it has left?"

"It has," Paul says.

"Fine. I think this conversation is over." I stand up, but he pulls me back down by my nightgown.

"Go ahead. Hit me. You're just like your sister and your mother," I say.

Once you put that kind of shit out there, you can't take it back. I've chinked his armor now. The same as he did mine the night he called me an alcoholic like my mother and all those mornings he stayed outside with Susie instead of coming inside and comforting me. He threw a canon ball through my armor by taking Madeline away this morning. I'll never be able to make love with him again.

I turn to Hope like a wheedling nine-year-old. "Did he tell you he's been cheating on me too?"

She keeps her face neutral. No confirmation or disconfirmation there.

"What? What do you want?" I yell. I spring off the couch. I

run upstairs with Paul in hot pursuit. I make it to our bedroom in time to shut and lock the door. He kicks it. The bottom of the door flexes in.

"Fuck you, Paul," I yell, stripping off my nightgown and dressing in a flurry. Shit. My car keys and wallet are downstairs in the backpack. Essentials are thrown into an overnight bag: jeans, a shirt, a dress, deodorant, toothbrush and toothpaste. I'll worry about whatever else I need when I get where I'm going.

"Meg, open the door or I swear by God I'll kick it in." He kicks it hard, wood splinters.

"Fuck you. You're the one who needs help."

He kicks the door again, jiggles the doorknob.

Hope is in the hallway, soothing him, telling him to let me cool off for a minute. Telling him to let me go. I wonder how other people ever got so much power over our marriage when it's only the two of us who get into bed together every night.

Grabbing my spare house key from my nightstand, I wish my spare car key was in there too. I step into the shower, open the bathroom window. There's a small roof that drops down to the first-story roof. I'm scared of heights. Why don't we have a single-story house like everyone else in Florida? I can barely climb a ladder, much less think of jumping off the roof.

I picture Maddie's face getting slapped by his sister. How could Paul be so irresponsible? Who's going to protect her? I lift my right leg out the window, then my left. I'm shaking. The worst thing that can happen is that I break my arm or leg. But I could snap my neck if I fall just the right way. I mean the wrong way. I shuffle to the edge of the roof. It looks like a long drop.

Once my bag lands on the ground, I have to move fast in case they see it out the kitchen window. "Ahh," I say out loud as a way of calming my nerves. I used to do that on ski trips when Paul would take me on a run that was steeper than my skill level. Throwing the bag past the first-story roof, I squat and back over the roof, hanging on by my hands. It's probably worse to go this way, but I feel like it will be a smaller drop. I hyperventilate and let go, landing on the lower roof on my left side. Several barrel tiles crack under me. I gotta keep going. Edging up to the first-story window, I do the same maneuver. I land on my feet this time. Thank God I have sneakers on. As I rise from my squatting position, I see Paul's surprised face looking out the kitchen picture window.

"There she is," he yells.

I grab my bag and run, tossing chairs and tables up and out of my way like a hurricane wind.

chapter twenty-four

Careening between houses, I race through block after block. My lungs feel like they're burning from the inside out. I enter Paige's yard through the hole in the fence. Knocking on her front door is out in case Paul is watching for me. I'm not even sure if he knows where she lives. But Susie would be willing to tell him.

Kira and Paige are at the breakfast table. I knock on the window I used to climb through. Paige points to the side door.

"You can knock on my door like everybody else, you know," she says, opening the door. When she sees my face, she says, "What's the matter? You look scared."

"Has Paul been here?" I say, placing my hands on my knees, catching my breath between words.

"Why, no. What's going on? Where's Maddie?"

"The sergeant went and talked to him. They took Maddie away."

"Who took Maddie away?" she asks.

"Paul's sister. She's taking her to Utah."

"Oh my." She places her hands on my shoulders, steers me into the kitchen. It's nice to have someone's hands on my shoulders who isn't trying to hold me down. She sits me down in a chair, takes the bag from my hands.

"Paul and his psychiatrist did what they called an intervention on me. Paul made love to me last night and just like that took Maddie right out from under me while I was sleeping this morning."

"You're talking too fast, dear. Kira, pour Meg a soda please."

"Will you drive me to a friend's house in Fort Lauderdale?"

"Of course," she says.

"Can I use your phone? I'm not sure if he's talking to me anymore."

Paige hands me the mobile phone, gesturing to the den, she says, "Take it in there for some privacy."

I dial Al's number, holding my breath. He picks up the phone. I can hear an extra question mark when he says hello. He must have Caller ID.

"Al?"

"Emily?"

"Yes."

"Please don't call me anymore."

"Why? I thought…" My head is swimming. It's one rejection too many.

"You make plans, you don't show up. Call me when you leave your husband." He pauses. "Ok?"

"Will you help me?" The "me" comes out as a high-pitched squeal.

"What's wrong?"

"They've flown Maddie out to Utah. They've taken her away from me." I hold my breath, wait for a response.

"I can't do this, Emily."

"Al, please. I need a friend. I need you."

I can hear him breathing. Finally, he says, "Who are they?"

"Paul. His psychiatrist. His sister. All of them."

"Where in Utah?"

"Park City. To his sister's house."

"Why?"

"I'm so screwed. Oh, God."

"Where are you now?"

"At a friend's house."

There's a pause. Then he says, "I'll come get you."

"No. She said she would bring me to you."

"What do you want to do?"

"I want to fly out and get her back, but I don't have any money. My wallet is at home."

"You can't get on a plane without a license. You have to go home and get your wallet first."

"Then I'll just drive out there."

"Emily, you want to get your daughter back quick or do you want to spend two or three days driving?"

"Shit. Shit, how does this kind of stuff happen to me?"

"Look, calm down first, then go get your wallet. I'll wait here for you."

"Ok."

"Emily?"

"Yes?"

"You're really coming this time?"

"I'm sorry about last night. I can explain. I swear I'm coming. It might take me a while to get in my house, but I'm coming."

"See you when you get here."

I hang up the phone. Shit. All my lies are catching up with me. He's going to see my license now and find out I'm Meg and not Emily. A year ago, I was an upper-middle-class mother of two with a husband. Now I'm on the verge of being institutionalized. How did things get so out of hand? What did I ever do in my life to deserve this? Then I think of Al. I wonder why a man as attractive, intelligent and funny as he is is still available. Maybe he's only available to me because he thinks I'm unavailable.

"How can I help?" Paige asks when I walk into the kitchen. Kira passes me a soda.

"Thank you, Kira. I'm Meg."

"I know. Mom's told me about you." She smiles timidly.

"I need to get my wallet and car keys out of my house. If I can get them, I can drive myself to Fort Lauderdale."

"Who's going with you?"

"Just me."

"But you called a friend."

"Yeah. He is a friend."

"Good for you, honey. Remember what I said about minding your own affairs." She cuts a glance at Kira as she emphasizes the word "affairs."

"I will," I say.

"Kira. Run over to the Parkers and stay with them until I get home. Ok?"

Kira touches my hand as she leaves. She doesn't say anything.

We pass my house once. I slide down in the seat. My car is missing from the driveway. "I can't believe they've impounded my car."

"He's playing hardball with you," Paige says.

"Bastard."

"I'll take you to Fort Lauderdale."

"I still need my wallet."

"You stay in the car. I'll get it," Paige says.

She loops the block back to my house. I hand her my key, explaining where Maddie's and my backpack is.

She says, "Pity. I was hoping to climb through your back window one of these days."

We laugh.

"Use the key. You're more civilized than I am anyway." I hunker down to the floorboard. I feel like I could vomit my heart straight out. I wonder if Paul put my car in Susie's garage. Maybe he's driving around in his car and Hope is driving around in my car, canvassing the neighborhood for me.

I hear Paige knocking on the front door, calling out, "Hello."

Shit, just get in and out of there. I squeeze my eyes shut, hoping no one sees me.

A few minutes later, she flies back into her Lincoln SUV, throwing my backpack over the seat. She purr-revs the idling engine, hightailing it out of our driveway.

"Wooo," she yells. "Now I see how you felt in my house."

"Exhilarated," I say.

"Exactly."

"Was anyone inside?"

"Just the man I knocked out."

"No, really."

"I don't think so."

As I direct her to Al's house, I say, "Can I ask you something?"

"Sure."

"Do you think everyone cheats?"

"I never thought about it," she says.

"I used to think cheaters were the exception. But now that women are more free, it seems like the whole world is cheating."

"God, I hope not."

"But you're a cheater," I say.

"I wasn't always. After years of being hurt, I learned to hedge my bets with Cameron. I didn't want to get left with nothing."

"How'd you get into bed with him every night?"

She shrugs her shoulders. "You learn to shut off tiny pieces of your heart one by one until it doesn't hurt anymore. Then you wake up one day and find your behavior is no better than his."

"I want my whole heart open to the man I'm with," I say.

"How can you be such an optimist after everything that's happened to you?"

I laugh. "An optimist? Me?"

"Maybe you don't see yourself the way others do."

"It's not so much that I'm an optimist as that I think if two people commit to each other, they should work to make sure no one comes between them."

She gives me the eyebrow look, then says, "I'm taking you to Al's house and you're being self-righteous about my life?"

"Ok, you're right. But it's because Paul has pushed me too far. What about your doctor friend? Is he married?"

"God, no. I'd never date a married man," she says. "You do know too much about my life. He wants to get married. I trust him more than anyone I've ever been with, but I'm not sure what I want. I'll stay with him until I can't."

"Like it's that simple."

"You have to reduce things to their lowest component. You either stay or you leave. We're almost there. Are you sure you want to do this?" she asks.

"I have to." Maybe she's right. Maybe I make things more complicated than they need to be. I notice myself hyperventilating the closer we get.

"Calm down," she says.

"Listen, he thinks my name is Emily. So if he calls me Emily, don't say anything. I want to tell him myself."

"I won't even get out of the car. What kind of life have you been living, anyway? Breaking into houses, using a pseudonym with strange men. We are going to have to hang out more often when you get back."

"Definitely."

As we pull up, Al walks out on his front porch.

"Nice specimen," Paige says, looking him over.

I reach over the seat for my backpack and overnight bag.

"Listen. You've been so nice. I'm not sure why and I don't really know how to thank you."

She waves me off, saying, "Call me when you get back so I know everything's all right. I can refer you to a good lawyer, too. I think you'll need one."

My stomach jumps over the word lawyer. All these months, I've played with the idea of divorce, but now that it's a concrete thought, it makes me want to throw up.

We hug briefly. I get out of the car.

"Ta, darling," she says and whisks off.

Al steps down from the stairs, gives me a hug. It's so interesting how nurtured you can get from people you barely know.

I kiss his lips before he finds mine first. I want him to know part of me wants him. I pull away. "Nice to see you, Al," I say, before he has a chance to prompt me.

He takes my hand, leads me inside. We sit down on the couch. He has glasses of wine, cheese and crackers on the table. He passes me a glass.

"I really shouldn't," I say.

He nods towards the glass with his head. "Yes, you should, you've had a bad morning. We're going to get on a plane in two hours."

"We?"

"Yes. Drink up," he says.

"Where are you going?"

"With you."

"Where?"

"To Park City. You said that's where Madeline is. Did I get it wrong? I already bought the tickets."

"Are you kidding me?" I ask.

"No. It is Park City, isn't it?"

"Yes, but."

"Well, drink up. There's Mormons out there. Who knows the next time we'll get a decent drink again."

I take a sip. I take another sip, but it turns into a gulp.

"Easy there," he says, taking my glass away from me.

I spin the bottle so I can see the label. "Rosso di Montalcino. Italian?"

"Just like me." He kisses me again and again.

"Wait."

"I know, it's not the right time, but I just had to."

I start to laugh, loud hysterical laughter.

"What's the matter?"

"You're just being so nice."

"And that makes you laugh?" He has a mad look on his face, but I can't stop laughing.

"I'm sorry, I'm nervous and distraught and...and not used to a man being this nice to me anymore. Why are you being so nice?"

"Because I care about you."

"But you don't know me."

"Think about how well we'll know each other by the time we get Madeline back. Come on, eat something. I can make you some macaroni and sauce if you'd like."

"No, this is fine." I feel self-conscious. I realize I have been running all over the place this morning and I haven't even taken a shower. I shut my legs, hoping he can't smell the remnants of Paul on me.

I say, "You know what I'd like?"

"What?"

"A shower."

"At a time like this?" he asks.

"It's just I've had a hell of a morning and I didn't get a chance to shower. I can't get on the plane smelling like this."

"I think you smell great."

I just look at him.

"Ok. You are a little ripe. It's this way."

Picking up my overnight bag, I follow him down the hall, walking away from the wine. For once, the wine isn't calling out to me. He opens the door to a beautiful bathroom. The shower is part of the room, a drain in the center. There are shelves with candles at all different heights.

"Wow."

"I did the work myself. There's a hundred pounds of amethyst in the floor," he says.

"Amethyst is my favorite stone. I don't see it though," I look hard at the floor.

"No, it's under the floor."

"Why did you do that?" I ask.

"I wanted my bathroom to be a sanctuary. Amethyst is soothing. It will be there in the floor giving comfort years after I've sold the house."

"That's interesting," I say.

"You'll see. The spigots are over there. You can turn on both showerheads if you'd like." He gestures to showerheads at opposite ends of the wall. "Here's a towel and shampoo."

I think I'm going to have to fight him off, but he backs out of the room, shutting the door softly. He may look like Paul, but he's certainly different.

chapter twenty-five

"What name did you put my ticket in?" I ask Al.

"I just reserved both under my name and told them we'd sort the tickets out when we picked them up at the airport. The plane is almost full. I didn't think you'd want to fly standby."

"Good thinking."

"So now you'll finally tell me your last name?"

"Actually, I'll tell you my first and last name."

"What do you mean?" he asks.

"Emily isn't my first name."

"You go by your middle name?"

"No, I go by Meg. Emily was just a made-up name."

He looks out the window, keeps driving. At the next stoplight, he turns to me and says, "Any other surprises?"

"Well…" I start.

The light turns green. He stays in place.

"Come on, we have to get there, we're cutting it close." Cars start honking behind us. He starts off, then pulls into a gas station. "Al, please. I don't want to miss the plane."

"Are you married?"

"Yes."

"What's your real name?"

"Meg O'Hara."

"Meg."

"Right."

"You look more like an Emily. Get it over with. What other skeletons are hiding in your closet?"

I flinch over the word "skeleton." "You don't want to know," I say.

"If I'm going to take off and go halfway across the country with you, I think I have a right to know."

"Look, I didn't ask you to come with me."

"Then why didn't you get your friend to take you directly to the airport?" he asks.

"I don't know. I was confused. I wanted to see you."

"Let's put it all on the table."

"I can't."

"Emily, I mean Meg. Whoever you are. What are you hiding?"

"Just take me to the airport. I'll go by myself."

"What could be so bad? I already know you're married."

"I killed my son, ok?"

"What?"

"I'm fucked up, Al. You should leave now. I'll get a taxi." I put my hand on the door handle, but I don't really want to go. With Paul, I always walk out when we get in a fight. With Al, I somehow know that he would never put up with that. If I get out of the car, it's the end. I stay planted in my seat.

"You killed your son? How? When?" he asks.

"Six months and twenty-seven days ago. I can give you the hours if you want them."

"How?"

"I hit him with my car. He was on the front lawn with Paul. He chased his ball into the street. I was watching Paul. I never saw him." My voice is totally deadpan, like I'm reporting details on someone else's life.

"Why didn't Paul catch him?"

I shake my head no. To tell Al that Paul was watching our

next-door neighbor's shorts climbing up her ass as she gardened would be a betrayal. Even though he betrayed me by taking Maddie away, I just can't do the same.

"God, that's awful." He puts the gearshift in park and hugs me.

His hug makes me burst into tears.

"I can't even face my own son. I haven't visited his grave since the day of the funeral. That's the kind of mother I am."

"I see you with Madeline. You're a great mother."

"I try, but I'm not. There's a million things I should do different."

"We better get to the airport."

I place my hand on top of his as he moves the gearshift from park into drive. "Wait. You might as well hear the rest," I say.

"There's more? I'm sorry, go ahead." He puts his arms around me again.

I wish he weren't so nice. It makes it harder. I take a good deep breath, stepping off the edge into a full confession. I'm prepared for him to open the car door and shove me out with his foot when I'm done. Really, it's what I deserve. Why would anyone be nice to me when I'm so fucked up?

"It's a long story," I start.

"I have time."

I take another deep breath. "Suffice it to say my mother killed my father and my brother in a car accident. She was a drunk. It was all my fault because I wanted this stupid bedspread. They'd still be alive if it weren't for me. I'm teetering on the brink of being a drunk myself. Hell, I think I am one. I took Maddie to a cancer support group and let people think she had cancer because I just needed people to be nice to me and I know Paige because her husband got in an accident at the same place my son did and I couldn't save him. I was caught breaking and entering, well, actually sleeping in Paige's house. I almost got arrested, but Paige was nice enough not to press charges and that's why Paul took Maddie away from me. Did I mention he's cheating on me with our next-door neighbor?

Al has taken his hands from around me to cover his face with his hands. "You can't be serious."

"This kind of shit, Al, you do not make up."

"I don't even know where to start."

"I can get a taxi if you'd rather."

"Have you had counseling?" he asks.

"Not until the intervention this morning."

"Intervention?"

"Paul's psychiatrist came to our house so he could confront me on all the bad things I've done."

"Emily, I'm sorry."

"It's Meg." I knew he wouldn't be able to take the truth. "I understand." I open the door.

"Where are you going?"

"I thought you wanted me to leave."

"Christ, no. I'm just sorry you've had such a shitty life."

I lean over and kiss Al. He kisses me back.

"Can we get to the airport?" I ask.

"Of course. Hey—thanks for being honest," he says.

"You shouldn't have to thank me. It should be the natural state of things."

"I'm glad you think that."

On the plane, I take the center seat, giving Al the aisle. The plane is full and cramped. The seats seem closer together than ever. I feel like everything is closing in on me. I wish I had had one more glass of wine before leaving Al's house.

A woman stands beside us, jockeying her purse and a huge canvas bag from her shoulders. She indicates the window seat is hers. It takes her five minutes to move in completely.

Al holds my hand on takeoff. I feel protected.

"Can I ask you some questions?" he asks.

I look over at the woman next to me. She's looking out the window, but I can tell she has her satellite dish ears trained on our conversation.

"Later, when we're alone and have Maddie back. Ok?"

Between having to stop in Dallas, landing in Salt Lake City and renting a car, it takes us all day to reach the perimeter of Park City. The snow-covered mountains are dappled with beautiful evergreens and Aspen trees. There's a free feeling in the air here. Maybe it's because there's so much open space. Park City reminds me of a college town that's trying to grow into a resort town. There's a mixture of clapboard houses and ski chalets perched on the side of the mountain. We find a 7–11 that I think must be the only one in town. I look Paul's sister up in the phone book, jot down her address and ask for directions.

The man behind the counter eyeballs me. "You a friend of Julie's?"

"I am," I say. I don't want to tell him I'm her sister-in-law. If he knows her by her first name, he might just call ahead and warn her.

"She's expecting me."

He glances out the window to Al waiting in the car. I smile at him.

"Are you friends with her too?" I ask.

"All the year-round residents in this town are friends."

"The directions?"

He grudgingly gives them to me. I know he's going to call as soon as we pull out. "Al, drive fast. This guy knows Julie. Go up here to the light and go through it."

I guide Al through the sequence of turns. "It's down here on the left. The gray house. Hurry."

"It's ok, we're almost there. Make sure you're calm when you knock on the door. Let's not escalate things right off the bat."

It's dark. As we approach the house, I see a black and white sign hanging to the left of the door that reads "Beware of God." Why would she put up a sign like that? She's even more nuts than I thought. I can't believe Paul sent Madeline here for protection from me.

"Do you see that sign?" I ask.

"What? The "Beware of Dog" sign?"

I look again. Al's right. It does say "Beware of Dog". "Yes," I say.

"All the more reason to be careful. What kind of dogs do they own?"

"I don't know."

He puts the car in park, kills the engine.

"Maybe you should leave it running in case we need to get away quickly," I say.

"No. I'm coming to the door with you."

"No. Please, let me go in and get her by myself."

"Ok. Be careful." He pats my back as I get out.

I examine the "Beware of Dog" sign while I wait for an answer to my knock. Julie's husband answers the door. I can hear their teenage boys fighting in the background. He turns and yells, "God dammit, shut your yaps. Meg. What are you doing here?"

"I've come for Maddie."

He looks past me to the car. "Is that Paul in the car? What are you two up to?"

"Nothing. I just want Maddie."

"Who is in the car?" he asks.

"Where's Maddie?"

"Honey, Paul had Julie paged when she was on her layover in Atlanta and told her to bring the baby back."

"What are you talking about?"

"What the hell's going on down in South Florida with you two? First Jordan, now you don't even know where your own daughter is?"

He's just trying to make me crazy. I push past him, run from room to room.

The boys stop wrestling, saying, "Hi, Aunt Meg," when I burst in their room.

"Where's your mother?"

"She went back to Florida," the younger one answers.

"What are you doing here?" the older one asks.

"I want answers," I yell. "I'm the one asking the questions." A dog starts barking in the backyard. "I'm sorry for yelling. Your mother didn't come home with Madeline?"

"No. She was supposed to, but then I thought you called and had her come back."

"Oh God." I run out of the house.

Julie's husband is leaning in the car window, talking to Al. I jump in the passenger seat. "Let's go. They took her back."

Al says, "That's what he's telling me. Nice meeting you." He puts the car in reverse. Julie's husband straightens up.

"Remember what I told you," the husband says.

Al nods at him, backing out of the driveway.

"I can't fucking believe it," I yell. "Do you think we can get a flight out?"

"Not until the morning. They don't have red-eye flights out of here. I asked when I made our reservations. Look, let's get something to eat and figure out our game plan."

"Sure there's no way for us to fly out tonight?"

"I'm sure."

"Maybe if we drove to another airport somewhere else?"

"I don't even know where the next big airport is. I know you want to get Maddie back, but maybe it's better. This way, everyone can cool down."

"I don't want them thinking I don't want Maddie."

"Don't worry, I'm sure Julie's husband is on the phone telling everybody who will listen that you came out here with another man."

"What was he saying to you?"

"Nothing, just a talker."

"What did he say?"

"That you're nuts."

"They beat their kids and I'm the one who's nuts? That's just great. Who did you tell him you were?"

"I said I was a concerned friend of the family."

We end up at an Italian restaurant named Grappa. Al looks at the wine list, then shuts it. "What do you think of having soda with our meal?" he asks.

I smile at him. "Not very romantic, but ok."

"Romance is between two people, not something that's poured out of a bottle."

"Where the hell did you come from?"

"I'm just a regular guy, Meg."

The food is wonderful, the company even better. We check into The Woodbridge Inn. It's a bed and breakfast. I've never stayed in one of those before. The innkeepers, Joyce and Jay, are very gracious. Joyce shows us to our room, clicks on a little fountain on the table, tells us about the Jacuzzi tub in the bathroom that fits two people. She shuts the door saying, "I'll see you at breakfast in the morning. We serve between 7:30 and 9:00."

I turn towards Al. "So now what?"

He kisses me, starts lifting my dress up over my head. I don't want this right now, but don't know how to tell him to stop. He stands back, looking at me standing there in my bra and panties. "Lovely." He kisses my neck. His hands are unbuttoning his own shirt.

"Wait, stop."

"What's wrong?"

He kisses me, I kiss him back.

"Wait," I say again.

"It's ok, it's all going to be ok." He starts with my panties.

"No. It doesn't feel right." I think of my conversation with Paige. She'll think I'm stupid for not sleeping with Al. But I can only be who I am. I still want my family together.

"You don't want to be with me?" Al asks.

"I do."

He kisses me again, sliding his shirt off. His chest is lightly tanned with no hair. I can tell he works out.

"Just not now." I look away from his body.

"You're hot, you're cold, you're hot, you're cold."

"Don't be mad. I just don't want to remember the first night we were together as the day that Maddie was taken away from me."

He sits down on the bed, pulls my arm so I'm standing between his legs.

"Ok?"

"Yeah, ok," he says.

"Would you just hold me? I'd really like that."

"Sure." He stands up, taking his jeans off. He doesn't wear any underwear. I try to not notice his hard-on. I walk around the bed, sliding in on the other side. I leave my bra and underwear on as armor.

chapter twenty-six

Al wakes me at 5:00 AM, by spooning up behind me. I can feel his morning hard-on. I roll over. "Good morning."

"Nice waking up with you."

I smile, don't say anything. The realization of yesterday creeps back into my consciousness. He props himself up on his elbow, strokes my hair.

"Tell me today is going to be better than yesterday," I say.

"It will be. Remember? I'm with you."

I touch his face.

"Our tickets are for a nine o'clock flight, but I think we can get on an earlier flight if we hurry," he says.

I toss the covers off. "Let's do it."

He gets up, opens the drapes. The hint of morning light outlines his naked body.

We're able to switch our tickets without incident. This flight is empty. I switch my seat for a middle row with three empty chairs I can lay across. I grab a pillow and a blanket, hoping to shut the world out with sleep.

Al wakes me before we land in Atlanta. "Sleepy?" he asks.

"Yeah."

"Avoiding the day?"

"Yeah."

"I promise, it will all work out."

"I don't think it can anymore. Things have gotten so crazy." I wonder why he's being supportive of me working things out with Paul.

"I have a friend who's a lawyer. He can help."

"With what?"

"Well, your divorce."

Why is it that everyone is pushing me towards divorce? What ever happened to people working things out? "Oh, I don't know."

"You can't be serious."

"What?"

"You are getting a divorce after what he's put you through, aren't you?"

I squinch my face up. "Can we talk about this after I get Maddie back?"

He turns, walking back to his seat. The stewardess's voice comes on telling us to prepare for landing.

The landing is bumpy. Al's seat is towards the front of the plane. He doesn't wait for me to come up the aisle. When I get to the jet way, he's not there either. I can't take it that this many people in my life want everything and nothing from me all at once.

I stop at a bar on the way to my next gate. I wonder if Al will be on the plane. I order a glass of wine. All they have is the cheap stuff that's guaranteed to amplify the headache I already have. I drink the wine in one swallow.

"Another?" the bartender asks.

I start to say yes, but then say, "I better not. On second thought, yes I will have one more and the check."

"I hate to fly too," the bartender says, placing the bill on the bar.

It's assumptions like that one that make you end up in a cancer support group and then end up with your baby being taken away. Ahh, shit. Paige is right. I have embraced the victim mentality. If I'm going to be a mother and a role model to Maddie, I better straighten up my act. I leave the second glass of wine on the bar untouched.

Racing through the airport, every man that looks like Al makes me slow down. He's not at the gate. I get on the plane as they call for the last seating. Maddie is my priority.

I stow my overnight bag under the seat. Close my eyes. Maybe I can sleep again. Maybe I'll just sleep the rest of my life away. I hear them shutting the outer door. My heart sinks a little. It was so wonderful to feel like someone really believed in me and wanted the best for Maddie and me. We taxi down the runway, away from Al.

I wish I had a book to read. I look over at the book the woman next to me is reading. There's a quote from Thich Nhat Hanh, whoever that is. But there's something that attracts me to the quote. It says, "The rhythm of my heart is the birth and death of all that is alive." I say it in my head again and again until the woman turns the page.

I think about the state of my heart. It's not in good shape. But there's still a space for Jordan. "The rhythm of my heart is the birth and death of all that is alive," I recite. There's a space for Maddie and in spite of myself, I have to admit there's a space for Paul.

I deplane in Fort Lauderdale. I'm happy and scared to be back home. Passing the bar where Al and I first met, I see him leaning against the column smiling at me. I keep walking. He hustles to catch up.

"Hi. You look just like this woman Meg I met here before," he says, walking fast beside me to keep up.

"I'm sure you have me mistaken for someone else."

"Maybe with a woman named Emily," he says.

"Yeah, sure. Whatever you say."

I ride down the escalator, walk to the curb and hail a taxi.

"Meg, stop this. I can give you a ride home."

The taxi driver opens his window, says, "Where are you going?"

Al says, "She's coming with me."

"Must be you two are married for too long," the driver says in a Jamaican accent.

"We're not married at all," I say.

"Then you should get married, long as you're fighting like this." He smiles and pulls up to the next couple waiting on the curb.

"See?" asks Al. "Even the cab driver thinks we should be together."

"You left me."

"I'm sorry. I was angry."

"Well, don't just leave me like that again. I can't stand it." I think of all the times I walked out on Paul and how he used to beg me not to leave when I was mad. I've been awful to him. I'm going to go back and be every woman I never was with him. Paul won't even recognize me, I'll be so good.

"Can I at least take you home? I want to make sure everything is ok."

"It will only complicate matters for me to show up with you."

"I'll drop you off down the block."

"I can't," I say.

"You're coming with me anyway. I want to make sure you and Maddie are fine."

"How will you know?"

"I'll wait down the road. If you don't come back out, I'll know she's home and you're with her."

"Ok."

He takes the overnight bag from my hands.

True to his word, he stops a block away from my house. "You're down the road on which side?" he asks.

"The left side."

"What's the house number?"

"It's the pale blue house. It's the only blue house on the block." Fingering the door handle, I breathe out hard.

"Just be calm and talk through things," he says. "They can't take her away permanently without a court order."

"That's what I'm afraid of."

"I'll wait right here."

I reach for my overnight bag.

He says, "Let me keep it. It has some of my stuff in it and that way I know I'll get to see you again at least one more time."

"Thanks for everything." I kiss his cheek and back out of the car. I turn when I'm three houses away. He waves. I start to run towards my house. Whatever's waiting for me will be ok if I can just see Maddie. My car still isn't in the driveway. I try the front door, it's locked. I fumble for my house keys. I run through the whole house. No one is home. I run next door to Susie's house. Paul and Hope are probably commiserating with her. I knock, then bang on the door when I don't get an answer. Her dog barks and bangs against the window. I sit down on her front stoop and cry.

Al's car rolls by, he hesitates at the bottom of my driveway, taking our house in. He spots me over at Susie's, pulls into her driveway. "Get in."

I don't move. He gets out of the car, holds his hands out for me to take. "Come on, get in."

I can't get a hold of myself. I'm crying and crying. It's like my head and my heart and my uterus are all splitting open at the same time. I'm breaking apart from the inside out.

"Where do you think they'd be?" He touches my shoulder.

"I don't know."

"A friend's house?" he asks.

"No. We've kind of insulated ourselves. We don't really have any friends."

"Well, they have to be somewhere. Is there a favorite

restaurant you have? Maybe they just went out for a bite to eat."

Then it dawns on me. "I know where they are."

"Where?"

"The cemetery."

He sighs. "Where is it?"

"Up in Boca."

"Do you think you can handle it?"

"I'll have to."

He drives at an urgent speed without being reckless. We pull off the main road into the side entryway.

"Let me go by myself. Ok?" I ask.

"Ok. I'm here if you need me."

I approach Jordan's headstone like it's going to rear up and bite me. Paul and Maddie aren't here. Dead roses wrapped in florist paper are on the ground in front of it. Paul must have been here within the last week; the red color hasn't drained completely from them.

I look at the little lamb etched on the blue stone. Leaning down, I trace my fingers over Jordan's name and his birth and death dates. Such a tiny life.

"The rhythm of my heart is the birth and death of all that is alive," I say out loud, lying down on the grass, petting the headstone, rocking myself back and forth in the rhythm of my heart ebbing and flowing. "Jordan, I miss you, my little man. Mommy is so, so sorry." Tears are running down my face, but I feel a calmness wash over me.

I hear voices approaching. I raise myself up on all fours. It's Paul and Susie and she's holding Maddie. I fly up off the ground at them, startling them.

"Mama, Mama," Maddie cries with her arms outstretched towards me. Susie turns around, starts walking back to the main parking lot.

"Where do you think you're going with my daughter?" My voice is calm.

Susie says, "Meg, let's not do this in front of her. You need help."

"And you don't? Sleeping with everybody's husbands."

I grab for Maddie, Paul lunges for my arms, but misses.

"Stop," I say.

"You've gone too far, Meg," he says.

Maddie wails, "Mama, Mama's home. Mama."

"Give her to me," I swipe Maddie from Susie's arms and gallop away.

"Dammit, Meg, get back here before you hurt her," Paul yells.

I'm running and running. The grass is uneven and we stumble a few times. The road is in view. I'm all turned around. I don't know which way Al is anymore.

"The rhythm of my heart is the birth and death of all that is alive." That's what it means—it's the old ashes to ashes, with a reincarnation spin. In death we are released to a better, happier life. In death—but that's only half of it. Maybe it means that we have to breathe in and out our acceptance of the full circle of life and death as a natural state of being.

I totter on the edge of the roadway. I wait until I see a big, dark blue car driving towards me. Susie and Paul are coming up behind me now. They're both yelling "STOP."

Maddie is grasping the front of my shirt with all the might in her little hands. I wait until the car is almost upon us, step out into the road. In my peripheral vision, I see Al pulling out of the side entryway towards us. He has a surprised look on his face. I can see his lips saying, "NO."

I sprint as fast as I can, veering around the honking, skidding car, running towards safety with Maddie in my arms. Running towards Al.